The Possession of Mr Cave

By the same author

The Last Family in England
The Dead Fathers Club
Shadow Forest

The Possession of Mr Cave

MATT HAIG

VIKING

VIKING
Published by the Penguin Group
Penguin Group (USA) Inc., 375 Hudson Street,
New York, New York 10014, U.S.A.
Penguin Group (Canada), 90 Eglinton Avenue East, Suite 700,
Toronto, Ontario, Canada M4P 2Y3
(a division of Pearson Penguin Canada Inc.)
Penguin Books Ltd, 80 Strand, London WC2R 0RL, England
Penguin Ireland, 25 St. Stephen's Green, Dublin 2, Ireland
(a division of Penguin Books Ltd)
Penguin Books Australia Ltd, 250 Camberwell Road, Camberwell,
Victoria 3124, Australia
(a division of Pearson Australia Group Pty Ltd)
Penguin Books India Pvt Ltd, 11 Community Centre, Panchsheel Park,
New Delhi – 110 017, India
Penguin Group (NZ), 67 Apollo Drive, Rosedale, North Shore 0632,
New Zealand (a division of Pearson New Zealand Ltd)
Penguin Books (South Africa) (Pty) Ltd, 24 Sturdee Avenue,
Rosebank, Johannesburg 2196, South Africa

Penguin Books Ltd, Registered Offices:
80 Strand, London WC2R 0RL, England

First American edition
Published in 2009 by Viking Penguin,
a member of Penguin Group (USA) Inc.

Publisher's Note
This is a work of fiction. Names, characters, places, and incidents either are the
product of the author's imagination or are used fictitiously, and any resemblance to
actual persons, living or dead, business establishments, events, or locales is entirely
coincidental.

ISBN-13: 978-1-61523-530-8

Printed in the United States of America

To Andrea

If there is anything that we wish to change in the child, we should first examine it and see whether it is not something that could better be changed in ourselves.

Carl Gustav Jung,
The Development of Personality

But the deep deep tragedies of infancy, as when the child's hands were unlinked for ever from his mother's neck, or his lips for ever from his sister's kisses, these remain lurking below all, and these lurk to the last.

Thomas De Quincey,
'Suspiria de Profundis: The Palimpsest'

Of course, you know where it begins.

It begins the way life begins, with the sound of screaming.

I was upstairs, at my desk, balancing the books. I recall being in a rather buoyant mood, having sold that afternoon a mid-Victorian drop-leaf table for a most welcome amount. It must have been half past seven. The sky outside the window was particularly beautiful, I remember thinking. One of those glorious May sunsets that crams all the beauty of the day into its dying moments.

Now, where were you? Yes: your bedroom. You were practising your cello, as you had been since Reuben had left to meet his friends at the tennis courts.

At the time I heard it, the scream, I had already lowered my gaze towards the park. I think I must have been looking over at the horse chestnuts, rather than the empty climbing frame, because I hadn't noticed anyone on East Mount Road. There was some kind of numerical discrepancy I was trying to solve; I can't remember what precisely.

Oh, I could hold that scene just there. I could write ten thousand words about that sunset, about that park, about the trivial queries of my profit and loss accounts. You see, as I write I am back inside that moment, I am back there in that room, wrapped up warm in that unknowing contentment. For this pen to push that evening on, to get to the moment where the sound of the scream actually meant something, seems a kind of crime. And yet I have to tell you how it was, exactly as I saw it, because this was the end and the start of everything, wasn't it? So come on, Terence, get on with it, you don't have all day.

The scream struck me first as a disturbance. An intrusion on the sweet sound of whatever Brahms sonata was floating to me from your bedroom. Then, before I knew why, it caused a kind of pain, a twist in my stomach, as if my body was understanding before my mind.

Simultaneous with the sound of the scream, there were other noises, coming from the same direction. Voices unified in a chant, repeating a two-syllable word or name I couldn't quite catch. I looked towards the noise and saw the first street lamp stutter into life. Something was hanging from the horizontal section of the pole. A dark blue shape that didn't immediately make sense, high above the ground.

There were people standing below – boys – and the hanging object and the chanting gained clarity in my mind at the same time.

'Reuben! Reuben! Reuben!'

I froze. Maybe too much of me was still lost in my account books as, for a second or so, I did nothing except watch.

My son was hanging from a lamp post, using the greatest of strength to risk his life for the sake of entertaining those he thought were friends.

I felt things sharpen and began to move, gaining momentum as I ran across the landing.

Your music stopped.

'Dad?' you asked me.

I rushed downstairs and through the shop. My hip knocked

into something, a chest, causing one of the figurines to drop and smash.

I crossed the street and ran through the gate. I crossed the park at the pace of a younger self, flying over the leaves and grass and through the deserted play area. All the time I kept him in sight, as if to lose him for a second would cause his grip to weaken. I ran feeling the terror beat in my chest, behind my eyes and in my ears.

He shuffled his hands closer towards the vertical section of the post.

I could see his face now, glowing an unnatural yellow from the lamp. His teeth bared with the strain, his bulging eyes already knowing the insanity of his mistake.

Please, Bryony, understand this: the pain of a child is the pain of a parent. As I ran to your brother I knew I was running to myself.

I stepped on the park wall and jumped down to the pavement, landing badly. I twisted my ankle on the concrete but I fought against it as I ran towards him, as I called his name.

Your brother couldn't move. His face was twisted in agony. The glare of the light blanched his skin, releasing him of the birth mark he always hated.

I was getting closer now.

'Reuben!' I shouted. 'Reuben!'

He saw me as I pushed my way through his friends. I can still see his face and all the confusion and terror and helplessness it contained. In that moment of recognition, of distraction, the concentration he needed to stay exactly where he was suddenly faltered. I could feel it before it happened, a kind of gloating doom leaking out from the terraced houses. An invisible but all-encompassing evil that stole every last hope.

'Reuben! No!'

He fell, fast and heavy.

Within a second his screaming had stopped and he was on the concrete pavement in front of me.

Everything about him seemed so hideous and unnatural as he lay there, like an abandoned puppet. The crooked angles of his legs. The accelerated rhythm of his chest. The shining blood that spilt from his mouth.

'Get an ambulance,' I shouted at the crowd of boys who stood there in numb silence. 'Now!'

In the distance cars sped by on Blossom Street, heading into York or out to the supermarket, immune and unaware.

I crouched down and my hand touched his face and I pleaded with him to stay with me.

I begged him.

And it seemed like some kind of deliberate punishment, the way he died. I could see the decision in his eyes, as the substance of life retreated further and further from his body.

One of the boys, the smallest, vomited on the pavement.

Another – shaven-headed, sharp-eyed – staggered back, away, onto the empty road.

The tallest and most muscular of the group just stood there, looking at me, a shaded face inside a hood. I hated that boy and the brutal indifference of his face. I cursed the god who had made this boy stand there, breathing before me, while Reuben was dying on the pavement. Inside the desperate urgency of that moment I sensed there was something not quite right about that boy, as though he had been pasted onto the scene from another reality.

I picked up one of Reuben's heavy hands, his left, and saw his palm was still red and indented from holding onto the post. I rubbed it and I kept talking to him, words on top of words, but all the time I could see him retreating from his body, backing away. And then he said something.

'Don't go.' As if it was me who was leaving and not him. They were his last words.

The hand went cold, the night gathered closer and the ambulance came to confirm it was too late for anything to be done.

I remember I saw you across the park.

I remember leaving Reuben's body on the pavement.

I remember you asked me, 'Dad, what's happening?'

I remember saying, 'Go back, Petal, go back home. Please.'

I remember you asked about the ambulance.

I remember I ignored the question and repeated my demand.

I remember the boy in the hood, staring straight at you.

I remember I became insistent, I remember grabbing your arm and shouting, I remember being harsher with you than I had ever been.

I remember the look on your face and I remember you running back home, to the shop entrance, and the door closing. And the knowledge below the madness that I had betrayed you both.

As you know, for much of my life I have spent my time mending broken things. Repairing clock dials, restoring old chairs, retouching china. Over the years I have become accomplished at removing stains with ammonia, or a dab of white spirit. I can remove scratches from glass. I can simulate different grains of wood. And I can restore a corroded Tudor candlestick with vinegar, half a pint of hot water and a piece of fine wire wool.

To buy a George III mahogany dressing table suffering the scars and strains of two centuries, and then return it to its original glory, once gave me such a thrill. Or equally, to have Mrs Weeks come into the shop and run her informed fingers over a Worcester vase without detecting the cracks, not so long ago filled my soul with happiness.

It gave me a kind of power, I suppose. A means of defeating time. A way of insulating myself against this foul, mouldering age. And I cannot explain to you the desperate pain it gives me to know that I cannot restore our own private past in quite the same way.

Here is something you must understand.

There have been four people in this life I have truly loved, and out of those four, you are the only one remaining. All of the others died of unnatural causes. Son, wife, mother. All three before their time.

You love three people and they die. It hardly warrants a public inquiry, does it? No. How many would you have to love and watch die before people grew suspicious of that love? Five? Ten? A hundred? Three is nothing. A fig. Three is just plain old bad luck, even if it is three-quarters of all you have ever cared for in the world.

Oh, I have tried to be rational. Come on, Terence, I tell myself. None of these deaths were your responsibility. And, of course, my defence would hold up in a court of law.

But where are the courts of love? And what possible punishment could they enforce that was worse than grief? I came to believe, after Reuben died, that there was something wrong with me, and with the love I had to offer. I had failed Reuben. I let him die among friends I had never met.

I had loved him, but I always imagined there would be some later day when I could make everything up to him. I couldn't accept that these later days would never come.

Of course, the death of a child is, for any parent, always an impossible fact. You hear the opening bars of a familiar sonata and the music stops but you still feel those silent notes, their beauty and power no less real, no less complete. With Reuben I had been ignoring the tune. It had been there, all the time, played continuously for his fourteen years, but I had switched off, stopped listening. I was always concentrating on the shop, or on you, and left Reuben to his own devices.

So what I once ignored I strained to find, and if I strained hard enough I caught flashes, brief bursts of the life that was transformed but did not truly end. Notes returning not in pretty sequence, but as a cacophony, crashing over me with the weight of guilt.

The morning of the funeral I awoke to the sound of buzzing. A rather angry, sawing noise that cut its way through the darkness. I opened my eyes and raised my head from the pillow to see where it was coming from. The room, softly lit by the morning sun that filtered through the curtains, was all there. The framed photograph of your mother, the wardrobe, the Turner print, the French mantel clock. Everything, apart from the noise, was normal. It was only when I sat up further, propped on my elbows, that I identified the source. Low above the bed, over the section of blankets that covered my legs and feet, I saw what must have been five hundred small flies, hovering, just hovering, as if I was a sun-rotten corpse in the desert.

For a moment, there was no fear. The sight of these creatures, moving in short oval swirls, at first had a mesmeric effect. Then something changed. As if suddenly aware that I had woken, the flies began to move in one cloudlike motion further up the bed, towards my face. Soon they were all around me, a dark blizzard, with their angry, unstoppable noise getting louder every second. I dived down, deep under the blankets, hoping the flies wouldn't follow and with that sudden movement the noise stopped completely. I waited a second in the warm and cushioned dark, then resurfaced.

The flies had all disappeared, leaving no trace. I looked around again and, although the creatures had gone, I couldn't help but feel that the room was different, as if every object had shared my delusion.

I remember Cynthia and me talking in the car, patching our grief with small nothings, as the funeral procession rolled through the old Saxon streets. At one point she turned to you and said: 'You are doing so well.' You returned your grandmother's sad smile and I muttered an agreement. You were certainly remarkably composed, as you had been for much of the week. Too composed, I had thought, worried you were keeping it all locked in.

I tried to keep my thoughts on your brother but found

them gravitating towards you, and to the effect your twin brother's death was having on your behaviour.

You hadn't played your cello all week. This, I told myself, was understandable. You had gone to the stables every evening, to take care of Turpin, but you hadn't ridden him since the day before Reuben died. This too was as might be expected. You had lost your twin brother and you were stranded now, an only child of an only parent. Still, something troubled me. You had been off school, and I had closed the shop, yet I don't think we had talked properly for the whole week. You had always found an excuse to leave the room (to check the iron, to feed Higgins, to go to the toilet). Even then, in that slow-moving car, you felt my eyes upon you and you seemed to wince, as though there was a heat to my gaze, scorching your cheek.

Cynthia's hand squeezed mine as we approached the church. I noticed her nails, decorated with their usual black varnish, her face painted in her macabre style, and remembered her tear-stained joke that morning about how the one useful thing with regard to her sense of fashion was that she never had to think what to wear for a funeral.

We pulled up at the church. We left the car with faces filled with the grief we felt, but also knew we had to show. As we walked past those cramped old graves of plague victims I thought of all the dead parents, separated from their children. Do you remember Cynthia's old ghost story? About the plague boy who had been buried outside York's walls, in line with the new laws, and the spirit of his mother rising up from the graveyard to search in vain for her son? She told you both it when you were younger, walking back with your oranges and candles from Christingle, and Reuben laughed at you for being scared.

It is strange. I feel myself sinking. You remember one thing and there is always something else, lurking below, pulling you under. But I must keep my head up. I must stay gulping the fresh air.

You may wonder why I need to relive these things, when you were there too, but I must tell you everything as I saw it, for you know only your side, and I know only mine, and hopefully when you read this account you will look behind what I have done and a kind of truth will emerge somewhere in that space, that airy space, between your reading and my writing. It is a vain hope, but the last I have, so I will cling to it, as I clung to you as we walked up the path.

Peter, the vicar, was at the other end of that path to meet us, ready to give sympathy and the necessary instructions. He said something to you, and Cynthia butted in on your behalf, defending you against any obligation to speak. It was then that I turned round and saw the boy who had been there the night Reuben died. The boy whom I had hated instantly, for the blank indifference I had seen in his face. His hood was gone. He stood in a cheap suit, wearing a black tie, yet I must admit he had a striking appearance. The pale skin and black hair and those eyes that seemed to contain a dark and brooding power. Something violent, and dangerous.

I don't know if you had seen him. Had you? I spoke a word in Cynthia's ear and walked past those antique graves towards him.

'May I ask what you are doing here?'

He didn't say anything at first. He was wrestling with the sudden fury that was marked on his face.

'Ah'm Denny,' he said, as if it should have signified something.

'Denny?'

'Ah were one of Reuben's mates.' There was a rough arrogance to the voice, something confrontational that seemed wholly inappropriate to the occasion.

'He never mentioned you.'

'Ah were there when he . . . You saw us.'

'Yes, I saw you.' I bit back insults and accusations. It was not the time nor the place. 'Now, why are you here?'

'The funeral.'

'No. You weren't invited.'

'Ah wanted to come.' His eyes pressed harder than his words.

'Well, you came. And now you can go.'

He looked past me, over my shoulder. I turned and saw you still struggling with the vicar.

'Go,' I said. 'You're not welcome here. Leave us alone.'

He nodded. A suspicion confirmed.

'Right,' he said, through a tensed mouth. As he turned and walked away I had the most strange and unpleasant sensation. It was a feeling I can only describe to you as a desertion, some essential part of my soul being pulled away, leaving me for a moment uncertain of where I was. My vision darkened, my brain fuzzed with a strange energy, and I grasped the stone gatepost for support.

My memory jumps at this point to inside the church. I remember the slow trudge behind the coffin. I remember the vicar's vague niceties. I can see Cynthia, up at the lectern, delivering the bit she had chosen from Corinthians with none of her normal theatrics. 'For since death came through a human being, the resurrection of the dead has also come through a human being . . .'

Even more sharply, I remember myself looking out as I struggled to start the poem I had chosen. I saw so many faces, all wearing the compulsory expressions of grief. Teachers, customers, undertakers. And you among them, on the nearest pew, staring over at your brother's coffin. I looked down at the sheet in front of me, the sheet Cynthia had printed out so neatly from her machine.

For a while I couldn't speak, I couldn't cry, I couldn't do anything. I just stood there.

I made those poor people live lifetimes inside that minute. I could hardly breathe. Peter was already heading towards me, raising his eyebrows, when I finally pushed myself into it.

'To sleep,' I said, the words echoing off the cold stone walls. 'To sleep.'

I kept saying it – 'To sleep' – turning the key to an engine in my mind. 'John Keats.'

> *O soft embalmer of the still midnight!*
> *Shutting, with careful fingers and benign*
> *Our gloom-pleas'd eyes, embower'd from the light,*
> *Enshaded in forgetfulness divine;*
> *O soothest Sleep! if so it please thee, close,*
> *In midst of this thine hymn, my willing eyes,*
> *Or wait the 'Amen', ere thy poppy throws*
> *Around my bed its lulling charities;*
> *Then save me, or the passed day will shine*
> *Upon my pillow, breeding many woes;*
> *Save me from curious conscience, that still lords*
> *Its strength for darkness, burrowing like a mole;*
> *Turn the key deftly in the oiled wards,*
> *And seal the hushed casket of my soul.*

I sat back down. Peter concluded the service. I watched the feet of the pall-bearers as they turned down the aisle. The left shoes crossing the right. Four pairs of feet moving in perfect time, like the beginning of a macabre dance routine.

My eyes slid up and reached one of the faces, trying to hide the strain it took to shoulder the coffin's weight, struck by a grief it didn't feel.

I looked at you and told you, 'It's all right.'

You said nothing.

Outside, five minutes later, and soft rain pattered on the large black umbrella that I held to shelter you and your grandmother. After a week of silence, your tears came, bringing Cynthia's with them. Only my eyes remained dry, even though my heart must have wept. I'm sure it must have.

I still hear Peter's voice.

'We have entrusted our brother Reuben to God's mercy, and we now commit his body to the ground.' The pall-bearers lowered the coffin, releasing the black straps in steady motion. 'Earth to earth, ashes to ashes, dust to dust.' The comfort of repetition, of ritual, did nothing to calm your sobs. 'In sure and certain hope of the Resurrection to eternal life through our Lord Jesus Christ.' The coffin reached hard ground, settled, and was still. 'Who died, was buried, and rose again for us. To him be glory for ever and ever.' And then at last there was the collective 'Amen', spoken so low it seemed to come from the earth that would bury him. The earth that made us believe he was gone.

The police were going to do nothing to his friends.

'He wasn't forced up there.'

Such a primitive notion of force, and accident, and responsibility.

I never told you this but I went to see them. The boys. They hung around the disused tennis courts, so, after I had dropped you at the stables, I went to voice my feelings.

They were there. All except him, Denny.

I pulled up to the kerb and wound down my window.

'I hope you're happy,' I said, leaning out. 'I hope you had fun, watching him die. I hope you sleep the innocent sleep, knowing you are soaked in his blood.'

They stood there, behind the crossed wire, like thugs in a Bernstein musical. The shaven-haired boy with the sharp eyes made a rude gesture, but said nothing.

'Murderers,' I yelled, before screeching off.

And I didn't leave it there. The next evening I yelled the same accusation. And the next, and the next, but I never saw him. I never saw Denny there. Indeed, by the fourth time, I couldn't see any of them. I was yelling into nothing, accusing the air. Guilt had made them evaporate, I told myself. My words had moved them on. The strange thing is I felt no satisfaction at this. My heart fell when I realised they weren't there, and my anger sank swiftly back to despair.

From his early school reports it was clear that your brother was not going to be a high achiever in an academic sense. There were none of the 'outstandings' or 'exceptionals' that always rained down on you, never a 'pleasure to teach' or a 'joyous addition to the classroom'.

Reuben had no interest in books in the way you had. For him, reading never rose above the level of a necessary chore. He enjoyed my night-time stories of Dick Turpin and all those other old rogues, as you both did, but once he had heard one story he wanted to hear it again and again, whereas you always craved tales you had never known before.

I see him now, at the window, his finger making patterns in the condensation. 'A quiet boy.' 'Easily led.'

Money, in this blind century, has become the measure of love. A crude outsider would tell me I exercised more care for you because, from the age of eleven, I paid for your schooling.

Yet what could I do? I could only pay for one of you – should you have both suffered for the sake of equality? Was it my fault the Mount was a girls' school? Would it have been better to send Reuben, who had never shown any interest in his education? No, St John's was the obvious choice for him.

Yet, of course, I must admit this was not the only extravagance I afforded you. After all, you wanted to ride, so I paid for a horse and for it to be at livery. You wanted to play music, and I paid for you to have violin and then cello lessons at the college. You wanted a cat, specifically a coffee-cream Birman, and I bought you Higgins.

Yet you were actively interested in these things. They weren't acquired out of any fatherly overindulgence, or if they were I would gladly have shown the same indulgence to your brother if he had only requested such presents. Where were Reuben's interests? I never had any idea. He wanted a bicycle and the one I bought wasn't good enough. He wanted all this technological claptrap that he knew I wouldn't allow before he asked. No, we must never forget it, your brother was not easy. Even in my grief I could not ignore this. Indeed, my grief required me to remember it very well, for I already knew how sentimentality can flood in and drown memories, leaving the true person beyond recall.

I wanted to remember him as he was. I wanted to remember his incessant screams through the night as a baby, his later tantrums, his insatiable appetite for jellied sweets. I wanted to remember how cross he got when you used to read from the same picture book together. I wanted to remember the rows he had with you, even the one where he tore up your sheet music.

I wanted to remember the way he used to sit and watch television, with his hand covering the birthmark on his face. I wanted to remember the cigarette incident, the shoplifting incident, the smashed vase incident. I wanted to remember the early Sunday mornings when you would both go with me to an antiques fair, and he would grumble all the way down the A1.

Yet the memories of him were always hard to relive and restore. When I thought of him a thought of you would swiftly arrive in its place. When I tried to picture you as babies, as your mother last saw you, I wouldn't be able to see his screaming face. There was always just you, lying placid by his side, lost in your innocent unworded dreams. A dream yourself.

Now, that first day I opened the shop after his funeral. Your first day back at the Mount. I kept myself busy polishing the ewers and tureens and all the other pieces of silverware. All day I was there in my white cotton gloves, filling the shop with the smell of polish, my curved reflection staring back with manic eyes.

Customers came in and I scared them out of spending their

money. I made mistakes. I gave people the wrong change. I dropped a Davenport jug. I was feeling dreadful.

'Come on, Terence, pull your socks up,' said Cynthia, helping out behind the counter. 'You've got my granddaughter to feed.'

I know I used to grumble to you about how she scared away the customers with her witch's nails and wardrobe and forthright manner, but really she was a great help.

She tried to get things back, for your sake. For all our sakes. Not just helping with the shop but arranging things. I remember that first fortnight, how she bombarded us with events. They were something to hold on to, ledges in the cliff-face, and the calendar became full of them. Her writing took over July, August, September, bursting out of date boxes with its capital letters and excessive punctuation. Bryony's Cello Lesson! Harrogate Antiques Fair!! Knaresborough Horse Show!!!!

Then there was her special meal she was already planning for no specified purpose. 'I'm inviting my old am dram friends,' she said. 'We're going to the Box Tree. It's got a Michelin star, apparently, and just had a refurbishment. You have to book months in advance, so if I want it for August I'm going to have to arrange it now. Do you both want to come?'

You were on the sofa, in your jodhpurs, ready to go to the stables. 'Yes, I'll come,' you said, much to my relief.

'Yes, Cynthia, of course,' I said, realising how important it seemed to her. 'I'd love to be there.'

'Very good,' she said. 'I'll write it on the calendar.'

You said little in the car, en route to the stables. I remember leaving you there, and feeling what I had felt at the funeral. That strange sensation of departing myself, a leaking out of my soul, complete with the darkening sense of vision. And then on my return, of course, I saw him. Denny. It was getting dark and so, when I turned towards the paddock and saw this sweating figure in running clothes, shining pale in the car headlights, I thought it might be a hallucination. I blinked him away but he was still there, staring straight at me.

I got out and told him to leave. He walked away, giving me a look of steely resolution, before continuing his run. Then I called to you, do you remember? And we had that row as we walked Turpin back to his stable. Apparently you had no idea what he was doing there. Apparently you hated him just as much as I did. Apparently he'd never been to gawp at you before.

You were perfectly convincing, and I was perfectly convinced, even if I had the sense that I had been woken up to something. There was so much that was precious in my life that I had been leaving open and undefended. 'I'm sorry, Petal,' I said. 'I shouldn't have raised my voice.' And you nodded and watched the houses slide past, perhaps wishing you were behind their square, golden windows, happily lost in another girl's Tuesday night.

I remember trying to sort out your brother's belongings. I sat there, on his bed, and felt the foreignness of the room. Posters of films I had never heard of. Unfathomable technology I didn't even realise he owned. Magazines covered with women who didn't look like women, women who looked so inhuman they might have been designed by an Italian sports car manufacturer.

I went through his school bag and found a letter he never gave me. It was from his headmaster, informing me that he had missed two of Mr Weeks' history lessons. The letter dated from March, before Mr Weeks had lost his job. I remembered him from the time he had come into the shop with his wife and his son George, to buy the pine mule chest. A tall yeti of a man who could have been quite a bully in the classroom, I imagined.

It was strange, being in his room. Reuben's presence was so real, contained as it was in all those objects, those possessions that reminded me how little I had understood him. With Cynthia's help we eventually packed a lot of stuff away in the attic. You helped with some of it, didn't you?

Though the thing I really need to tell you concerns his bicycle. As you know, I popped an advertisement in the window, offering it for twenty-five pounds. Within a day a woman had called and arranged to come in and buy it for her son. A Scottish lady with a long face that reminded me rather of the aboriginal statues on Easter Island.

I was retrieving the bicycle from the shed when the darkness crowded around me and I again felt that peculiar sensation at the back of my brain. Only this time it was stronger. It was as though someone was turning a dial in my mind, sliding it across frequencies, trying to find a different station. The feeling was at its most intense as I patted the saddle and let the Scottish lady wheel the bicycle away from me. I stood there for a while, in this kind of vague trance, watching her roll it down the street. I stayed there until the bicycle disappeared, and the sensation stopped, leaving my mind restored to its comforting mode of sadness.

*

As your former hero Pablo Casals once put it, to be a musician is to recognise the soul that lives in objects. A soul that may be made most visible by a Steinway or a Stradivari, or may be most well expressed by a Bach or a Mozart, but that is always there, in every thing of substance.

Of course, I am not a musician. I sell antiques, but the same knowledge applies. You sit all day in a shop, with the old clocks and the tables and the chairs, the plates and the bureaus, and you feel just like them. Just another object that has lived through events it could not change, crafted and transformed, forced to sit and wait in a kind of limbo, its fate as unknown as all the others'.

A customer came in one afternoon – a bullish man of the Yorkshire mould. The sort of chap within whom arrogance and ignorance compete for top billing. He grumbled his way around from price tag to price tag, telling Cynthia and myself that he'd be very surprised if we'd get this much for an art nouveau figurine, or that much for a reading table.

'Oh,' said Cynthia. 'But it's rosewood.'

'Makes no difference,' the man said.

'And it's early Georgian.'

'Early Mesopotamian wouldn't justify that price.'

By that point, I'd had enough.

'There are two types of customer for antiques,' I told him. 'There are those who appreciate an object's soul, and understand that, truly, even the smallest items – the sauce ladles, the thimbles, the silver barrel nutmeg graters – can only ever be undervalued. These I would call the true aficionados, the people who appreciate all the lives that have grated with, or worn, or poured, or sat at, or cried near, or dreamed upon, or cried against, or fallen in love in the same room as such things. These are the people who like to frequent an establishment such as Cave Antiques.'

He stood there, mirroring Cynthia's widening mouth and eyes, as unlikely to interrupt as the figure in his hand. The Girl with a Tambourine, decorated in green and pink enamels. I had bought it originally as part of a pair. The other one had dropped and smashed when I had collided with the chest on my way to reach Reuben, the night he died.

I continued: 'Whereas the other type, the type I might just see before me now, is the customer who sees an object as the sum of the materials with which it has been made. The customer who does not understand or acknowledge the hands that went into its making, or the centuries-long affection which various and long-dead owners have bestowed upon said item. No, these people are ignorant of such matters. They don't care for them. They see numbers where they should see beauty. They look at the face of a brass dial clock and see only the time.'

The man stood there, almost as bemused as myself by this outburst. 'I was going to buy this for my wife's birthday,' he said, placing the art nouveau figure back where it came from. 'But with service like this I think I'll take my custom elsewhere.'

After he left I had Cynthia to deal with. 'Terence, what on earth has got into you?'

'Nothing,' I said. 'I just didn't like the way he was talking to you.'

'Good God, Terence. I'm old and ugly enough to look after myself. We just lost a sale there.'

'I know, I'm sorry. It wasn't about him. I'm sorry.'

She sighed. 'You know what you need, don't you?'

I shook my head.

'You need to get away. You and Bryony. A holiday. I could look after the shop for a week.'

A holiday. Even the word seemed preposterous. A dancing jester at a wake, handing out picture postcards. It prompted a fleeting blink of a memory. Heading south on a French motorway with you and Reuben asleep in the back, your bodies curved towards each other like closed brackets.

'No, Cynthia, I don't think so,' I said, but all afternoon the idea grew and grew.

Maybe it wasn't so preposterous after all. Maybe this was our opportunity to restore things. To pick up all the broken pieces and put things back the way they once were. Yes, this was the chance to heal our fractured souls.

Ever since the funeral I had been aware of slight changes to your behaviour.

Instead of the sombre strains of Pablo Casals, or your own cello, I would hear a different kind of music coming from your room. A violent and ugly kind of noise that I would ask you to turn down almost every evening.

You rarely practised your cello, now. You still went to your lesson at the music college every week, but when I asked how it went I'd get shrugs or small hums in return. A friend I had never heard about – Imogen – suddenly became someone you had to call every evening. Your bedroom door would always be closed and I would some-times stand there behind it, trying to work out if you were on your bed or at your computer. I noticed, once, when you stepped out, that you'd taken your poster of Pablo Casals down from the wall. The old cello maestro who had always been such an inspiration.

It seemed incredible. I thought that man was your idol.

You had adored his interpretation of Bach's cello suites. You had even ordered that old footage from the library. Pablo, aged ninety-four, conducting a special concert at the United Nations. The tiny old man, his time-creased face reflecting perfectly the strain and emotion of the orchestral movements until there seemed to be no difference between them, the man and the music, so that each refrain heard in that grand hall seemed to be a direct leaking of his soul.

You had devoured his memoirs, and told me to read them too. The story I remember now was when he and a few companions walked up Mount Tamalpais near San Francisco. Pablo was in his eighties, and had felt very weak and tired that morning, but to the bemusement of his friends had insisted that he still wanted to climb the mountain. They agreed to go with him but then, during the descent, disaster struck. Do you remember that story?

A large boulder had become dislodged further up the mountainside and was now hurtling towards them. The boulder missed all of his companions but, having seen it, Pablo froze. As it shot past, the giant rock managed to hit and smash Pablo's left hand, his fingering hand. His friends looked with horror at the mangled, blood-soaked fingers, but Pablo showed no sign of pain or fear. In fact, he was overwhelmed with a kind of relief, and thanked God he would never have to play the cello again.

'A gift can also be a curse,' wrote the man who had felt enslaved by his art since he was a child. The man who had anxiety attacks before every single performance.

This last fact that had always comforted you when playing in public. And so it made no sense, with the annual York Drama and Music Festival not too far away, that you would want to take down his poster. A trivial issue, I suppose, but one I viewed as symptomatic of a broader change.

Maybe I should have been firmer with you then.

Perhaps I shouldn't have let you shut yourself away. At the time, though, I imagined this was your way of grieving. In tribute to the life of your brother you were shrouding yourself in the same mystery.

What I didn't realise was that this retreat would continue, that you would slip further and further away from me until the point at which I couldn't call you back.

As I flicked through the travel section of the newspaper I saw it – a weak black-and-white photograph of the Colosseum. 'Price includes flights and six-night stay in the Hotel Raphael.'

The city of faith and antiquity and perspective, the place

people go to mourn and accept the transient nature of human life, where old temples and frescoes outlive us all. Such was my thinking.

Oh, pity the folly of a desperate mind!

Do you remember that sunny evening we walked to Cynthia's and I had to stop halfway down Winchelsea Avenue? You asked me what the matter was and I told you I didn't know, that I just felt a bit dizzy. It was the feeling I had experienced at the church, and when selling Reuben's bicycle. A darkening of vision accompanied by a kind of tingling towards the rear of my skull. Similar, I suppose, to pins and needles, only this felt warmer, as though tiny fires were raging through the dark spaces of my mind, generating sparks that wriggled and danced before losing their glow. And these fires were burning those parts of me that knew when and where I was, leaving me for a moment deprived of all identity.

I turned to see the house I had passed, number 17, and it looked as depressing as all the others on the street. I told myself to keep my head. It was only a dose of the shudders, I reasoned. A result of frayed nerves and poor sleep, nothing more. Although if you ever wondered why we never walked that way again, you have the reason.

By the time we reached Cynthia's bungalow I was feeling much better, and quite hungry. Although of course one can never be quite hungry enough for one of Cynthia's curries.

'It's an authentic Goan recipe,' she said, as it slopped onto our plates. 'I printed it out from the computer. It was meant to be mild but I'm worried I might have overdone it a little with the chilli.'

'Oh, I'm sure it's fine,' I told her, as I tried to avert my eyes from the charcoal sketch of a nude on the table. We must have arrived before she had time to frame it. A study of creased female flesh from one of her life-drawing classes.

'Mmm, it's lovely,' you said, enjoying your first mouthful. You actually sounded like you meant it.

Cynthia smiled at you, and seemed for a moment mildly entranced. 'Oh good. Good. Not too hot?'

'No,' you said, although within five minutes you were in the kitchen topping up your glass of water.

'I've thought about what you said,' I told Cynthia, in a hushed tone, as you ran the tap. 'And I think you might be right. I'm going to book a holiday.'

'Good, Terence. Good. Have you told Bryony?'

'No,' I said. 'I'm going to keep it a surprise.'

'Well, maybe you should consult her first.'

I shook my head. 'She's always loved surp—'

You were back, drinking from your glass, feeling our admiring eyes upon your neck. Two old ducks in awe of a swan.

Somehow, we made it through the curry. A feat of endurance on all our parts I imagine, and Cynthia tried to humour us with some of her old am dram stories. 'It was on the opening night of *The Glass Menagerie* . . . Ray was in his toga . . . I was sitting in the green room . . . It was the third act . . . There I was, queen of the fairies . . . And someone broke wind in the audience . . . Oh, our faces!'

And then she went quiet, keeping her dark lips in position even after her smile had died. For quite a while she

26

stared into some indeterminate space between us, as the sadness shone in her eyes.

'It was less than a year ago, wasn't it?' she said, after a while. 'When Reuben did his work experience at the theatre?'

I tried to think. Yes. It must have been. You had spent a week at the music college, arranged weeks in advance, while Reuben was still unsorted right up to the last moment. If it wasn't for Cynthia having a word with David wotsit then he'd have been in all sorts of trouble at school.

'Yes,' you said. 'It was a year ago.'

Your grandmother gave a sad laugh. 'Poor boy. Having to do it the week of *Joseph and the Amazing Technicolor Dreamcoat.* Stuck outside looking after a donkey every day!'

'Yes,' I said. 'Yes.'

'Did you ever see it?' Cynthia asked me. 'You weren't there, were you? When he was struggling to push that bloody creature on the stage?'

'No,' I said. 'No. I had a meeting, I think. A dealer. I can't remember.'

You smiled a distant smile. 'I was there.'

'Yes,' Cynthia nodded. 'Yes, you were. You were.' She saw you looking at her unframed sketch and waited for the silence to run its course. 'Now, I must tell you what happened at life drawing . . .'

Two days before the end of your term we sat upstairs, eating breakfast together. You were in the same uniform you had been in the previous morning, your hair in an identical style, yet as you sat there eating your limp cornflakes I couldn't help but notice that you looked transformed.

'Dad? What's up? You're creeping me out.'

I couldn't speak. I couldn't tell you that I was made numb, made petrified by your sudden beauty.

Of course, you had always been a pleasure on the eye. I had never been able to ignore the way strangers had shied away from Reuben's frowning, birthmarked face to focus on yours. Nor had I been surprised when Mrs Weeks had wanted to paint your portrait. Yet rather than a source of pride, that morning I must confess your face triggered a startling fear.

Someone had overfilled the cup. You were never meant to look quite this way. Oh certainly, your mother had been a gorgeous creature in her youth, yet her beauty was an acquired taste. Like Bow porcelain. Or art nouveau. When I first met her she required a certain Byronic imagination to render her wholly perfect. Those slight, asymmetric flaws were part of her charm.

What troubled me was the obvious nature of your loveliness. In that tiny last skip from girlhood to womanhood, in that most subtle overnight alteration, you had bloomed from a limber elf-child into a Juliet, a Dido, a Venus. My fear was about the impact this beauty would have on the male population. After all, boys don't acquire such taste. It is there from the start, formed in the bliss of their womb-warmed dreams, their sole incentive for being born.

I knew that this spelt trouble. I knew that you would soon be inspiring the wrong kind of attention. Boys would buzz around you and I feared you would enjoy that buzz, welcome it, walk like a novice beekeeper straight into it, unaware of any potential sting.

'Dad. Stop staring. It's impolite.'

Tell me, how do you respond? 'My daughter, my darling Petal, you must never leave the house again.'

No.

28

'Your eyes,' I said. 'Have you done something to them? Are you wearing make-up?'

'A bit.'

'For school?'

'You can wear make-up to school now, Dad. It's not 1932. It's not a nunnery.'

'Green eyeshadow?'

'It's two days before the holidays. Nobody cares.'

I knew I shouldn't have been overly concerned. After all, there were only girls at school. But what about afterwards? What about your walk home? You must surely have crossed paths with the lowly specimens from St John's. In my mind I saw you laughing. In my mind I saw an anonymous boy's anonymous arm around your shoulder, steering you down a leafy, houseless path. And then the vision became less anonymous. It became him. It became that boy, Denny.

'I will drive you to school. And I'll pick you up.'

'Dad, why? You haven't driven me to school since I was twelve. It's only up the road.'

'I worry about you, that's all. Please, let me drive you. And let me pick you up. Cynthia will be here to look after the shop. Please.'

I squeezed so much into that final 'please' that a flash of your old self returned. You probably realised I was thinking about Reuben, that I was feeling guilty for letting him slip beyond my radar so many times.

You shrugged. 'Do whatever you like.'

In the car I told you about Rome.

'Rome?' You said it as though it were the name of a former friend who had let you down.

'I booked it last week.'

'Why didn't you tell me?' I could feel the blast of your stare, even as I kept my eyes on the road.

'Well, I thought it would be a rather jolly surprise.'

'I'm meant to be going out with Imogen next Monday.'

'Going out?'

'I mean, going around. To see her.'

'Well, can't it wait? I'm sure she'll still be visible the following Monday.'

'When do we come back?'

'On the thirtieth, so the world won't end. And anyway, you always told me you wanted to go to Rome. You've wanted to sit on the Spanish Steps since you were ten. Since *Roman Holiday*. Or have you changed?'

You scowled. 'What does that mean?'

'It means: have you changed?'

'Since I was ten?'

'No. Since . . . never mind.'

Two boys crossed at the lights, nudging and staring, making wild simian noises at the sight of you. You scrunched your nose in disgust but I detected the smile. Embarrassed, flattered.

'You still want to see the Sistine Chapel, don't you?'

You shrugged. 'I suppose.'

'And Petal, I couldn't help noticing, why have you taken the poster down from your room?'

'What poster?'

'The Pablo Casals poster. I thought he was your hero.'

Another shrug. 'It gives me the creeps.'

'What?'

'At night. I feel like he's looking at me. I feel his eyes staring at me.'

It felt like blasphemy. Those harmless eyes of that former

ambassador for peace, those eyes that had to be closed every time he played to a public audience. My anger was tempered by a guilty memory of me standing in your doorway, watching you sleep.

'Well, I don't see why you couldn't have put it on the opposite wall,' I said.

'What's the big deal?' Your voice was fading now, the anger at a dull pitch, as though a part of you was already beyond the school gates, inside the day you had to live.

'There's no "big deal." Anyway, I think Rome will be the perfect tonic, for both of us. Don't you?'

You never answered. I pulled up by a lamp post, you stepped out of the car and I fought to let you go, for you to leave that sanctuary and get sucked in, like a weak molecule, towards that swarm of girls making their way to the school entrance.

'Bye, Bryony. Be careful.'

And then I stayed there a second longer, gripping the steering wheel as though it was the last solid thing in the world, and found the courage needed to ignore the black flies and Reuben's whisper in my ear – 'Look, Dad, I'm getting stronger' – and drive home.

Every life, as with every story, has its various turning points. Often they are clearly marked as such. The symptoms of dizzy nausea that signify first love. A wedding. A graduation. A sudden windfall. The death of those we need so much we take them for granted.

At other times the turning point is less clear. Something shifts, and we may sense it shifting, but the cause is as invisible to us as a swerve in the wind.

Do you remember how hot Rome was? Do you remember that argument we had in the queue to get into St Peter's? That Vatican policewoman had handed you a paper cape, so God wouldn't take offence at your naked shoulders.

You'd accepted it with a smile, of course, as you hadn't changed so much as to be impolite to strangers. But the moment she was gone you said, in a quietly forceful tone: 'I'm not wearing it.'

'I don't think you have a choice.'

A year, or even three months before and that would have been enough. You would have put the cape on and smiled at how silly you looked and forgotten all about it once you were inside the basilica. We would have wandered around with pilgrims and other tourists – some caped, like yourself – and marvelled together at Michelangelo's dome and all the other Renaissance treasures contained inside.

But no, you were adamant. 'I'm not wearing it,' you kept saying. 'I'm not wearing a lime-green cape. I'll look like a tent.'

Never in your fourteen years on the planet had I seen such a look of resolution on your face.

'Bryony,' I said, 'don't be ridiculous. No one's going to care what you look like.'

'I'm not Catholic,' you said.

I drew attention to a Japanese woman, in front in the queue, putting her cape on without complaint.

'I doubt she's Catholic. Now come on, don't be childish.'

Don't be childish. Ironic, of course. If you had been six or seven, then you would have wanted to wear the thing. If you had been eight or ten or even twelve then none of God's police officers would have found your bare shoulders guilty of any offence.

I can see your face. Too childish and too grown-up all at once, still saying it like a mantra, mumbled through your lips: 'I'm not wearing it, I'm not wearing it . . .'

People were looking at us now. More people than would have ever looked if you'd have worn the cape. Among the gazers were two American boys, who I surmised were about three years older than you. They had no parents with them, and I suppose you had noticed them too. Maybe this was why you didn't want to wear the cape. They were laughing, anyway, and their laughter flushed your cheeks. I turned and stared at them, for your sake, but they didn't notice me. They just carried on in hysterics: their long, clumsy limbs falling on and around each other, like reincarnated puppies.

One last time, your voice in a whisper: 'Please, Dad. Don't make me wear the cape.'

I turned back to your face, half in my shadow, and in a moment of weakness I decided not to argue.

'I can wait for you there on the step,' you said, answering my unvoiced question.

I think this was the moment I told you about Florence Nightingale's experience of St Peter's. Of course, when you were younger the Lady of the Lamp had been one of your heroines, and you had even turned your room into a

Crimean battlefield, dressing the wounds of Angelica and all your other dolls. But when I told you that no event in Florence's life had ever matched her first visit to St Peter's you were unmoved, and by this point we were close to the entrance.

'I'll be over there,' you said, handing me the cape.

Before I knew it you were walking off, assuming it had been agreed. By this point I was being motioned through a metal detector by a surly, and armed, member of God's constabulary. I suppose I could have still followed you, and made even more of a scene, but I somehow managed to assure myself you would be all right.

I think I imagined that you would sit there and brood about how foolish you had been to neglect such a chance of enriching your mind. I thought of it as a kind of lesson, something that would highlight the mistake in your behaviour and correct it.

So I went inside, told myself you would be all right, and tried to feel the splendid glory of the place.

I remembered the last time I was there, with your mother. Then, we had been moved with a mutual emotion that seemed as overwhelming as the architectural proportions themselves. That almost paradoxical feeling of diminished human scale, paired with a sudden swelling of the spiritual self, had been like nothing we had known on this earth. We had marvelled at the dome, and then climbed up to the lantern to see Rome as God might see it, a beige bowl of intersecting histories, rendered so beautifully coherent your mother had tears in her eyes.

This time though, I stayed at ground level and felt the empty terror of the place. I just shuffled along with the other tourists, and paused for a short while in front of Michelangelo's *Pietà*, staring at the sculpture through a sheet of bulletproof glass. It still had an impact though. Indeed, the glass added another layer to the narrative. It seemed to suggest the distance between the dying Christ and the modern world, a distance brought about by the desire to protect.

An equivalent desire was there in the face of the Virgin Mary, sitting strong and father-like, with the feeble-bodied child across her lap. I wished you had been there by my side to see it. The foundation of a religious faith expressed as a parent's tragedy. A parent whose son had gone away from her, out into a world that killed him. And then too late he was returned to the safety of the parent's lap. A safety that meant nothing now.

I stayed there for a short while, as tears glazed my eyes. Tourists stood all around, with star-struck faces, ready to tick off another sight before moving on. Of course, none of them displayed any understanding of what Michelangelo was trying to say. They just made the same pleasant mumbles as they had when they stood in the Sistine Chapel, casting their eyes down from the ceiling through the Last Judgement and an underworld that stopped above their heads.

Michelangelo's message to me, standing in front of the *Pietà*, was clear. Agony awaits if you let your child out into a world of lost souls. You must protect her, and you must never let her go.

I walked away, without seeing anything else. No chapel, no altar, no memorial or papal tomb could steer me from my course. I went outside and took a moment to find you. For a second I thought you had gone. There were too many people to make sense of the scene, but then my eyes found the column, and the step, and you sitting exactly where you had said. I rushed over, and didn't notice the two American boys until the last moment. I can see that appalled look on your face as I approached. A shame so intense it spilled into hatred.

'Bryony, shall we go?'

You rolled your eyes, and the boy-pups laughed and said, 'See you later.'

'See you later?' I asked, as we walked past the Egyptian obelisk towards the Via della Conciliazione.

You shrugged, and said nothing.

A figure of speech, I told myself, as I glared again at your bare shoulders. Nothing to sweat about.

And yet, in that delirious July heat, it was impossible not to sweat. 'Right,' I said. 'The Forum's the next on the list. I don't think you'll require a cape for that.'

I fell from the heavens through a night-blue sky, dropping fast as my body gained form and mass. It felt like an eternity, waiting for the flat earth to come into view. A dark carcass of land bleeding moonlit lakes and oceans. I was heading straight towards the water but landed in my bed feeling worse than ever. Knowing something was wrong, I got up and left the hotel room to go and knock on your door.

There was no answer, so I tried again.

Nothing.

Try to put yourself in my shoes – although, to be precise I was barefoot – as I stood out in that hallway. 'Bryony,' I said your name softly at first. 'Bryony, it's me.'

The silence scared me, so I kept knocking it away. Voices from other rooms told me, in numerous European languages, to shut the whatever up. I stopped knocking, went downstairs, and explained to the old man behind the desk that something could be the matter. He blew a long sigh, as though I were a regret he had just remembered, but eventually he gave me the key. When I got back upstairs and opened your door I sank at the sight of your empty bed. I scanned the room, and sent your name into every corner. There was nothing but clothes and magazines and all those other empty parts of you.

For your tenth birthday I had bought you a selection of films. *Whistle Down the Wind. The Railway Children. Meet Me in St Louis.* And your mother's favourite, *Roman Holiday.* It became your favourite, too, and I saw no problem with that at the time. 'Suitable for all' was the advice of the British Board of Film Classification. Now, though, I hold Audrey Hepburn at least partially responsible for your antics in the Eternal City. A young princess escaping her responsibilities by heading off into the Roman night, to find love and freedom and Gregory Peck. The message of that film clearly infected your vulnerable mind. Why else would you leave your hotel room in that same city to search for whatever adventure you thought was out there?

I walked those ancient streets without direction, for how could I know which direction to take? You could have gone anywhere.

I remember heading down the Via Condotti, where mannequins in designer dresses stared out from dark windows.

A girl about your height turned the corner and I called your name. She was coming towards me, a walking silhouette, but didn't answer. My heart died as I realised it wasn't you, but a grubby-faced street urchin carrying a baby. Not even the baby was real. A plastic doll, which she threatened to throw towards me. She hissed at the same time, and then said something in a language I'm sure wasn't Italian.

'Money,' she clarified, realising I couldn't understand. 'Mun-eeee.'

I kept on going, at a quickening pace, while the ragged

gypsy girl stood in the street hissing curses, snake words, to poison my luck.

I alternated between a walk and a jog as I trod those streets, feeling a rush of hope at the sight of every moving shadow, at the sound of every new footstep, only to plunge into deeper despair when you were not the source.

This went on for hours, this jogging after every new hope, asking drunks and homeless emperors and men stocking up newspaper kiosks if they had seen you. Of course, it was all futile. Really, I should have returned to the hotel and waited for you in the foyer.

Light came, and the city slipped slowly into its daytime colours. The jaundiced yellows of the old and dying.

I had to head back to the hotel. I knew that. But I also knew that if you weren't there I would fall into a nightmare beyond all imagining. 'Bryony,' I called, down every deserted street. What despair your name contained when it was unanswered!

What if you had been kidnapped? I know this sounds ridiculous to you now, and maybe even to me, but I did not know where you were. There was no note in your room to explain where you had gone, and in the absence of explanation the mind torments itself with all manner of horrendous things.

I walked back slowly, as time and hope were equal partners in this, through the Piazza di Spagna, passing the deserted Spanish Steps and the house where Keats wasted away. As I walked by the fountain I sensed his ghost, alone and palely loitering at the window, trapped for eternity in the city he thought would heal him. But not even Keats, that great interpreter of the human soul, could offer me any clue or comfort.

I returned to the hotel and asked the man behind the reception desk if he had seen you.

'I am sorry, sir, but I am only just beginning,' he said, as oblivious to my pain as to the strange poetry of his words. He was a younger man, a less obvious misanthrope, but such was my delirium that I had thought it was the same one as before.

I was, by this point, quite dizzy with fear, and again my mind was beginning to fuzz and tingle.

I must have muttered some kind of thanks and then climbed the stairs up to the third floor, as an ashy darkness tinged away at the periphery of my vision.

If you were there, in your room, I was going to hug you and kiss your forehead and stroke your hair. I was going to tell you 'I love you' and you were going to tell me 'I'm sorry, I didn't mean to worry you' and I wasn't even going to think about telling you off. The relief was going to be so much, so perfect and so complete, that it would be impossible to scold you. It is peculiar, isn't it? The way our minds bargain with fate when every future possibility still hangs in the balance.

I knocked on your door, as the darkness crept closer. Were you asleep? The seconds ticked by without you answering, and I felt the corridor tilt under my feet. I had to steady myself by placing a hand against the wall. I knocked again. 'Bryony, are you there? Petal? Bryony?' This time no one told me to be quiet, although I doubt I would have been aware if they had. The rest of the world could have slipped out of space and time and I wouldn't have noticed. The only thing that mattered was concealed behind that door, 305, and I was about to go back down to the reception desk and get the man to give me the key when I heard something. You. Your feet padding across the carpet. 'Bryony?' The door opened and you were there, rubbing the dreams out of your eyes.

Had you been asleep, or were you just pretending? Was that delay in answering a part of the act? Were you aware that I was aware? Oh, the heavy weight of trivial questions!

'Dad?'

I can tell you, in all honesty, that I have never felt so much love for you as I did inside that moment. To see you standing there, alive and intact, was all I had wanted. And there you were, in that baggy Picasso-print T-shirt, yawning like a baby. I know this must be hard for you to believe, given how things progressed, but I swear it is true. I wanted to hug you, I wanted to thank you for being such a miracle, but then I said it.

'Where were you?' and I kept saying it, the question backing you into the room. 'Where did you go?' My head was heating up, the mental bonfires raging away at my being, and the sunlit room was sliding into shade. I felt something rising within me. A violent force that weakened me, causing me to lose control.

'Nowhere. I've been here. I've just woken up.' Your lies, your lies, your lies. 'What are you on about? You're mad. I've been here. I've been asleep.'

I caught it, on your breath, something corrupt beneath the toothpaste. 'You smell of smoke. And drink.' Then you laughed. You shouldn't have laughed, Bryony. And you said a profanity, which I will euphemistically put as 'go away', the word I cannot write so ugly and vile in your mouth that when I did it, when I struck your face, I wasn't really striking your face but the word on your tongue, this alien thing that had got inside you, this new presence that wanted boys and didn't want your father. And the fuzziness cleared, along with the dark, as though the outside force that had been pressing in suddenly fled like a villain. And I know this was it, I know this was the pivotal moment when the wind swerved in our story, and even now I can still hear your sobs and see your hand on your reddening cheek and I said it then and I'll still say it now, 'I'm sorry, I'm sorry, I'm so, so sorry,' but I know these words are worthless healers and cannot restore a single thing.

*

Oh, this is useless. I should stop right now. What is the point? I can see that look of sickened disdain on your face. If only I could put my soul into these words, if only I could make you feel precisely what I felt, then you would see the truth.

I suppose I expect too much. Every writer, every artist since the first cave painters has been trying to find a way to articulate their experience and are we any closer to seeing ourselves as we truly are? No. The distance we have to travel is exactly the same as it always was. So how can I expect to do what no writer has ever managed?

People say that humans are the superior species on this planet because we have minds that are conscious of their own existence, and therefore we have the capacity to create a culture, to create an art. I look at sheep, at peace on the moors, and wonder exactly how much of a delusion are our arrogant souls prepared to share?

There may be no bovid equivalent of a Michelangelo but there is no need for one. They accept their existence in a way we never will. They do not try to build artistic mirrors – books, paintings, orchestral symphonies – by which to capture and reflect their own nature. Even if they could, they wouldn't. They have that understanding in-built. All these human things, all these arts, these religions, these sciences, what are they really but ways of trying to make up that difference? If we could accept like animals then there would be no Sistine Ceiling, no *Madame Bovary*, no Fantasy and Fugue. Out of our mistakes, out of our pain, arrives everything we love in this world. All that humans create serves solely to lessen the terror of existence. The terror that Beethoven and Keats and Van Gogh and every supreme artist has ever felt, the collective terror of a humanity that still stumbles around, looking at dark and untrustworthy shadows rather than true reflections.

If we found a perfect art, a perfect mirror to reflect our plight, one which helped us see ourselves from every angle, then it would mean the end of all creative endeavour. Art would have killed itself. Or it would live on in the way it lives in horses and cats and sheep. The art of living, and letting live, that our human souls have yet to learn.

It was a week after Rome that I first met Imogen. I say 'met' although I realise this is somewhat of an overstatement. It would be more accurate to say that I spotted her in various locations around my house, the way a birdwatcher might spot a chaffinch in his garden. Every time I got closer, trying to identify her chief characteristics, you both immediately took flight.

Now I was close-up, I didn't like what I saw. What had happened to your other friends? What had happened to Holly, for instance? I used to enjoy hearing your mini string section when you practised together. Or what about that girl from the stables? Abigail, was it? That good old-fashioned hearty girl, who loved looking around the shop. I always thought she was lovely.

These were studious, freshly aired girls. The type of friends that justified your school fees.

Imogen was something different. How different, I couldn't quite tell, but I needed to find out.

'You must be Imogen,' I said, to the face behind the fringe, when I cornered you both on the stairs.

'I must,' she told the carpet, and then you gave me that unforgiving stare you had recently cultivated, as if I had violated some secret pact simply by identifying your friend.

Did she know about what had happened in Rome? I have no idea what you had told her about me or what you said to each other in your room. Your music drowned out your voices, and that was probably its point.

Did you ever read the book on philosophy I bought you for your birthday? If you did you might remember the section on Plato's cave. Well, let me tell you that to be a parent is to be permanently confined to that cave, forever trying to understand shadows on the wall. Shadows that only half make sense, and may be easily and disastrously misunderstood. You can never understand what really goes on in the world your child keeps from view. The reports you hear from her mouth are the shadows against the rocks, shadows that can't be interpreted without stepping outside, into the light.

'Terence?' Cynthia was calling me from the shop. 'Terence? Terence?'

You see, that is what I had decided to do. Ever since Rome I had decided to stop trusting your mouth and start trusting my eyes.

'We're going out,' you told me, that Wednesday afternoon.

'Oh?' I said. 'May I ask where?'

'Terence?' called Cynthia, her voice rising now to a theatrical pitch.

'In a minute,' I called back. Then softer to you: 'Where?'

'Around the shops', you said, in the minimalist fashion I was becoming used to.

'Fine,' I said. 'Fine.'

You expected more, I could see that. Some kind of obstruction. But I gave you nothing.

'We'll be back,' you said. 'Later.'

'What time?' you expected. But I gave you: 'Fine.'

The defiance that had creased your forehead softened into blank confusion.

'Okay,' you said, almost as a question. 'See you . . . later.'

'All right. See you later. And see you too, Imogen.'

You left and I watched you walk out of the back door, into that fearful day.

I ran into the shop.

'Cynthia, can you look after everything here for a bit? I won't be long.'

Your grandmother gave me one of her unforgiving looks. That tight, crinkled mouth offset with those tough eyes that once had her cast as Hedda Gabler. 'Terence, where have you been? I was calling you. Mrs Weeks came in wanting a word.'

'I was upstairs. Listen, I've got to nip out.'

'But, Terence –'

And so I left the shop and followed you, out of Cave Antiques, out into the light. I followed you down Blossom Street, through the city walls and down the length of Micklegate. I held my distance when you disappeared inside a clothes shop. I held my breath when you crossed over the road, turning your head in my direction. You didn't see me.

You carried on, over the river, on to Ousegate. I bumped into Peter, the vicar, and he blockaded me with mild smiles and charitable words. He asked how we were bearing up.

'Fine,' I told him, although the anxious looks over his shoulder probably gave a different story. 'Honestly, we're getting there. We have our bad days but . . .' I saw you turning left, heading out of my view. 'Listen, I'm terribly sorry, Peter, but I'm in a rush. Another time.'

I ran towards Parliament Street and saw two crowds of youths loitering around the benches near the public toilets. The nearest group was made up of boys sitting on stationary bicycles. Or standing: eating chips, sucking on cigarettes or typing into their mobile telephones. Boys wearing the kind of clothes Reuben always wanted. Trainers, tracksuits, their faces shaded by caps or hooded tops. The warm fuzziness inside my mind returned for a second.

I recognised one of them as the small boy I had seen vomiting his innards out onto the pavement the night Reuben died. He nudged his friend and nodded over to the other group. The boy had his back to me but turned, smiling. The smile died as he looked across. It was him. It was Denny.

I followed his gaze over to the others. I scanned this

second tribe. Boys with odd haircuts, dressed for the French Revolution. A rather rotund girl with a painted Pierrot tear on her cheek. T-shirts with macabre designs and Gothic fonts. The Remorse. The Pains of Sleep. The Cleopatras. Daughters of Albion. Instructions for My Funeral. Teenage Baudelaires, plugged into music machines or eating bagel sandwiches.

My heart fell as I spotted you, right at the very centre.

The boys buzzing around your beauty as I had feared. I saw one of them talking animatedly to you and Imogen.

He seemed older than the rest, rake-thin, dressed in tightest black, and despite the weather he was wearing a blood-red scarf. He had a long, pale, fleshless face with sleepy eyes. A cadaverous face, Dickens would have said. What was he saying to make you both laugh? I itched – no, burned – to know.

There was someone else, on the furthest fringe of that group. A boy I recognised but didn't know why. A tall, over-weight boy trying loudly to fit in. He had blond hair with a pinkish fringe and wore thick-lens glasses. And then I realised. It was Mrs Weeks' son George.

Up until recently he had always accompanied his mother on her Saturday-morning visits. The reason it took so long to place him was that George Weeks had always struck me as a quiet, studious kind of child. For all his heft it had been easy to imagine him bullied, what with his bad breathing and shy manner. And having had his father teach at the school wouldn't have helped matters. I remember once trying to get Reuben to talk to him, as George was a year above him at St John's, but your brother slipped away and made an excuse, as was his fashion. (I remember the letter I had found in his schoolbag. Perhaps Reuben resisted George because he hated Mr Weeks. Or perhaps it was simply out of allegiance to his tribe. I don't know. I have no answers.)

I wondered if Mrs Weeks knew her son mixed in such circles. I wondered if she knew her asthmatic child was a smoker. I wondered what she would do if she did know these things.

Anyway, there he was, being loud and boisterous, trying like all the others to steal your attention. And there I was, peeping around the corner of Marks & Spencer, as invisible to both groups as the thousand shoppers and tourists that swarmed around.

It would have been a risk to move any closer so I had to stay there, unable to hear a word except for those of the African lady with the loudhailer, filling that carless street with the Book of Revelation.

'The kings of the earth, and the great men . . .' she raged with her fundamental anger, giving proof of nothing except its own doubt.

Denny's group began to laugh at the woman, and throw chips at her. All except Denny himself, whose dark, unreadable eyes were still staring at you.

'. . . and the rich men, and the chief captains, and the mighty men, and every bondman, and every free man, hid themselves in the dens and in the rocks of the mountains . . .'

I saw Denny walk away from his group, past the doors to the toilets and over towards you. The boy with the cadaverous face, the Uriah Heep face, turned and said something that Denny ignored. And then Denny spoke to you and you spoke back and I wished I could have read your lips, but all I had were the words of warning boomed angrily in my direction.

'. . . And said to the mountains and rocks, Fall on us, and hide us from the face of him that sitteth upon the throne . . .'

The words bulging her eyes, her eyes bulging her words.

'. . . and from the wrath of the Lamb: for the great day of his wrath is come, and who shall be able to stand?'

Uriah Heep pushed Denny away and Denny pushed him back, as the others tightened around them. Chips and insults flew through the air. Denny won the push and Uriah fell at your feet. I saw another of Denny's tribe wade in. It was the shaven-headed boy whom I had seen at the tennis courts, kicking Uriah in the stomach.

You looked at Imogen, scared, stranded in the middle of all this.

I had to do something.

I started walking, towards you, but things calmed.

Denny's tribe pulled the skinhead away as Denny himself disappeared out of the scene. Imogen helped Uriah to his feet.

I stood stuck to the ground as you walked away with your companions, to the rising cheer of Denny's friends. Any moment you were going to see me and I would have no excuse for leaving the shop. None that you would have believed. And, after Rome, I couldn't afford to push you further away. Inside the sun-red darkness of a blink I saw Reuben, crooked on the ground, and I took this as a final sign.

'God shall wipe all tears from their eyes.'

My watch told me it had been an hour. And enough of the old Terence was there to return me to the shop, to help Cynthia on this busy afternoon.

'Where on earth have you been?' she asked me, in a hiss quiet enough not to disturb the old couple having a browse around the furniture.

I found it difficult to answer. 'I had to . . . I went to . . . Bryony was . . .'

Cynthia closed her eyes and released an exasperated sigh. 'You didn't follow her, did you?'

The old couple glanced towards us, and made their silent decision to leave.

'Yes,' I said. 'Yes, I did. I followed her. But I'm back now, aren't I?'

'I don't know. Are you? Are you *back*, Terence?' The 'back' was given further emphasis with her ascending eyebrows.

'What is that supposed to mean?'

Cynthia inhaled, preparing for a verbal onslaught, but she changed her mind. Her tone softened. Her eyebrows lay back down. She stared over towards the spot where the old couple had been standing only moments before. 'Nothing, Terence. Nothing. I just think you might need someone to talk to.'

'Someone? What someone? About what?'

'A third party. A bereavement counsellor. Someone you don't know and can open up to. I found it so helpful, you know, when Helen . . . Knowing that I could go somewhere every Tuesday afternoon and sit and blubber away and make a show of myself.'

'No,' I said. The idea of sitting on a plastic chair in a room filled with mental-health leaflets and the smell of cheap instant coffee, talking to a total stranger about all this – well, it was abhorrent. 'No, I don't think so.'

She smiled, hopeful. 'Well, perhaps you should talk to me. Perhaps we should talk together. Perhaps it would do us both some good. It's not healthy, you know, to keep it all caged in. You can make a monster of your emotions by ignoring them. You need to open the doors every now and then. You need to let some air in.'

I sat down on the wooden stool, while Cynthia remained seated in the chair. 'Perhaps,' I said. And it was a faint but sincere perhaps. A soft echo of the old Terence, the Terence who knew what good advice was and how to take it.

'He was such a kind boy,' she said, the breadth of her smile increasing in line with the sadness in her eyes.

'Yes,' I said. 'He could be.'

She chuckled at something. 'I remember when he was at the bungalow and he said, "Grandma, why do you have all these twigs in vases?" And I gave him that book to look at. Andy Goldsworthy. Do you remember? He liked the ice sculptures. "Wow, that's well cool. How did he do that?" It's so strange, isn't it? It must have only been about two months ago. A Sunday. He still wanted a toffee after his meal though, didn't he? Oh no, he was never too old for a piece of Harrogate toffee!'

'No,' I said, struggling to remember that same Sunday. 'No, he wasn't.'

Cynthia filled the afternoon with anecdotes and stories from that finished and irretrievable world. I smiled and nodded and mumbled but had little to contribute. In truth, I was too busy thinking about you, and praying you would stay safe.

The prayer was rewarded. You returned at five to five, alone and intact, hating me no more and no less than when you had left.

'Your father and I have had a good chat, haven't we, Terence?' Cynthia told you, as you stood in the hallway.

'Yes,' I said. 'We have.'

Cynthia's widened eyes and nodding head gave my words an unwarranted endorsement.

You smiled, for your grandmother's benefit. 'Oh,' you said. 'Right. Good.' No more than that, I think.

And you trod softly upstairs, away from us, while Cynthia's whisper tried its futile best. 'See, there's nothing to worry about. She'll be all right. She'll find her own way home. Now, come on, be a good boy, Terence. Why don't you make us a lovely pot of tea?'

*

If you had always been a dream of a child, then Reuben was the dark sleep I could never comprehend. I struggled to compete with Cynthia's anecdotes, partly because even while he was alive Reuben never let me in. I had to pick up whatever clues I could, fragments of evidence that never gave me the complete picture: the vague comments of teachers; the half-formed mono-syllables that rumbled at the back of his throat; the sound of his feet walking across his bedroom; the friends he used to visit but never talked about. Yet there were occasions when I would gain a sharp glimpse into his state of mind. One incident, in particular, I remember very well. Now when was it?

You were practising for a school concert, so you still weren't home. That would make it a Wednesday, wouldn't it? Yes. And I'm reckoning it was about a week before you both turned fourteen. Yes, I'm sure it was. Anyway, the other details are much clearer.

I was in the shop, aware of Reuben's presence only as a series of sounds. The turn of his key, the slow clump of the back door as it closed behind him. I'm sure it was at this point I said, 'How was your day?' or something of equivalent non-significance. He didn't answer. Hardly unusual. He was probably lost in his own world. He might simply have been ignoring me. Whatever the reason, I thought nothing of it, as I was having a bit of a nightmare with the bureau I was trying to restore.

After however long, I heard feet leave his room and head for the bathroom, then the sound of running water from upstairs. He had the tap on at full blast.

I left the bureau and went upstairs. Pausing on the landing I heard something else, above the water.

Now, to describe it. The noise.

A kind of panting, I suppose. What sounded like fast and

heavy breathing but accompanied by an occasional whimpering. In retrospect, I realise I should have opened the door sooner. But I didn't. This inaction, I hasten to add, was not due to any kind of parental lethargy but was rather a father's intuition. When a man happens to hear his adolescent son panting heavily in the bathroom it makes certain sense to hold back from intervention. So, I held back, and tried my very hardest not to think too much about it. You see, at that time I still believed there were some things that a parent shouldn't enquire about. I imagined I was protecting my son from his own shame.

It was only when his whimper became more pronounced that I decided to intervene. 'Reuben? What are you doing in there?'

He didn't hear me. Or, at any rate, he didn't answer. The water kept on, so I spoke a little louder. 'Reuben? Do you really need that much water?'

Now I was closer to the sound I realised it was one of pain and not pleasure.

He switched the tap off, and I heard his heavy breath.

'Dad,' he said. 'I'm just . . . I . . . I won't . . .'

Panic and pain competed in his voice. I tried the door. He hadn't locked it. Maybe he'd forgotten. Or maybe, subconsciously, he'd wanted this to happen. Maybe he wanted me to swing the door open and see what I saw, what I still see as vividly as if it was a second ago.

Your brother, in front of the mirror, turned towards me with wide-eyed dread. There was something in the basin, but I didn't notice that at first. What I noticed was the blood. It began in a deep shining scar by his left cheek.

'My God, Reuben, what have you done?'

He didn't answer. I think he was too ashamed, but the information I needed was in the basin. His toothbrush, cradled there, its bristles pink with diluted blood.

'You did this to yourself?'

I looked at the scar again and realised its purpose. He had been trying to rub off his birthmark. He had been standing there, all that time, brushing away at his own skin.

'Reuben,' I was speaking softer now. 'Reuben, why would you –'

The smack of shame, the pain, the leaking blood, were all working to weaken him. He turned pale and wilted sideways in a kind of half-faint. I moved fast, and held his body.

I saw to his wound. I pressed a plaster onto his face. I gave him a paracetamol.

'I don't want Bryony to know,' he said.

'I won't tell her,' I said. 'We'll just say you had an accident playing rugby.'

'I don't play rugby.'

'Football, then.'

(You never believed that, did you? At least now you know the lie wasn't Reuben's.)

I asked him, obviously, why he did it, but never heard an answer.

The standard parental condolences were offered and, in my arrogance, I believed they might have had some effect. In truth he probably just wanted to leave the bathroom, and the eyes of his prying father, as soon as he could.

I stayed there, and washed the last remnants of blood from the brush.

Even after it had all gone I kept the tap running, not caring a fig about the wasted water, and found a strange therapy in the sound of it blasting through the white bristles and down the drain.

*

Come on, Terence! Drag yourself out of the quicksand before you sink any deeper.

Right, the next incident: Cynthia's grand meal out.

Yes. You didn't go, do you remember?

'Bryony,' I called. 'Bryony, your grandmother's here. Are you ready?'

Cynthia was standing in front of the mirror, combing her hands through her freshly dyed black hair, and running through various thespian poses. 'Liz Taylor, eat your heart out,' she said.

I kept calling you. 'Bryony? Bryony?'

'Oh, Terence, hasn't she told you?'

'Told me?'

Cynthia pointed a black nail up towards your room. 'Other plans,' she whispered.

'What?'

'She phoned me an hour ago.'

'Phoned you?'

'On her mobile.'

'Phoned you on her mobile telephone? When?'

'I told you,' Cynthia said, exasperated. 'An hour ago.'

'Well, I'm afraid, Cynthia, you've been misinformed. She promised you she was coming and she's coming. Now, Bryony? Bryony?'

The taxi honked outside.

'Bryony? Bryony?'

Your voice, somewhere above: 'What?'

'Why did you tell your grandmother you weren't coming with us?'

'I'm going to Imogen's,' you said with cool defiance.

'Imogen's?'

At which point Cynthia's fingers played a quick four notes

on my arm, her nails shining like onyx jewels.

'Apparently her friend's very upset,' she whispered. 'She's just split up with her boyfriend and wants to have a girls' night with Bryony. You know girls like sleepovers, don't you? Now, come on, Terence, don't make a big hoo-ha.'

I went upstairs and you handed me a piece of paper you had already prepared, complete with Imogen's address and telephone number. You assumed, no doubt, that I would do nothing with this information.

A third baritone blast of that taxi horn and Cynthia's voice: 'Come on, Terence. We'll be late.'

And me looking directly in your eyes saying: 'So, it's just going to be you and Imogen?'

Your eyes conjured their wide innocence. 'Uh-huh.'

'And how, may I ask, are you getting there?'

'Imogen knows a pimp who works this part of town and he's kindly offered me a lift,' you said, before puncturing your tease. 'Imogen's mum. She's picking me up.'

'All right,' I said, thinking of Cynthia. 'I trust you.'

Even if that had been true, I would have still spent the night in panic.

In the taxi, we passed an accident near the racecourse. A mangled car, high and hunched like an angry cat, nosed up with the barrier.

'Poor soul,' Cynthia said, as a raised shape in a blanket was pushed into an ambulance.

'Yes,' I said, and wished I had your grandmother's empathy. Wished I could feel for a faceless victim, rather than my daughter, in the back of a stranger's car, driving to a house I had never seen.

At the Box Tree I smiled and nodded my way through the meal, giving myself indigestion as I wolfed down my grim-lipped turbot, listening to the tale of when Cynthia tripped over in a long-past production of *The Tempest*.

I hardly remember anything about those people.

Her old am dram friends.

Well, no, I can remember one or two. I can remember Ray. An infuriating man with a face like a toby jug who found great sport in vulgarising my name: 'So, Terry . . . is that right, Tel? . . . pass the wine, would you, Tezzer?'

He kept on testing me with quotations, as his wife cringed and shrank by his side.

'"He who aspires to be a hero, must drink brandy,"' he said, as he leaned back in his chair and stared at the wine list. 'Dr Johnson, in case you didn't know. Are you a brandy man, Telly?'

'No,' I told him. 'No spirits for me.'

He stroked his preposterous chin and looked at me in a rather smug fashion. 'Didn't think so,' he said.

I believe it was at this point Cynthia started talking rather loudly about her life-drawing classes.

'Would you ever take your clothes off, Tel?' asked the toby jug. 'For art's sake, I mean.'

'No. Would you?'

'Well, if old Ollie Reed saw no shame in it I don't see why I should,' he said.

A man next to me came to my rescue. That homosexual chap. Snowy-haired, canary-sweatered, facially reminiscent of a neatly groomed camel. I think you've met him before. You saw his Widow Twanky in the *Aladdin* pantomime years ago. Michael. Is that what they call him?

'Oh, Ray, I don't know,' he said. 'Aren't you more Ollie Hardy than Ollie Reed?'

The table burst into wild guffaws and the toby jug threw a stern glance at his giggling wife.

Later, Michael's sombre voice in my ear: 'Cynthia has told me everything. I'm so sorry. It must have been impossible for you. I met him at the theatre once. He was on work experience, wasn't he? Having trouble with that damn donkey.'

'Yes . . . yes . . . ,' I said, staring down at the fish skeleton on my plate. All the time, in my mind: where were you? What were you doing? Were you in the car yet? Were you strapped in? Were you going where you said you were going? And I felt rather ill with it. With all those people between us. All those people occupying the physical space between you and me. All those personalities. All those narratives we had no part of, who wouldn't care if you stopped existing. 'You'll have to excuse me . . .'

I remember going to the toilets and calling the house to see if you had gone, and listening to that depressing bleat of the ringtone for over a minute. Then I tried your mobile telephone and was informed by a female replicant that you were unable to answer.

Back at the table I couldn't cope with it. With the oppressive lightness. With the nothing-talk of those guests. With the sickening cheesecake or my palpitating heart. I wanted to go. I wanted to leave. I should never have gone there. I was so out of place. A miserable caterpillar among the social butterflies. What was the point of it? I had only gone out of duty to Cynthia, after all her help, but now other duties were taking over.

It must have been eleven thirty by the time we eventually arrived back. Cynthia insisted on coming in for a late coffee but I couldn't settle.

'I have to call Imogen's mother,' I said.

'Oh, Terence. Don't be such –'

'I'm sorry, Cynthia. I'm phoning her. I just want to speak to Bryony, that's all. I just want to check she's safe.'

Cynthia shrugged a surrender. 'It's your daughter. Do what you want.'

'Right,' I said, picking your note out of my pocket. 'I think I will.'

We drove out of York and fast through twisting country lanes.

Cynthia was furious. I was over the limit. 'In more ways than one,' she added. But what was I meant to do? As there had been no answer to the number you had given me I was spiralling fast into thoughts of car accidents, rapes, abductions. Now we were heading towards the address, hoping beyond hope you had written the correct one down.

I had told Cynthia I could have dropped her off at home, or called for a taxi, but she had decided to come too. 'I don't want you doing something silly, Terence.'

Ah yes, something silly.

Before we reached the village where Imogen supposedly lived, we detected a dull golden light somewhere ahead of us. Turning the next corner we saw it: a fire in a field, with people dancing around. It was a scene from before civilisation, or after it, beyond the apocalypse. A ceremony of victory, or initiation, or sacrifice.

We pulled in to the side of the road and waited a while. 'She's there,' I said.

'Oh, Terence, you don't know that. Come on, let's keep driving to the house.'

'No, look, she's there.' I pointed towards a girl, a dancing silhouette against the fire. It was you, and Cynthia knew it.

She sighed. 'Leave her.'

'What?'

'Leave her. You can talk to her later. Tomorrow.'

'Are you joking?'

'No. I'm not. For God's sake, think about it, Terence. If you went over there now she'd never forgive you. These things stay with a child, you know.' She said this mournfully, and I wondered briefly at the humiliations her own childhood had brought her.

'I'm sorry, Cynthia,' I said, 'but I want to deal with it now. She's my child. What if something happens to her, tonight, while she's in that state? Fire, alcohol, boys. It's hardly the most comforting combination.'

Cynthia turned to me, light words passing her dark-painted lips. 'You don't know if she's in any kind of state. Now, come on, Terence, let her enjoy herself.'

I was getting crosser. 'Look. Look at them. For Christ's sake, look. They're out of their minds.'

'They've probably had a bit to drink. They're teenagers. It's a Saturday night.' She leaned in close, and spoke in a deep whisper. 'Be not afeard: the isle is full of noises./ Sounds and sweet airs, that give delight, and hurt not.'

Cynthia mistook my frown for a query.

'*The Tempest*,' she said.

Maybe she was right. Maybe I was being over the top. Maybe her wise witch's face was about to win me over. But then I heard it. The scream. A scream that gave me the same ache as when I heard your brother, hanging. Indeed, now I am reliving that scene I do not hear your scream at all. I hear Reuben's, in its place, but at the time I knew it was you and

I knew precisely what it meant. You were in trouble, terrible danger, and we were the only ones who could protect you.

'That was her,' I said.

'What was her?' Your grandmother's question pursued me out of the car. 'Terence, I think you're making a terrific mistake.'

I ignored her, and clambered over the fence. Cows were close to the road, away from you and your friends. They were lying down, sleeping their empty sleep.

I called your name.

'Bryony!'

My voice axed its way through the boys' laughter. What were they doing to you? I had no idea. No, not true. I had ideas. And these ideas pushed me again.

'Bryony!'

Three girls, four boys. Throbbing orange by the fire. Standing there, like the world's last survivors, and turned towards me.

'Dad? Dad?'

'It's all right,' I said. 'You're all right.'

Laughter of a different kind now. Trapped and tight, like flies in a jar. I looked among them. I saw Uriah Heep, with his thin, child-catcher arm around Imogen. The other boys I'd never seen. And George Weeks, laughing loudest of all, raising his bottle like a trophy.

You walked fast, towards me. Then your face was there, full of anger and shame, flashing gold.

'What are you doing?' Your tone was disbelieving, betrayed.

'I heard you scream. Were they trying to hurt you?' I pointed to the nearest boy. 'Was he trying to hurt you? That boy? Who is he? Was he trying to hurt you? You were upset, I thought you were hurt.'

'I can't believe it,' you said. 'I can't believe you. Just go away.'

Disgust made a stranger of your voice. You sounded like you hated me.

I was numb.

I couldn't speak.

Behind you, the fire crackled, and drunken conversation began to bubble. You wanted to be with them. You wanted me to disappear.

'You said you were at Imogen's. I phoned and there was no answer. Your grandmother and I came to look for you.'

Not even a shrug.

'I heard you scream.'

You looked away and said it again. 'I can't believe you.' As though I could evaporate with the right evidence.

'I thought you were in trouble.'

'Just leave. Please, Dad, just leave.'

'Yeah,' shouted one of the boys. 'Just go away.'

'I'm not leaving without you. It's midnight, for God's . . . what time were you planning to go home?'

'Never.' You were drunk. I could see it now. Hear it. Smell it.

The wind switched, and brought smoke towards us.

I grabbed your arm. 'You're coming with me, young lady.'

You slipped my grip and ran further towards them.

And then the changes. The tingles. The sliding between stations. The dark on top of dark. It was as though everything, even the fire, was set behind black gauze.

I tried to follow you, but felt strangely off balance. A short way into my pursuit I tripped over something, landing close enough to the fire for a spark to singe a hair off my hand.

I turned to see George Weeks, an ominous white vision through the dark veil. A grotesque colossus above me. A juvenile Nero, blond and overweight, a baby swollen to a man. So near the fire his face had a monstrous appearance, with his white pallor rendered devilish red and his eyes invisible behind his glasses. Two gleaming squares of light.

I pushed myself up off the grass and stood facing him, trying my best to ignore the sensations in my mind. 'George Weeks, does your mother know where you are? Does she know you are smoking and drinking and tripping adults into fires? Does she . . . know?'

At which point, as you may recall, he insulted me loudly. '—— off.' He was inebriated beyond all reckoning, and he thrust forward.

'Have you lost all respect for your elders, George? What's . . . what's happened to you?'

My dulled senses stopped me dodging his hands. He pushed me, I staggered back, but didn't topple. George looked around for laughter that never came.

'Leave him alone,' you said.

'Leave it, Georgie, you dumb ——,' said another of them. A boy. The vulgar, archaic word hit George like a stone, and he retreated from me.

In his place you appeared. My beautiful girl. Slowly, the black gauze lifted.

'I won't forget this,' you said.

We walked back to the Volvo. Behind us, one of the boys made a noise like a dying aircraft.

'I'm your father. It's my job to look after you, even when you think you don't need looking after. One day you will thank me.'

Your grandmother was initially silent when we got to the car. She didn't understand any more than you did.

'You did say you were going to Imogen's,' she eventually

said, without conviction. 'Your father was worried about you. He didn't mean to make a complete show of himself.'

I glanced into the rear-view mirror and saw you stare out at the dark fields and farmhouses. At unseen primitive lands, enclosed by drystone walls, where fathers once commanded without question.

'I heard you scream.'

'From ten miles away?'

'I phoned Imogen's mother and there was no one there. We were worried.'

Cynthia sighed, for your benefit. Discomfort at the 'we', I suppose. She decided to stay with us, in order to 'keep us on our leads', but said she had to disappear early the next morning. Life drawing, or something. When we arrived back home you went straight to bed. I don't even think you used the bathroom.

I sat down on the sofa and Higgins strolled onto my lap.

'Happy?' your grandmother asked, before sipping her glass of brandy.

I sighed. 'It's not a question of happiness.'

She laughed. A laugh sadder than her usual cackle. I looked at her. I looked past the cabaret singer's make-up and the aged skin and sensed your mother there, sharing a joke that shone inside those eyes. 'No. So, Terence, tell me, what exactly is it a question of?'

I couldn't answer that, so I answered something else instead.

'You're different,' I said. 'You're a different type of person.'

Of course, this prompted a Cynthian scowl, and an audible eruption of disapproval. 'Oh yes? Enlighten me, Terence. What *type* am I?'

I trod carefully. 'The coping type. You cope. You get by. You've got a – I don't know – an "inner peace", I suppose.

An acceptance. I don't have it, you see. I just don't have that capacity.'

You would have thought I had slapped her. Red anger over-powered her make-up, and those dark heavy eyelashes widened like dangerous plants. 'Oh, listen to yourself. Honestly. You don't seriously think there has been one single day in the past fifteen flaming years when I haven't woken up and yearned for her still to be here? You don't think I ever accepted that I lost my daughter, do you? Or Howard? Or that I am in any better position now to cope with the loss of my grandson? I've cried myself to sleep God knows how many times. I wake up in the middle of the night and feel like I could scream with it all. Nobody accepts these things, Terence. But what can we do? What can we do? These things have happened. We will never know why – if there is a "why" to know. I get up in the morning and get on with things because what's the choice? What is the alternative? But don't you dare think for one little minute that when I climb into an empty bed, or when I think of my poor daughter lying on that floor, or when I see a tin of Harrogate flaming toffees, that it's any easier for me. The only thing I accept is that I am still alive, and other people are still alive, and while we are still sharing that same crack of light we ought to be making things easier for each other. That's my *type*, Terence. That's my bloody type.'

This tirade exhausted her, and had frightened Higgins out of the room. A long silence was left in its wake.

'I'm sorry,' she said, at the end of it. 'I didn't mean to shout. It's probably just the brandy.'

'No, Cynthia,' I said. 'No. You're absolutely right. It was a stupid thing to say. *I'm* sorry.'

And I meant it. I really think I did.

'Well, the main thing is we don't let Bryony suffer,' she said.

'Yes,' I said. 'Of course. You're right.'

And I went to bed that night feeling I was truly able to turn over a new page, a blank one, and write a better future for us all. But of course, and as always, I was wrong. The next day was written in the same descending style I was growing accustomed to, with Terence the Tormented Tormentor about to take a further plunge into his designated role.

I dreamt it was you. I dreamt you were there, where he was hanging from the lamp post. You lost your grip and I woke up, knowing I had to keep you close, keep you safe.

When Cynthia had gone to her art class I went into your room.

I tried soft words. I tried to offer an olive branch. 'We were both partially to blame,' I said. 'I know I shouldn't have embarrassed you in front of your friends. I'm sorry. And I am sure you were aware that you shouldn't have lied to me.'

You didn't want to listen. You didn't want me there, at the foot of your bed. 'Please, Dad, just leave me alone.'

'I just think you should say sorry that's all. I've said sorry and I'll say it again. Say sorry and we can forget about it.'

'No.'

'Apologise. You lied. Bryony, if you don't tell me where you are how can I know you're safe. Apologise.'

'No.'

'A. Pol. O. Gise.'

At which you disappeared back under your covers and made a sound like a near-boiled kettle.

I became angry. Something switched inside me and suddenly I found myself losing control. I sat there, listening to my own tense words, and wondered what had got into me. At that moment a new plan occurred to me. A plan fuelled by desperation, by anger, and by this new dark force closing in on my soul.

'Well, Bryony,' I said. 'It is a tragedy for me to accept it, but it seems that we have now reached a point where firmer action is required. If you are unable to be honest with me, or to admit your own mistakes, or to show any remorse for these mistakes, then it seems I am left with absolutely no choice but to lay down some rules for you to abide by. Rather than risk the excuse of a memory lapse, I will write these rules down and I will stick them in the kitchen for you to read. Now, I want you to remember that these rules are to be followed to the letter or there will be strict consequences.'

'Huh!' Your response, dulled by the tight blankets that lay over you.

'Well, Bryony, there is no point setting rules unless there are consequences for the rule-breaker and I assure you that if these rules aren't followed or are wilfully misinterpreted then you will be punished accordingly.' I hesitated, while my mind turned to the possible punishments I could inflict. 'If you persist in breaking the rules then I will be forced to sell Turpin. Or I will move you to another school. Or I will forbid you from leaving the house. Do you understand me?'

I left you and went to my desk. I looked ahead at the curtains I never pulled open any more, and then I took the fountain pen from the lacquered case as its Pre-Raphaelite nymphs watched me with concern.

My hand, trembling with this sudden and alien anger, pressed the nib to the paper and began to write.

1. You must not visit Imogen. If Imogen must be seen at all it is to be on these premises.
2. You are never to be out of the house after 7 p.m., except on cello evenings, or when you are being chaperoned by myself or your grandmother.
3. You must always eat your meals at the table, so we can enjoy a little conversation.
4. You must refrain from playing the noise you euphemistically refer to as music, unless you can do so at a civilised volume.
5. You will not inform me of an imminent departure when I am with customers in the shop. You will give me prior warning, and details of where you are going, and then I will consider if I approve.
6. You will not leave the house for longer than one hour at a time without a significant reason. Such as when you are at school, the stables or the music college.
7. You will not walk home from school. When term begins you will be picked up by myself every day, without complaint.
8. You will help in the shop on Saturdays.
9. You will not watch television of a corrupting nature, or communicate with strangers or males of any kind via your computer.
10. You will not drink alcohol.
11. You will not spend mine or your grandmother's pocket money on magazines or other corruptive forms of literature.
12. You will not travel in motor vehicles unless they are driven by myself or a driver approved by me.

13. You will not enter into a physical relationship with a member of the opposite gender until I am satisfied that you have reached the requisite level of emotional maturity.

A few days later Mrs Weeks came into the shop to buy the Arabian dancer. In all honesty I was sad to see it go, as it was by far the oldest item we had on sale.

'Is this an authentic Franz Bergman?' she asked me.

'Yes,' I told her, through her nods. 'The Dancing Arab Girl. Late 1880s. An amazing period for the decorative arts in Austria. The detail is quite exceptional.'

Her pretty mouth twitched in a manner that reminded me of an inquisitive mouse. She raised the small bronze beauty to eye level.

'I have a Barrias from around the same period,' she said. 'Winged Victory. Not quite as vulgar as many of his others. This might complement it rather well, I feel.'

I can see her standing there, with her neat blonde bob and wicker basket, as she contemplated the purchase.

I remember feeling a kind of savagery inside me, knowing that I was about to trouble this proud golden fieldmouse with some truths about her son. Yet Mrs Weeks had to be told. I owed it to her, you see, as a fellow parent. As a trusted ally against the unseen forces that were corrupting our children. Oh, it was horrible though, the actual act of telling. To watch her face as she stood there at the counter, struggling as it tried to keep its pretty dignity in place. I felt such a vandal.

'I'm sorry, Mrs Weeks. I just thought I had to tell you.'

'George? . . . George? . . .' Her eyes, normally so precise, slipped away to stare at some vague point behind me. 'Mr Cave, I must apologise for my son's behaviour. I admit he has been acting strangely recently. The separation between his father and myself has not been particularly pleasant. George has suffered a great deal. I will talk to him, be sure of that.' This was delivered as if in a kind of trance, as though I were a hypnotist prying for details of her childhood. 'Goodbye, Mr Cave.'

She placed the brown paper parcel delicately in her basket and walked – or, as it seemed, floated – out of the shop. I saw her face through the glass as she stood on the pavement. She sniffed the air and seemed to give a tiny shake of the head, a gesture that made me think of Higgins flicking away water.

And then she was gone.

You obeyed my rules, but you still found ways to punish me. Silence, that was your first weapon during those early days. You would sit opposite me at the dining table, pushing your carrots around, and speak only when you saw fit.

I looked at you, my child, and wanted you to understand what I was trying to do. All I wanted, all I ever wanted, was to protect you from changing, from losing all that made you special. To protect you, in short, from turning into me.

'So then, how are your cello lessons coming along?'

Blank stare.

'Turpin seemed a little stubborn today, when I picked you up. Was he difficult to ride?'

Indifferent sigh.

'Are you going to finish the rest of that?'

Poisoned glance.

And if you were selective about what came out of your mouth, you were also rather choosy about what went into it.

Up until Reuben's death I had been so proud that I had managed to raise a daughter who never bothered to check the calorie content of a raisin before she dropped it into her mouth. A girl with a healthy figure, who didn't aspire to be like the skeletal clothes horses and starving pit ponies of the magazines.

It had been a steady decline. A slowing down of your jaw as it chewed. A mild flinch of regret as you swallowed. A silent reading of ingredients and daily guidelines, assessing the numbers with the studious eyes of a stockbroker.

Once the rules were in place the decline steepened. And I was left wondering how we were going to find a way back up that slope. Yet every time I thought about reconciliation you did something to further my anger.

Angelica, for example.

Now, I understand what I said when I saw her face staring up at me from the kitchen bin but you must appreciate the shock it gave me.

To see an 1893 Heinrich Handwerck bisque doll's head detached from its body and lying on a bed of carrot shavings in a plastic bin liner would be quite a test for even the most hardened antique lover. Of course, I shouldn't have gone on about how much it had cost a decade before, or its current worth now. This wasn't truly the point.

The point was this: Angelica was a special part of your childhood. You had chosen her yourself, at Newark Antiques Fair. I had gladly risked a tantrum from Reuben and sacrificed the chance to buy a pair of second-period floral-encrusted Aberdeen jugs in order to see the smile on your face.

For years you mothered this doll – giving her a name, combing her hair, removing and reattaching her handwoven cape, talking to her as a living thing, nursing her on imaginary battlefields, reading her extracts from *Black Beauty* or *Little Women*.

I understood that these activities stopped a long time ago and it would be a very foolish parent who would want them to continue towards womanhood. Time, I know, is a rolling boulder we can't hold back. Yet are we really to aid that boulder in its destruction? I wasn't expecting you to still be playing with a doll in your teenage years, yet to discard such a valuable treasure, such a piece of your own past, was beyond my immediate comprehension.

'Bryony, I don't understand it. Why would you do such a thing?'

You didn't answer me.

'Are you trying to hurt me? Punish me for something?'

A word quivered your lips. 'Why?' you eventually said. 'Why? Why? Why on earth? Why?' It was as if you didn't know anything about it. As if you thought I was responsible.

'Is this about Reuben?' I asked, but got no further reply.

After you stormed upstairs I reached into the bin and held the pretty head in my trembling hand, as though it were Yorick's skull. Those large blue eyes seemed to acknowledge our sorry fates. Both of us, like the doll: broken, discarded, lost from their complementary parts. All the tragedy and violence of time, staring out from the palm of my hand.

I arrived late at the stables due to my desperate attempt to restore the doll, but gave up, unable to find the rest of her. You weren't there and I panicked. The sky didn't help. Purple-black clouds pressed down onto a horizontal stretch of yellow, as though God's scarred palm was crushing the day.

I switched off the engine and climbed out of the car. I walked over to the gate. There was no sign of you. There were hoof-prints heading out of the stables towards the road and I worried for a minute that you had gone out on a solitary hack, rather than staying within the fenced paddock as I had always instructed.

I opened the gate and stepped into the yard. It gave the eerie impression of a Nevada ghost town, for there wasn't a horse nor a human to be seen. Then I noticed something even more troubling. Turpin's stable door was wide open, with no Turpin visible inside. As I walked closer I heard a noise, a sobbing, and knew instantly it was you.

'Bryony?'

I ran into the stable and saw you sitting in the dark shade, on the hay, with that boy's arm around your shoulder.

'Get off her,' I said. 'Get off my daughter.'

Denny stood up. He was in his running clothes. 'She's upset. There were some trouble with the horse –'

'I can see that. Now go. Get out of here. Get out, get out, get out.'

He looked at you and you looked back with your damp red eyes. You gave the smallest of nods and he left.

'Where's Turpin?'

You said nothing. This in itself wasn't a surprise. After all, you'd hardly said a word since I had given you the rules. Yet, even so, I pressed for answers.

'What was that boy doing here?'

'He –' Your answer peeped outside, before cowering back in silence.

I looked around. 'Where's everyone gone?'

You stood up, trembling, and followed me back to the car. It was only later, when I received the phone call from the stable manager – what was her name, the speed-talking Irish one? Claire? – that I eventually heard the truth. How was I to know what had happened?

How was I to know that boy had sought so hard to become your hero that he had actually risked his life? But don't you think I wouldn't have confronted your bucking horse and carried your petrified self out of the stable? Of course I would have. Yet, I wasn't there and he was.

Everywhere you went, I had to watch you and guard you against the bleak curse that was still infecting our family.

*

I woke with a jolt.

There was a noise, outside.

Or perhaps it wasn't a noise, perhaps it was another kind of sensory intrusion, something less easy to explain.

Either way, I awoke, and felt the need to step out of bed and part the curtains I never opened. At first I saw nothing. But then, across the park, the street lamp flickered. My eyes lowered their gaze and strained to see through the dark to interpret the large shape in the distance.

I gasped.

There, precisely where Reuben had fallen, was something else standing on the pavement. A horse, a chestnut Trakehner, under the street lamp.

It was Turpin, staring (I imagined) straight at me.

I didn't dress. I didn't wake you. I simply put on my slippers and my dressing gown and quietly locked you in the house. The town was dead so nobody saw my strange figure cross the park towards him, the horse that stood still under that stuttering light as if he had something to tell me.

When I reached the street he leaned his head away from me and began to walk towards Micklegate. I followed, breaking into a jog as I went under the Norman archway of Micklegate Bar. A strange sensation of being watched as I came out the other side, as if traitors' heads were still looking down from their spikes. Richard, Duke of York, sneering at another mad sight in the city of ghosts.

I picked up speed as your runaway horse began to canter, but I lost a slipper. 'Turpin! Turpin! Wait! Come back!'

A night taxi smoothed in towards me, lowering its window. 'Y'all right, mate?' The overfed driver, his swollen face leaning over an empty seat.

'Yes. No. My daughter's horse. I'm following my daughter's horse. Do you see it? You just passed it.'

He frowned and glanced down. Finding some kind of warning in my naked foot he drove away. As for myself, I retrieved my slipper and kept up my pursuit, following Turpin over the stagnant river and through the streets, losing sight of him at each corner but following the clatter of his hooves.

A lunatic tramp was in the market square. He had jumped out from nowhere and his giant hands now wrestled with my dressing gown. I tried to twist away and keep sight of the horse, but I had lost him.

'Leave me alone,' I told the tramp, but he wouldn't. I pushed him away, my hand pressing into his scarred and ancient face. There was a brief tussle, concluding with him falling onto the cobbled ground and crying out in pain.

I ran on, but it was no use. Your horse was nowhere. The hooves had faded into silence. I wondered what, precisely, I was doing. Even if I had caught up with Turpin, what could I have done with a horse with no harness? I can only tell you that I followed not out of thought but instinct, a decision of the soul rather than the mind, as though I had little choice.

Then I heard those iron-shod hooves again, trotting near the Minster.

There was a growing tightness in my chest as I reached the south transept of the church, its golden limestone rendered pale under the floodlights. I stood still, caught my breath, and admitted defeat. I strained to hear the horse but there was nothing.

It was at this point that I heard Reuben behind me. He was standing in the dark, rubbing his toothbrush against his cheek, just like that day I had interrupted him in the bathroom.

'Where's my horse?' he said, the violence against his own face not causing any apparent pain.

'Reuben, I don't understand.'

'Petal wants a horse. Petal gets a horse.'

I wanted to see him more clearly, so I stepped closer. 'You didn't want a horse.'

'I asked for a horse.' His voice soft and quiet, with only the faintest trace of resentment.

'You were never interested in horses. I got you other things. I bought you a bicycle.'

'You sold my bike. Where's my horse?'

'Reuben, please.'

'Horses aren't bikes.'

'Reuben?'

In the reflected light from the church I saw the blood on his cheek shine black.

'I loved you, Reuben. I still love you.'

'Horses aren't bikes.'

'Oh, stop it, Reuben. Please.'

'You didn't love me.'

I thought of the horse that had nearly killed you. The horse that had been there, precisely where Reuben was standing.

'It was you, wasn't it? You got inside Turpin.'

He said nothing, but kept on brushing his cheek.

'You're trying to get inside me, aren't you? Please, don't, Reuben. Please.' I pleaded, I fell to my knees. I closed my eyes, and prayed aloud: 'Reuben, please, please, I'm begging you, don't hurt your sister.'

I rose to my slippered feet, scanned around the empty paving stones. 'Reuben, where are you?'

I looked towards the Minster, a structure men devoted entire working lives to make look this bold, this solid, this arrogant.

'Where is he?' I shouted up towards the church, towards the Rose Window. 'Where is my son?'

A fleeing echo, and then nothing.

Just the true dead quiet of limestone and glass.

Such troubled nights weakened my resolve. I felt like Odysseus crossing the River of Fear, too weak and confused to be fully in control.

The rules I had given you gradually seemed harder to enforce, as my worries grew about your brother's unseen intention. Yet wasn't it precisely because of Reuben that I had to keep you where I could see you? Even so, I couldn't help loosening my grip.

You would nip out on errands that would take far longer than required. You would test the phrase 'civilised volume' to the limit. Imogen would walk out of your bedroom and I would smell tobacco, but could never find any other evidence that you smoked.

Of course, Cynthia was small help.

'You need to finish with these rules, Terence,' she said one afternoon, as she sat in the shop polishing a tray.

'No, Cynthia, I don't. They are working perfectly well.'

She screwed up her nose, as though my words smelt as bad as the ammonia that was filling the shop. 'Oh, Terence, you don't believe that, do you?'

'With the greatest of respect, I really feel it is up to me and me alone how I choose to deal with my daughter.'

Her nose took particular offence to the 'deal with' part of that, if I remember correctly. 'And what would Helen think, I wonder?'

The Helen card, the ace in Cynthia's pack.

'Helen wanted me to protect her children,' I said. 'No matter what, that is what she wanted. I've already failed half of that task, I'm not going to lose Bryony as well.'

A long silence followed.

I was tired and emotional and sometimes I found that your grandmother's manner, much like her use of ammonia, was a little heavy-handed.

'It's her birthday coming up,' she said eventually.

I remembered Reuben talking about his bicycle the previous night. 'I *know* it's her birthday coming up.'

By this point I had already asked you what you wanted and you had shrugged a 'Nothing' in response. I think you meant it, too. I think you wanted the whole day to drop off the calendar.

It was always going to be a difficult occasion, I knew that. The first birthday that wasn't a shared event. Yet I knew also that it would be a good opportunity to try and put things right again, between us both. A way of showing you that I really did have your best interests at heart.

'Why don't you take her clothes shopping?' Cynthia asked, as Higgins jumped onto her lap.

I winced. 'Shopping? I don't know. It could be a recipe for disaster.'

Higgins' slow blue gaze echoed Cynthia's look of disappointment.

'Not if you *made the effort*, Terence,' she said, emphasising the 'made the effort' part. 'It will be good. You won't have to choose anything. I doubt your sartorial judgement will be in high demand,' she added, with a sly look down at my beige, cotton twill trousers. 'All you have to do is nod your head and tell her she looks lovely.'

I had no alternative. I didn't have a clue what to buy you. In previous years this had never been a problem. It had always been so easy to know what to get, as there was always something you had specifically wanted. A doll's house. A trip to the ballet. A holiday to Catalonia, to see Pablo Casals' former home.

A horse.

Now the things you wanted were hidden from view, part of the mist that had gathered around your whole being the evening Reuben died.

But this was it, I realised. An opportunity to clear the weather, and bring back my blue-sky girl.

'All right,' I said. 'All right, Cynthia, we'll give it a go.'

And she smiled, and seemed proud, and I felt your mother's own pride somewhere beyond, behind those dark painted lips and eyes, and I felt stronger, just for that moment. A man repaired, who could shield us from whatever Reuben had in store.

That night, with Cynthia's words still fresh in my ear, I cooked you your favourite childhood meal – shepherd's pie followed by apple charlotte.

'Bryony,' I called. *Ma cherie! À table!* You stayed in your room. I wrestled to keep calm. 'Bryony, please, come into the kitchen.'

Eventually you appeared, my starving waif. Your nostrils visibly quivered at the smell, but you tried not to look anything other than in a sulk. You sat down. Your lips were in a pout. Your arms hung limply by your side, like oars in an abandoned boat.

'Look.' I pulled the shepherd's pie from the oven.

'I'm not hungry,' you said.

I decided to defrost your mood by telling you about the shopping trip I had planned.

Your pout twisted in consideration. 'What, I can buy any clothes I want? Not long flowery dresses or polo necks or anything? I can buy things I like?'

I extracted a reluctant 'Yes' from my mouth. 'Within reason.'

You seemed mildly impressed, perhaps wondering if this was going to be part of a wider change, and sat down to contemplate your shepherd's pie. Then, before you had taken a mouthful, the telephone rang and you sprang up to answer. Judging from your light tone I knew it must be Cynthia. You chatted for a while, giggling occasionally.

'Really?' you kept saying, as I strained to catch Cynthia's weak murmur on the other end of the line.

'Da-ad,' you said, after five minutes or so. You hadn't sounded this pleasant for weeks. 'Grandmother wants to know if I can go to her house for my birthday. She says I'm allowed to have some friends around.'

I struggled to hide my fury. How dare Cynthia undermine my authority! Why hadn't she mentioned this alongside the shopping suggestion? I grabbed the telephone. 'Cynthia? What's this?'

She groaned, like a runner who had just realised she'd entered a longer race. 'Now, listen to me, Terence, I thought it would be nice for her to have a little party.'

'A party?' I spat the word. 'So I'm meant to sit there all night listening to horrendous music?'

'No, Terence,' Cynthia told me firmly. 'You're not meant to sit there all night doing anything. You're not invited. It's girls only.'

As the conversation went on I could see your eyes pleading with me, and your palms pressed together in prayer.

'Now, is she allowed to come?'

I thought of Rome and all those other times I had pushed you further away from me.

'Yes,' I said, with slow solemnity. 'She's allowed.'

I placed the telephone down, and consoled myself with the 'girls only' part of Cynthia's plan. And at least you'd be under Cynthia's roof, rather than in a country field.

My lenience had a reward: the hunger strike came to an end. I watched with attentive glee as the minced beef and mashed potato disappeared into your mouth, and enjoyed my own meal so much more for knowing its taste was being shared. Cynthia telephoned again, later, after we had finished the apple charlotte.

'Well done, Terence,' she told me, and confirmed my hope. 'Helen would be proud of you.'

After the call I followed the tender sound of cello music coming from your room, as you practised your piece for the Drama and Music Festival. My head leaned against your door, my eyes closed, and I lost myself in the divine opening bars of Beethoven's *Pathétique*. The sound of love, the sound of grief; the helpless, hopeful tears of the human soul.

A love song was playing. A man was on a large video screen, creasing his young face with forced emotion.

'That's the problem,' I told Cynthia, pointing up at this unkempt crooner.

Cynthia gave me that look of stern confusion I was becoming increasingly used to. 'What? Music?' She seemed appalled at the suggestion.

'No. All this false love they're surrounded by. All this exaggerated emotion. It makes everything so difficult for them.'

'For who?'

I gestured vaguely around me, at the young girls, flicking their way through rails of boy-catching outfits. 'For children,' I said. 'They are sold love as if it was another must-have purchase. They're bombarded with all this fake feeling constantly nowadays. They can't escape it. It's incessant. They are drowning in it. It's precisely what D. H. Lawrence prophesied.'

Cynthia rolled her eyes. 'Oh yes, D. H. Lawrence. The great moralist. Enlighten me, Terence, please. What did he say?'

'He said something about it. Oh, I can't remember. Something about how it will drive people towards insanity. They won't know how to feel any more. They'll have all this counterfeit emotion and never know their own feelings.'

Cynthia closed her eyes and shook her head. 'Have you listened to yourself, Terence?'

'D. H. Lawrence,' I said. 'Not me.'

'No. You, Terence. You.' I caught my own distorted reflection in the ridiculous bangle she was wearing. 'But I know what this is really all about.'

I sighed. 'Do you?'

The knowing raise of those thinned eyebrows. 'Yes, I do. You're just worried. It's her birthday. Bryony's getting older and you can't cope with it.'

'She's turning into someone else,' I said. 'It's like she's been infected with all this modern rubbish she used to be immune to. I want her to be immune again. It's unhealthy. She'll end up doing things she'll regret, when she's older, when she knows better, when she . . .'

Cynthia was staring over at a stand of accessories where an array of belts were hanging down. On the top of the stand was a row of hands. Mass-produced sculptures, cast in black plastic, intended to hold jewellery. They made me think of dead spirits reaching out to the living.

'Aren't those belts fabulous?' Cynthia said. 'I think I might get one.'

'Cynthia, are you even lis—'

My words died. You stepped out of the changing rooms, wearing a look I can only describe as Harlot Caught in a Cyclone.

'Oh, it looks great,' Cynthia said. 'Isn't it fun? Doesn't she look great, Terence? Terence? Terence?'

A sharp elbow to my ribs.

'Yes,' I said. 'From the neck up.'

I caught a boy staring at you, behind his girlfriend's back. A famished longing that sent a shot of fear through me.

'Oh, don't listen to your father,' she told you, as if you ever would.

You disappeared back into the changing rooms and re-emerged to test Cynthia's opinion on a variety of combinations. Striped harlot. Knitted harlot. Polka-dotted harlot. I sat there and grumbled my fatherly way through each and every one of them. No. There was one I liked, wasn't there? The jeans with the green sweater. That was quite an easy combination to approve, given that it covered all the parts it should have, and didn't advertise your flesh like a pig's carcass in a butcher's window.

'Oh yes,' I said. 'That's more like it.' The kiss of death of course. You screwed up your nose and disappeared, re-emerging as Dracula's bride.

Still, it was a good afternoon.

We got along, with the aid of my credit card and Cynthia's warm witchcraft. We went for a drink and some walnut loaf at Betty's Tea Rooms, do you remember? You seemed happy, between the distant stares, to be with me. Out in town, on public view, with your father. Rome, it seemed, was forgotten. And so was the embarrassment I had caused in the field. We didn't speak of it. We let Cynthia lead the conversation, a narrow and happy path with the right kind of scenery. Reuben stayed in the bushes, even though we could feel him, ready to pounce on us at any moment.

'So,' Cynthia said to you, as a gleaming black talon addressed the crumb on her lip, 'are you looking forward to tonight?'

And she winked. Yes, she did. She winked. That saucy, theatrical descent of the eyelid closing me out of existence.

'Yes,' you said, smiling smirkishly. 'Yes. I am.'

Oh yes, that evening. Your birthday. It comes to me. The whole hideous shape of it perfectly intact. Except, of course, that one missing link.

I had dropped you off at Cynthia's and then loitered nearby, parked high on a kerb. My plan was to sit there a while, and see who had been invited. I saw Imogen arrive, dressed like a Victorian strumpet, but was relieved to see she had no boys in tow.

I was on the cusp of leaving when I saw it. The taxi. I sat there, watching, as it pulled up, gasped in unheard terror as it honked its horn and you and Imogen ran out, giggling, and climbed in the back.

Before I had fully appreciated the situation it was driving away. What could I do? There was no point rushing in and reprimanding Cynthia. My priority was to follow you, and make sure you were safe.

My first instinct was to speed ahead and overtake the taxi, forcing it to stop. But I remembered the way everything had deteriorated the last time I had embarrassed you in front of your friends. And what would have happened? You would have given me a boxful of lies and then sought even harder to defy me. No. I had to follow you. I had to find out all the answers for myself, and punish you later.

Yellow hovered through the foggy air. A kind of alien sickness spreading from the street lamps to infect the whole night. It made it no easier to see the car in front, transporting my daughter at speeds she wasn't made to travel at, but I held onto the chase, ignoring limits of speed and recklessness as I sped through the jaundiced vapours.

The taxi slid into the left lane and turned off at the next junction. I turned too, recklessly close. One twist of your neck and you might have seen the familiar headlights gleaming through the fog. To my infinite horror I realised we were heading towards Leeds, a city that cared as much for my daughter's well-being as a flame cares for the well-being of a moth.

I felt sick with anxiety. Where were you going at this time on a Friday night? The fog thinned out, and I slowed down to create more distance between the two cars.

All around me, the horror continued.

There are still Enlightenment thinkers among us who grasp

at the idea of Progress as stubbornly as a three-year-old holds onto a forbidden toy. The idea that society is at its most advanced is a preposterous one. Scientific progress – yes, maybe, perhaps. But moral progress? Aesthetic progress? Social progress? These latter-day Diderots should ride their gilded carriages into the heart of the English city centre on a Friday night and measure how far the humans have come. Oh, what advancement they will find! Look, there's Progress throwing a bottle across the street! Look, there's Progress showing the world the dark crevasse of its backside!

I stayed two cars behind, safely invisible, as the Victorian architecture loomed above the street lamps and bar fronts, dissolving like an irrelevant memory into the night.

Your taxi eventually halted under a railway bridge where a queue of strange-haired boys (I saw only boys) waited to enter a door in the wall with the word COCKPIT hanging over it, a word which conjured all manner of connotations in my fevered mind.

'Cynthia,' I muttered to the empty car. 'You foolish, foolish woman.'

I parked next to a loading bay for a pizza parlour and waited, eyed with humorous curiosity by an underage chef on a cigarette break.

Cities try to shame us into action, as they know stillness is the preserve of the destitute, the dangerous, the dead. But there was no point rushing. I wanted to stay where I was until you were inside that place, that unknown Hell I was soon to enter. After all, I had to stay hidden from you and then find out how best to protect you. I had to know what this night would consist of, without my interference, if I was ever to steer you back onto the right course.

A group of women passed the car wearing angel wings

and advertising their bad diets with the most ill-advised attire. They eviscerated a love song at high volume, a communal mating call uglier than any in nature, and blew me kisses. One held a large inflatable phallus and waved it in front of the car window.

I closed my eyes, and tried to fight him back, as the singing faded away into traffic. Then, taking a large deep breath of that sealed and untainted air, I went out, into the night, to watch my dear sweet lamb dance among the wolves.

The man at the door stared down at me from his giant boulder of a head.

'No, fella,' he said, 'Don't think so.'

I begged his pardon.

'Saint your scene.'

And which scene was it? I wondered. The pivotal turning point in Act Two, where a twist of fortunes is followed by the increasingly rapid descent towards tragedy?

'I have money,' I said. 'And I am more than prepared to pay the full cost of entry into your establishment.'

The boulder ignored me, looking behind and tilting left. A signal for the two young droogs next in the queue to enter the doorway. Meanwhile, my unstoppable mouth continued to plead with this rock-head, this St Peter on protein shakes.

'Listen, are you planning to let me pass, because I must inform you I have no intention of leaving.'

To which he responded with a most creative turn of phrase: '—— off, you ———— before I —— your face.'

I inhaled his words with dignity. 'Right, I see. Well, dear man, let me put it like this. You have just allowed a girl who is three years under the required age to enter your establishment. I know this because she happens to be my daughter. Now, as keeper of the gates, you have two choices. Either you persist in your present and rather offensive strategy and suffer the unfortunate consequences. Or you allow me to go inside and retrieve her. In which case I shall not be contacting your employer, or my close friends at the council.'

His eyes contemplated the parallel universe, devoid of councils and employers, where he was now merrily engaged in stamping my head into the tarmac.

'——,' he said, but let me through all the same.

A 'band' was 'onstage' playing 'music'. I saw a crudely designed banner indicating they were called the Cleopatras, which was strange as there were four Antonys to only one, impossibly angry Ptolemy Queen.

Did you know this band? Were you a fan? Was that why you were there?

It was like walking into a panic attack. No, that makes it sound too cosy. It was like walking into someone else's panic attack, someone I didn't know and didn't want to. Someone closing their eyes on a railway platform at a quarter past midnight, debating whether to end it all under the next freight train that passes through. (I once heard a Radio 4 nitwit say that if Beethoven were alive today he would be playing lead guitar in a rock band. No. He would be sitting on that railway platform, breathing into a brown paper bag as he prayed for the train that would finish him.)

I searched for you amid the groundlings, amid the jumping bodies that reached hungrily for the stage. The idea of you there, among these sun-shirking opium eaters, filled me with the same terror I had found when searching for you in Rome, a sense that I was losing you to evil forces of the night. Darkness and devils.

Cleopatra screamed as I pushed my way through. I turned to the stage and saw her wrestling with the microphone as though it were an asp, ready to sink its poison into her chest.

'Excuse me,' I said, but of course I had no voice. The music had stolen it. Indeed, that was probably what it was there for, to steal voices, to give flesh an easy triumph over conversation.

Yes. Bodies, bodies, bodies. The whole place was congested with them. That was all they were to me. Just bodies. What else could I see them as? What type of personality could have existed inside that place? The noise made thought and conversation impossible.

'Is there no way out of the mind?' asked the poet.

Yes, you go where youth goes. To the 'Cockpit' on the dying hours of a Friday. There you will find five hundred rocking heads becoming no more or less than the limbs below them.

Oh, Bryony, don't frown.

Please, don't shake your head in disgust.

I am ignorant in these matters. You think that, don't you? You think I have no understanding of what it means to be young. To want to abandon yourself entirely and dissolve inside a moment. To desire feeling instead of thought. Oh yes, I know to you I have always been there, as parents always have. I might as well have been erected by the Druids.

A standing stone, from the time before time.

You never looked into my eyes and saw the long-haired youth who had once slugged back a glass of absinthe midway through a reading of Keats' 'Hyperion' at the Young Restorers' Poetry Club.

*

Eventually, I caught sight of you in your new clothes, alongside Imogen and the rest of them.

I weighed my options. Go over and drag you out of there and lose your trust for ever? No. I would wait and intervene only if necessary. I would hang back out of sight, dissolve among the smoke and noise and keep my distance.

Oh but it was hard, standing there, being jostled and groped as I tried to keep my eyes on you. They stood on my feet, they elbowed my ribs, they blew their multi-scented smoke into my face.

I saw a tall boy lean over and whisper in your ear. It was Mr Cadaverous. Uriah Heep. Other boys were with him, and I recognised some of their faces from the day I'd followed you into town. There was no sign of George Weeks, though. His mother must have spoken to him, I decided, and I gained a drop of satisfaction from the thought. The drop evaporated when I saw Uriah's long skeletal hand upon your back, sliding lower.

At that moment, someone spilt a drink down my shirt, a purplish liquid in a beer glass that left a stain. I ignored the sticky wetness against my skin and kept watching as the hand tested its luck against your hip. To my amazement you offered no resistance. Did you like him? I couldn't tell, but made no hesitation when I saw him head to the toilets.

When I got there he was in one of the cubicles, struggling with a catarrh problem. I waited, staring at myself in the mirror. At the stain that was drying on my shirt, fading pink. A stain that seemed to signify what I was, who I had become. Terence. Latin root *terere*. To fade out, to use up, to rub away. To disappear.

The slide of the weak metal lock, the shuffle of his feet. He washed his hands at the sink, at first ignoring my presence.

I would talk to the boy. That was my plan. I would address him politely, and present him with a lucid argument as to why he should not continue in his efforts to seduce a fifteen-year-old girl.

Then something changed.

I had the usual sensations. My brain tingled, my vision darkened but then, suddenly, I wasn't there. I wasn't in my own mind.

Or, more accurately, I was thinking thoughts that had not originated inside my own mind. You see, that was the first time it happened. That was the first time I saw something, a memory, that I myself (Terence Cave) had never experienced. Suddenly I was riding a bicycle and I saw that boy's face, his long cadaverous face, laughing at me, and I noticed his bony hand was pointing in my direction as I pedalled. Then I looked down, inside the memory, and saw that the bicycle I was riding was the present I had bought Reuben for his birthday a year ago that day. This was your brother's bicycle that I had been riding. And this, I realise now, was your brother's memory that I was reliving.

There was no further detail in the scene. There was the laughing Uriah, and there was the bicycle that Reuben (I myself) had been riding. All other details – weather, physical landscape, people accompanying either one of us – were entirely missing. Yet I must tell you that it was sharply believable. Indeed, it was so sharply believable that the question of whether or not I should have believed it did not emerge. The pain I felt inside me was so real it had to have been lived.

But as I said, such rationality arrived afterwards. At that moment I was so lost, so faded, so rubbed out, that anything Terence Cave had planned to say or do to this boy was completely irrelevant.

As Uriah posed in front of the mirror – changing the angle

of his face, sucking in his already sunken cheeks, pulling his hair forward to cover one of those sleepy eyes – a strange force rose within me. My fists clenched as I tried to control this force. Yet I could no more steer it away than I could hold back dark clouds arriving in an empty sky.

I trembled with it, tingled with it, became dizzy with it, this relentless feeling of being pulled away from myself. And then, instead of the slow descending gauze I had known before, I suffered something more intense. A black flash – a completely dark blank – that I now recognise as the eclipse of my soul by another.

After that, there is the gap, the missing link.

I was there, staring at him in the mirror. And the next thing I can remember his face was bleeding in front of me as I pressed him by the throat into the wall.

There was a sudden flood of sound as the door opened and someone walked in. For a moment, I did nothing. I just kept the boy fixed against the wall. The door closed, and as Cleopatra's death cry faded I heard something new. A fuzzy, crackling sound. Radio static. Then a large and ominous shape entered my peripheral vision.

'What the ————— is this?'

It was him. The boulder-headed heavy on the door.

I was grabbed and pulled away, seeing the crack I must have caused in the mirror before being dragged past all the sweating bodies and thrust out of the nearest fire exit.

'I think I've lost a button,' I can remember saying, before being kicked in the back and laid low on the damp concrete.

Four more kicks to my soft flesh and he was gone, and I was gone too, aware of nothing but the pain and the nausea, and the air that had been sucked out of the world at that moment.

'Reuben,' I gasped, to my face's black shape in a puddle. 'It was you, wasn't it?'

And in the city's quiet grumble I heard a confirmation.

Water dripped into the puddle from a gutter high above. The dripping brought another memory to my foggy mind, this time my own.

When you were six I took you both to the Dropping Well at Knaresborough. Do you remember? That incredible place where water continually drops down from a high rock, turning all beneath it to stone.

Fragile and human things made tough. Made eternal. Of course, science stole most of the magic for me. The water is rich in calcium bicarbonate and has a calcifying effect on the objects it touches.

Calcium carbonate.

This is the reason why people used to flock with their tea towels and wellington boots and teddy bears and leave them there to hang like washing, knowing that in a year or so they would be permanent memorials of their former selves.

'Daddy, if I stand under the water will I turn into a statue?' I remember the look on your elfin face as you asked the question. A look that mixed a certain thrill of excitement with a terrible fear.

It comes to me, that conversation, perfectly formed.

'You'd have to stand there for a rather long time,' I told you.

'How long?'

'At least a year,' I said. 'But you'd have to stay very still.'

'How still?'

'Like this,' said Reuben, demonstrating.

'What is it like to be a statue?' you asked.

'I don't know,' I said. 'I've never been one.'

You frowned, as you considered. 'If I had an itch I couldn't scratch it?'

'No.'

'I couldn't go to the toilet?'

'No.'

'I want to leave something.' It was your brother, melting out of his statue pose to interrupt your train of thought.

'You've got nothing to leave,' I said. 'We should have brought something.'

By this point I'm sure Reuben had already taken off his wristband. The red-and-white towelling one he treasured so much. 'I could leave this.'

I'm pretty sure I objected, but eventually gave in, donating the requisite pound coin to Knaresborough tourist board and pegging Reuben's wristband to the rope. Of course, I had to peg it up there myself because the rope was high, but Reuben stayed next to me while I did it. I remember having trouble with the clothes peg. The water fell with quite a force, and the wristband was too small and thick to clip in place with any kind of ease.

It was next to a sandal. I remember that. A proper object, I thought. Something that they would keep hanging for years.

'Come on, Dad,' he said, in that insistent voice. 'What are you waiting for?'

All the time I was struggling with the wristband my trousers were getting soaked. At first I thought it was just the water bouncing off the stone, but then I glanced down and saw Reuben with his arm outstretched, an upward palm blocking the water's descent, splashing all three of us.

'It's on my dress,' you said.

'Reuben,' I snapped. My voice loud, above the water. Even on the best days he had a habit for mischief. 'Don't do that.'

The hand dropped back by his side and he watched in silence as I finally managed to attach the wristband in place. We stood back and looked at it. It was the smallest and most pathetic of all the objects. Drenched out of shape with water, it was hard to imagine that one day it would be as solid as the petrified rope it hung from.

By this time, Reuben was more interested in his hand.

'I can't move my fingers,' he told me. He sounded convinced. 'They're turning to stone.'

He had quite an imagination when he was younger. Can you remember how he used to walk around with an invisible dog at one point? He wanted a real one, of course, but that was unfeasible. Cats are so much easier. I've never been very compatible with dogs, have I?

As we walked back over to you, passing objects further and further transformed, he ran through the advantages a stone fist could bring.

'I could punch through walls. I could put my hand in fire. I could . . .'

We visited the museum. Do you remember?

We saw a tiny stone shoe that had once been worn by Queen Mary. A lace parasol that still looked delicate despite the effects of the calcite water. Crystallised teddy bears and cardigans. A hardened ribbon. Oh, and that top hat. You must remember the top hat. I tried it on and nearly sank

96

into the floor. You bent double in hysterics, while Reuben was still soliloquising about his hand.

He came over to show us his rigid fingers splayed like a starfish. 'Look, it doesn't move. My hand doesn't move. I can't move my fingers.'

You tried to bend them, and got worried when you couldn't. 'Stop it, Reuben, you're scaring me.'

'He's only pretending.'

'I'm not,' insisted Reuben. 'My hand is turning into stone.'

You began to cry. No, not cry. You made the face that always came before tears. I told Reuben off and he showed you his hand was not turning into anything.

After that, we continued with our afternoon. You learned all about Mother Shipton and found something new to be scared of – the old hag prophet who had predicted the Fire of London, the defeat of the Spanish Armada, the Siege of York and the date of her death. We'd signed up for a tour of her cave next to the Dropping Well and you clung onto my hand for dear life.

The tears that had readied themselves earlier finally ran down your face. We made our apologies and left, dragging Reuben with us. Out of the cave, past the Dropping Well, and along the bank of the river.

'I'm a statue,' Reuben said, in that repetitive way he had. He was getting jealous, I think, of the attention I was giving you.

'I'm a statue. I'm a statue. I'm a statue.'

'Statues don't talk,' I said.

'I'm a half-statue. My mouth didn't touch the . . .'

It faded, as I crouched there over that puddle at the back of the nightclub. And it fades now, as I try to bring it back. I can't hear him. I can hear the water but I can't hear him.

*

On with it. Terence, charge forth. No more digressions. On with that horrendous night in that vile city of beasts.

Eventually, I pushed myself off the ground, away from the puddle and the memories it contained. As I hobbled my aching body towards the car, I wondered if I had broken a rib. The pain in my chest was certainly at an intense pitch.

They laughed at me, all those young drunks. All those apes in striped shirts and miniskirts staggering out of Latin-titled wine bars. I reached the car, and checked my face in the rear-view mirror. The faintest of grazes next to my eye, where I had scraped it against the concrete. A piece of grit, still pressed in my cheek.

There I sat, the faded Terence, my hands trembling on the wheel.

An oriental man was selling flashing bracelets and artificial roses on the main road. People squeezed his face and kissed his cheeks but didn't buy his neon jewellery.

Another man, toothless, strummed his guitar at the passing hordes, running behind them like a puppy seeking love.

And then I saw him. The injured Uriah, walking out of the Cockpit with another boy. No. Other boys, plural. Two or three other boys. They are blanks now, if they weren't then. But I can still see Uriah's face, and those long fingers testing the wound on his forehead. A wave of guilt as I realised what my hands had done.

I sank down in my seat and opened the window slightly, so I could catch their voices.

'The old ——— thought I was into Bryony,' I heard him say.

'Aren't you, squire?' asked one of the blanks.

'Would make no difference if I was, now she's only into that lowlife. That Danny or Donny or . . .'

'Denny,' I whispered, to myself, as their voices faded.

I waited two hours before I saw you, and lurked safely behind as we headed out of that beastly city towards York.

What does it make you feel, to know I was there, without your knowledge? Your guardian angel, trying his best to ward off the corruptive forces of the night. It makes you hate me even more, doesn't it?

Oh please, Bryony, please don't hate me.

I can neither live nor die with your hatred. Please, you must understand I had no realisation of what I was doing, or that he was still there, still lurking at a further distance, disapproving of the love that dictated my every move.

Cynthia was unapologetic, to say the least. Indeed, she was furious with me when I told her that I had followed you into Leeds. Obviously I didn't tell her everything, yet even with a partial account she was quick on the offensive.

You were still asleep, with Imogen, in Cynthia's spare bedroom. It was about eight in the morning and we – your grandmother and I – were sat at that ghastly table of hers, watched by all her theatre posters and Klimt reproductions and her own charcoal sketches. The whole bungalow was a mess, even by her own standards. She had evidently been acquiring more twigs and popping them into vases, clogging up the hallway. The fruit bowl was a mouldering still life of black bananas and blue-tinged clementines, while the arts supplement of the *Telegraph* was doubling as a table mat.

She was eating her breakfast and taking her hawthorn and echinacea and her daily meadow of supplements, all the little bottles and packets scattered out on the table. I sipped the coffee she had made me, and tried to ignore the throbbing pain of all those unseen bruises.

'I'm sorry, Cynthia,' I said, 'but I'm not letting you off the hook.'

She was quick on the volley. 'It's not your hook,' she said, before washing down her last tablet with a swig of grapefruit juice. 'It's my hook, and you couldn't free yourself if you tried.'

We had an argument in whispers. I remember she came out with some of the psychobabble she had picked up from her years as a child therapist. She quoted Jung at me, as her daughter once had. Some tosh about internal dangers manifesting themselves as outward signs.

'And besides,' she said, 'it was a night for under eighteen-year-olds.'

That is when I learned I was not the only adult you were lying to. 'I can assure you, it was not for under eighteen-year-olds,' I said. 'I saw the people going into that place. Some of them must have been thirty.'

Cynthia scowled. 'Are you sure, Terence?'

'I'm absolutely certain. This was no children's party.'

'Well, I'll have a talk to her,' she said. 'When she wakes up.'

'No,' I said. 'No. Don't. She can't know I was there. Please, Cynthia. You mustn't tell her I . . .'

She was ahead of me. 'No, I don't suppose we can. But, Terence, you must stop doing this. You must stop stalking your own daughter. There are some things a parent is just not meant to know.'

I rubbed my eyes and made a false promise of my own. 'All right, I'll stop. I'll stay wrapped inside my ignorance. I'll believe her lies and do nothing.' I stared up at the wall, at Klimt's lavishly decorated lovers, locked in their eternal embrace, and wondered what he could mean to you. This Denny.

'Terence, are you all right?' Cynthia asked after a considerable pause.

'I don't know. I mean yes. Yes, I'm all right.'

'You don't look yourself,' she told me.

'Well,' I said, trying not to think of the blackout I had experienced, or the violence I had inflicted, 'I am myself.'

Her eyes assessed me sharply, as though I was a counterfeit. A replica Terence.

'Did you sleep?'

'I managed two hours,' I said, although it hadn't even been that.

'How are you going to handle a Saturday in the shop on only two hours' sleep?'

'I don't know,' I said.

'I can help you this afternoon, but I've got a hospital appointment this morning.'

'Hospital?'

She stared mournfully at the mini metropolis of pill jars and bottles. 'It's nothing. It's just a routine check-up. A stomach thing. It's nothing.'

'All right,' I said, and I left it at that.

It was at this point, if I remember rightly, that you emerged from the spare bedroom, pale-faced and wild-haired, to head to the toilet.

'Bryony?' I called. And then, sharper: 'Bryony?'

You looked at me from the hallway. You gave a glance of tired recognition, and disappeared inside the bathroom.

'Bryony?'

Cynthia tutted and scowled and sent me a stormy 'Terence' from across the table.

'What?' I asked.

'Ease off,' she told me, and repeated it with pressing eyes. '*Ease off.*'

Ah yes, the balcony scene.

Now, I could often tell the type of customer entering the shop from the sound of the bell as they opened the door. A brisk ting would normally signify a browsing tourist, with no intention of making a purchase, while a more lethargic sound would often indicate a more serious buyer, who opens the door with the slow caution of a poker player lowering his hand. I suppose doorbells, like all objects, gain personalities over time. You get to know them, and they to know you, and they communicate their knowledge as best they can.

We were back home. You were upstairs with your headache and I was out in the hallway, straining my ears to try and tell what you were doing. Then I heard it. The bell. So low and sombre it might have been announcing the dead.

I sped into the shop and he was there, Denny, staring straight at me with those brooding eyes. He held a grubby little package in his hands. A belated birthday present, I suppose. Something crudely wrapped in cheap blue paper.

'Espryin,' he said.

I confess I was exhausted from the previous night, but I had absolutely no idea what he was talking about. What, or who, was this Espryin? A magician? A Dacian god? A password for a secret sect?

'I'm sorry?'

And he said it again, this time with the requisite pauses: 'Is Bry in?'

Shakespeare was mistaken. A rose by any other name is not as sweet.

'No,' I said. 'Bryony is out. Bryony is away. Bryony is far, far away.'

'Where?' He was not one for taking hints, this boy.

'I have not the faintest idea.'

He looked around the shop, as if I might have been keeping you locked up inside one of the cabinets.

'D'you know when she's back?'

'No. I do not.'

The truth, Bryony, is that I hated him. I hated his arrogance. This boy who had watched your brother die without shedding a tear. This boy who stood there, with his overdeveloped body and his underdeveloped mind, imagining he had a right to exist on your plane. This boy who probably had never even heard of Brahms or Handel or Mendelssohn, this primitive with a dream so many miles above his station. To be with you – a girl who appreciated art and music and literature, who could talk easily on a million subjects, who could have had her pick of any boy in the land.

There was a sound, from upstairs. Had you dropped something? Or had you heard the boy come into the shop and made the noise on purpose? Either way, the effect was the same.

He looked up to the ceiling, in the direction of your room. I looked at his neck, with the preposterous Adam's apple. A thick, muscular neck, but one that could still be cut like butter.

'I want you to go,' I told him in a low voice. 'Bryony's not here, and if she was I can assure you she would have no interest in seeing you.'

'What?'

'Look at you,' I said, too fatigued to hold my tongue. 'Look at you. Look at you. Just look. What on this earth makes you think you are worthy of my daughter? You are preying on a weakened mind. Do you understand that? You stood back and let her brother die and now, in her grief, she is too confused to understand what kind of creature you are. I am grateful for what you did at the stables. Of course I am. Any father would be. But don't think for one moment that I don't understand your motives. Save the girl and then steal the girl. That was your plan, wasn't it? Wasn't it?'

There was a violence inside him. He wanted to hurt me. I could see that. His jaw clenched, holding back his primal impulse.

'No,' he said. 'There were no plan. Ah just heard a noise, that's all. When ah was out running. She sounded like she were in trouble.'

'Just leave,' I told him. 'Just leave and don't return. Just leave. If you care about my daughter at all you will leave her alone.'

He breathed deep, and then gave the smallest of nods before leaving the shop. As he left, and as I saw him walk past the window, I felt the darkness creep over me again. I closed my eyes and shook it away. 'Tiredness,' I told myself. 'I'm tired, that's all. It's not him. It's not him.'

Then I heard something. A noise, coming from the rear of the house. A kind of tapping. Pebbles against a window.

'Higgins?' I enquired, but the cat's blank eyes indicated his lack of knowledge.

Walking out of the shop, towards the stockroom, I saw Denny outside. He was in the backyard, staring up towards your room. You were there, a weary Juliet, leaning out of the window.

He saw me. He saw my watching eyes as I stood in the hallway and then he went, taking that scruffy parcel with him. What had he said? What had he arranged? Of course, you gave me no answers. You kept your secrets, as I kept mine, but I was going to know everything. Yes, indeed. Which is why, that very evening (while you were sleeping off the night before) I went into the attic to find the item that would help the most.

The vulgar plastic of the baby monitor was caked in dust after nearly fifteen years spent in a box in the attic. So strange, that of all those old and treasured objects we had on the premises, this was the one possession I only had to touch for the tears to fall.

Instantly, it came back to me. That hellish day all those years ago. The break-in. Those three sets of eyes, bulging with mad anger as they stared out from balaclavas. My selfish panic as one of our intruders picked up the nearest item – an Ebenezer Coker candlestick – and threatened to test the solidity of my skull if I wouldn't tell them the location of the inkstands. An impossible task, of course.

'Where the —— are they?'

'They were sold yesterday. Both of them. They're currently thirty thousand feet above the Atlantic on their way to a silver-ware collector in Massachusetts.'

'You're —— lying,' said another of them. He wore a bomber jacket. The holes in his balaclava revealed pale skin, intense dark eyes, and the fringe of a black moustache. 'What kind of —— do you take us for?'

'He's not lying,' said your mother.

I remember the silent despair of our exchanged glance. Only five minutes before she had been with you and Reuben. She had only come downstairs to the shop because I had wanted help in preparing for the miniatures fair I was going to the next day.

She had been worn out. Reuben had been hard to settle. She had just switched the baby monitor on when we both turned sharply at the sound of smashed glass.

I see her standing there. Her long dark hair pulled back in a loose ponytail, the sleeves of her baggy blue shirt rolled to the elbows. She was a strong and fearless kind, your mother. A hands-on, wade-in type. Qualities she had inherited from Cynthia, but minus the theatrics.

Despite the despair I could see in her face, her voice tried to sound calm. 'The inkwells are gone,' she told them.

Behaviour breeds behaviour, she had always told me. One acts calm, one creates calm.

'You can search the whole shop,' I added. 'I assure you they're not here.'

This was the truth, but I wished it wasn't. Oh, Bryony, I wished I could have handed the inkwells over. Truly, I would have done it in an instant. I would have handed them the Holy Grail if I'd had it. But the inkwells were gone.

I know I have never told the full story of what happened next but now I am compelled to do so. I must walk through this raging fire that exists in my memory, the fire that has burned for years in my soul, a fire that has devoured us all. Now, I must tend to those flames.

A week before the break-in there had been an article in the *York Daily Record* about my miraculous find at a car-boot sale in Wakefield. This was back when I would stalk into such low hunting grounds. I found a kind of predatory thrill venturing onto those car parks and school fields, the thrill of a wolf walking into a flock of ill-guarded sheep.

The silver inkstands, though, had been completely

unexpected. Toby jugs and the odd piece of broken furniture were more typical pickings. To find these matching treasures – their panels decorated with the most exquisite engravings (urns, horses, Bacchic heads) perched atop beautifully crafted lion-paw feet – had almost caused me to collapse on the spot. Below the arms and motto I found all my hopes confirmed: '*William Elliot. London, 1819.*' Of course, my good Christian upbringing made me point out to the seller – a trollish lady with a Birmingham accent – that these items might be worth considerably more than the eighty pounds at which she had priced them. She doubled the figure and I rounded it up to two hundred, and she smiled as though I was an imbecile. A day later I had them tested with a dab of nitric acid and valued at twenty-five thousand pounds apiece.

'They're ———— here somewhere. What about that box?'

While the Coker candlestick hovered above my head, one of the other intruders pulled out a cardboard box from under a table.

'"The possession of Mr Cave",' he said, as he read my handwriting. The box was full of small items I was planning to take to the miniatures fair at the Railway Museum the following day.

The contents of the box were tipped onto the floor and, when no sign of any inkstands appeared among the snuff boxes and scent bottles, the intruders became more desperate. They looked at each other, wondering what to do. And then the man who had been waiting silently by the door stepped forward, signalling for the one with the candlestick to stand aside. He came closer, whistling an ominous G flat.

'Now, Mr Cave,' he said, after the whistle. He was more well spoken than the others, but somehow his voice contained a deeper terror. 'You have a choice. A pair of fractured skulls or a pair of inkstands. It is your call.'

'No, please, no, we're telling the truth,' your mother said. Her calm was beginning to crack as her eyes darted between the three men.

It was at this point that Reuben began to cry. I remember your mother's words as she looked over at the baby monitor, its white plastic as obvious in the room of old objects as an open eye on a corpse. 'Be quiet. Be quiet. Be quiet.' I remember her pleading stare, as though Reuben could see her through the tiny black holes of the speaker.

The intruders looked to the ceiling.

'No,' your mother said. 'They're not upstairs. The inkstands, I mean. They're not upstairs.'

'Where's the babby, Mr Cave?' said the one with the candlestick.

'Sorry?' I managed.

'The babby.'

Babby. Infinite terror in the violated world.

The well-spoken one met my eyes again.

'What's it going to take, Mr Cave? Would you really swap the life of your baby for fifty thousand pounds.'

Of course, he was bluffing. He was not going to go upstairs and order one of his thugs to beat our babies to death with a candlestick holder. I knew it, and prayed for your mother to know it too.

My prayer went unheeded.

'Do something, Terence,' she said. That whisper haunts me still. You see, Bryony, I did nothing. Nothing at all, for those crucial seconds. The man in front of me, the well-spoken man with the low whistle, nodded for the other two to head upstairs.

Your mother ran to block their path. Her hands gripped the door frame on both sides of her. 'Leave my children alone,' she said. There was fury as well as fear in her now. Wild eyes and a flash of teeth. The animal instinct to protect. 'Leave them alone.'

I stood there, rooted, thinking too fast and acting too slow. Every possible action I envisaged ended in a violence I knew I couldn't allow to happen.

But, of course, the violence happened anyway.

A gloved hand reached for her, as though her head was a vase on a shelf, a precious object to be vandalised. It was the one with the moustache and dark eyes. He flung her out of his way and she travelled halfway across the room. Her whole self – this infinite mass of emotions and experience – all useless against such physical force.

We had a pine mule chest, at that time, in the middle of the shop. Your mother hadn't wanted it. She doubted we'd ever get a return on the eleven hundred pounds we bought it for. It was me who had insisted, believing it would be a helpful item in terms of display. Indeed, we kept all manner of objects upon it – figures, glassware, a couple of jardinières – although few people had shown much interest in the chest itself.

She caught her head on one of the top corners, a hard piece of wood cut into a sharp right angle that hung out from the body of the chest. She slid and landed and lay there on the floor, her sleeves rolled up for a task she'd never finish. I knew he had killed her, and all their eyes knew it too, filled with a terror so different from my own.

There was a siren.

Mr Nair, the Pakistani gentleman who used to own the newsagent's, had heard them smash the window and had telephoned the police.

The intruders fled and were caught within a minute. I learned that later. At the time I knew little at all. I had fallen into shock, apparently. I couldn't speak to anyone that evening – not the police, not the ambulance people, not even Cynthia (it was left to a rather wonderful lady officer to make that call).

I remember, at one point, being with you two. You and your brother. I remember you were still asleep, still deaf to his continuing cries. I remember holding my hands to my ears, desperately trying to close out the sound, a sound that seemed to be responsible for everything. I wished for dreadful things, that evening. Terrible exchanges of fate. For days, weeks, months afterwards I did not trust myself around him. There would be times when he would cry and I would know that he was crying because he hated me, because he had an evil inside him that resented his life and everyone else's. There would be times when I would have to telephone Cynthia for her to come round and I would shut myself away in the attic, or I would crouch behind the counter, scared of my own dark capabilities. One night I even called her at the theatre. I called during the interval and she had to leave the Tennessee Williams play she was in. Oh, they were terrible times.

Of course, I would never have done anything to hurt him. Yet at the time I did not trust myself. Part of me wanted to blame a crying baby for what was really my own responsibility.

'Do something,' she had said. Do something. Do something. Do something. But I had done nothing. I stood and did nothing and let her die. Never had I realised, before then, that I was this type of man. A coward. A man of fear and selfish instinct. So what else had I to discover about myself? What further shadows could be cast across my conscience? Such questions lead to all kinds of fears. Fears that did not cease when Andrew Hart, your mother's killer, was sentenced for his crimes.

He was a human. That was the hard thing to stomach. A human with a human name. In the courtroom, stripped of his balaclava, I had to acknowledge he was of the same species, a man with a strangely warm and stoic kind of demeanour. When I saw him, sitting there, with the intensity gone from the dark eyes, I knew I would never be able to trust a man's face again. A killer, I realised, can lurk in even the gentlest of smiles.

They sent him away, eventually. They locked him up in Ranby Prison.

And as for me? I was a weakened man, but a man who had got through. Even if I was never again able to look into my son's crying eyes without thinking of his mother's death.

My experience of grief has never been that of intense sadness, as people often claim to feel. Sadness slows things down, presses you into the sofa and drags out the day. Grief doesn't do that. Grief throws you out of a plane. Grief is terror, in its most undiluted form. The moment in the fall when you realise the parachute is not on your back. You pull the cord, but there is nothing. You keep pulling and pulling and pulling, and you know it is no good, but you can't stop because that would mean accepting the rather appalling fact of the ground, a fact that is moving at an impossible speed towards you, and that will smash you to pieces. And you want to stay whole, unbroken. But there you are, falling, and there is nothing you can do except keep believing in that parachute.

*

And so, there I was, two months after your mother died, pulling that cord.

I had gone to Nottinghamshire, for the Newark Antiques Fair, where I found myself at an arms and armouries stand. Amid the cutlasses, civil war helmets and Scottish dirks there was the usual collection of firearms, organised neatly along the front of the table. Normally, this was precisely the type of stand I would walk by without interest, avoiding the malodorous and ill-bred miscreants who crowd such places. Yet there I was, gazing with wonder at the fine and varied collection of pistols.

In particular I was staring into an open case, admiring the weapon lying on a burgundy velvet lining. A solid, powerful-looking percussion-lock pistol dating from the American Civil War, with intricately rendered leaf motifs engraved on the brass frame. '*New Haven Arms Co. No. 1. Pocket Volcanic Pistol with cartridges*' read the yellowing certificate, in Wild West font. The cartridges were still there inside a lacquered tin, untouched and patiently waiting for their moment.

'A beauty, isn't she?' said the man behind the stall. An over-weight specimen wearing a lumberjack shirt and drinking flask-hot coffee from a plastic cup.

'Yes,' I said. 'A beauty. Indeed.'

'She's a rare beast, that one. You won't find an American pistol from the 1860s in such a condition. Serial number 28 if you look at the grip. That makes it quite a collector's item.'

'So, it's in full working order?' I looked him straight in the eye and troubled him with the intensity of my gaze.

'Yeah. Yeah. It is.'

I laid it in my hands, and felt reassured by its weight. 'If I wanted to shoot, say, a rabbit at fifty paces I'd have no trouble?' I enquired.

He laughed, uneasily. 'Depends on your aim, I suppose. Not that I advocate actually using the weapon of course.'

'But I could?' I said, staring at the tin of bullets. 'Hypothetically. If Abraham Lincoln was shot today, in that same theatre, with this gun, he'd still die? Am I correct?'

He scratched his rough stubble. 'Yeah. You are.' Even within the unsavoury context of firearms collectors I could see I struck this lumberjack as a rather worrying character.

'Right,' I said. 'Good, good.'

You see, I was convinced it would happen again. Convinced there would be another break-in and I would be faced a second time with men in balaclavas threatening those I loved. 'Do something, Terence.' Her voice, in my mind, as I watched the man demonstrate how to clean the barrel and load the cartridges. The words still echoing as I pulled out my cheque-book and made the purchase.

'Now, be careful with her,' the man warned, as if selling me his daughter.

'Yes,' I said, as my free-falling soul slowed its descent. 'Of course.'

You've always been a deep sleeper. That was the first difference we noticed between you and your brother. You slept, he cried. Even so, it was a risk setting up the baby monitor while you were in bed.

Indeed, I begin to wonder if I took such risks purposely, as though a hidden part of me always wanted to be caught. Something inside that was always working against my conscious intentions even when Reuben wasn't there.

You didn't wake, though. I plugged the monitor into the wall socket behind your wardrobe and hid it underneath, directly behind your rolled-up poster of Pablo Casals. You turned, in your bed, and I waited at your door for you to settle.

That same evening, in my room, I tested the speaker. I could hear you, I was sure. The reassuring rhythm of your breath shaping the quiet crackle that came out of there, through the same holes that had once transmitted your brother's fatal wail.

I heard your voice through the baby monitor. You were talking to Imogen on your mobile telephone about me, and about that boy.

'He came around,' you said.

'My dad wouldn't let me see him,' you said.

'It's like living with Hitler,' you said. 'Or Stalin.'

'If there was a search engine for brains he'd be searching mine right now,' you said. 'If he wasn't such a Victorian and could actually use a computer.'

'I've got to see Denny,' you said.

'You don't understand. I've got to,' you said.

'All right, I'll tell you. It's like I've known him for ever,' you said.

'It's like, when I'm with him, nothing else matters. It's like playing Beethoven or something. Like it's real. Like the whole world is just a bad dream and when I'm with him I wake up, like into myself, and know that everything is all right,' you said.

'Don't laugh, that's how I feel,' you said.

'I don't care,' you said.

'Shut up,' you said.

'No,' you said. 'No.'

'It's not like that,' you said.

'You're filth,' you said. 'Pure filth.'

'I don't care where he lives,' you said.

'Well, I find ways,' you said. You were quieter now.

'Last week,' you said.

Your words sunk quieter still, hiding secrets in the crackle, but I stayed determined to uncover them.

So, the next evening, two nights after your birthday, I dropped you off at the music college and I pulled away only to park further down the street. After what had happened on your birthday, I knew I couldn't be too suspicious.

When I saw you leave the building just two minutes after entering, I got out of the car and followed you. Where had you left your cello? You must have stored it somewhere inside the college, I suppose. Was there another student, helping you in all this? Weren't you feeling just a modicum of guilt, or worry, with the York Drama and Music Festival just around the corner? I never knew. All I could know was what I saw. And what I saw was your back, walking away from me, walking fast towards Clifford's Tower.

I stood, in a darkened doorway on Tower Street, and watched you sit in your new clothes on the sloping grass, waiting for him. You sat there for ten minutes and then he appeared, wearing a padded jacket, and gave you that parcel he had wanted to give you the day before. You opened it. Something in a frame. Denny placed himself next to you on the grass. Light was fading, and I couldn't see you clearly, but he was talking to you.

What was he saying? I had no idea. Maybe he was congratulating himself on his 'heroic' display at the stables. Maybe this was how he had claimed possession of your heart. Indeed, what else did he have to win you over? I prayed for you to see through whatever spell he had put on you. True heroes don't seek rewards, I thought to myself. They protect from a distance, from a shaded doorway, and stay invisible.

A lofty aim in this city, of course.

I heard feet and voices behind me, walking up the street. A procession of some kind. I turned and saw a man in a mock-Georgian long-coat and a wild blond beard, holding a lantern. Behind him was a group of around twenty tourists, walking in a thin line of couples and loners.

I could hear the guide's voice as the procession got nearer. 'You can see Clifford's Tower up ahead. Now, according to at least thirty witnesses over the last century, anguished screams have been heard from within the tower. Often this mortifying sound has been accompanied by the crackle of fire, which suggests they are hearing the long-dead victims of the Massacre of March . . .

I stepped back further into the doorway, knowing that you would soon notice the lantern or the voice and look towards Tower Street. I also had the feeling I knew this voice, but my mind was too busy with the fear that you would spot me to realise who this man was.

It is strange, how deep this fear was. Any other father might have stormed right over to you and dragged you home. Yet I had tried that, hadn't I, that night in the field? And where had that got me? No. I needed to stay unseen, and watch you undisturbed. If you knew your secrets were exposed you would have only sought more elaborate lies, and I would have been struggling to catch up. This way, I would stay a step ahead. That was how I rationalised it at the time. Yet wasn't there another part of me that wasn't so rational, a part that needed to watch you so that . . . ?

Never mind.

The ghost tour was only metres away from me now. I held my breath as the man with the blond beard walked past. He was explaining about those twelfth-century Jews, suffering under the anti-Semitic practices of Richard I, who chose to burn themselves in the tower rather than face certain death at the hands of the mob.

Then, just as I thought I was safely out of view, I heard another voice.

'What's that? Is that some kind of ghost?' An American boy, pointing and laughing at me before his mother hushed him. It was too late.

The guide raised his lantern and looked back in my direction. Recognition flickered with the flame. 'It's you,' he said, a smile pushing through his beard like a highwayman from the bushes.

'No,' I said. 'No, it's not.'

'Mr Cave?'

'No.'

'Mr Cave?'

'Please,' I said. 'Just go. Just leave me.'

'Terence Cave?'

I felt so weak, so vulnerable, with my name bouncing off

those medieval buildings. His voice was so loud I was sure you, and half of York, must have heard.

It was Mr Weeks. George's father. Reuben's dreaded history teacher. I had seen him twice before. Once at a parents' evening, where he offered sympathy for my having such a difficult son. The other time was in the shop, with Mrs Weeks, when they had bought the pine mule chest your mother had died next to. The one I had only just put back on sale. I remember how quiet Mrs Weeks had been around him, too timid to show her usual interest. Such a strange pairing, I had thought at the time. The giant hairy yeti and the neat golden fieldmouse.

They had separated, of course. I hadn't been surprised when Mrs Weeks had told me. Indeed, she had already given the occasional hint of his unreasonable behaviour – a bullying tendency towards both her and George – and there had been that undisclosed 'incident' that had caused him to finish working at St John's. Yet it was still a surprise to see him reduced to leading ghost-hunters around the evening streets.

He leaned in, with the lantern, and I backed into the shop doorway.

'Listen,' I said, 'It's great to see you, but you're obviously very busy and I don't want to hold you up.'

He smiled at me, revealing a gap in his front teeth I had never noticed before. 'I hear you had a little trouble with George, Mr Cave.'

'Oh,' I said. 'It was nothing. Honestly. Nothing.'

'That's not what I heard, Mr Cave.' There was something bitter about his tone, a barely suppressed anger. I remembered the letter I had found in Reuben's bag.

'Well, it's over with now.' I smiled meekly at the audience of tourists, who were watching the scene with confused interest.

'It's not easy raising children, is it, Mr Cave? Especially boys. We understand them too well.' He tapped his forehead at this point. 'But of course, you know all about difficult boys.'

I closed my eyes and tried to remain calm, but knew Reuben was pressing in. The changes were happening quickly. 'My son is dead,' I managed to say.

'Yes, Mr Cave,' he said, as if my statement had been beside the point. 'I know.'

As his smile retreated back into his beard, the black veil descended.

'You useless, pathetic boy!' He was shouting, loudly, without even moving his lips. 'You hopeless child! Someone stole your homework but you can't tell me who? I'm meant to believe that, am I? What kind of idiot do you take me for? Sorry? Excuse me? Speak up, child! Speak up! You are a sorry case. A sorry case. Wipe that look off your ugly little face. Now, wait outside and I'll deal with you later. Class, stop laughing!'

And then, with his lips: 'Goodbye, Mr Cave. Right, everyone, on with the tour.'

I experienced one quick last wave of darkness and then he was back in view. The smile, the beard, the missing teeth. Reuben had left me, unable or unwilling to hold on.

Mr Weeks said no more and, with a wild beckon of his arm, turned to lead his people towards the tower.

'Bye, ghost,' the American boy said, as he passed.

I said nothing. I took their curious glances and stayed exactly where I was.

One foot forward and you might have seen me. Your gaze, surely, was now aimed in that direction. I had to wait quite a while before I could afford to peek my head past the wooden entrance and, when I did, the view was obstructed by the ghost tour making its way up the path towards the Tower.

Between the flicker of walking bodies I saw you and Denny, sitting so close you were one formation. He was kissing you, I was sure. A roving hand probably somewhere upon your torso. His new-found land. I felt appalled, repulsed, but did nothing except watch. My eyes strained against the distance and the growing dark, the procession passed you, and he was standing, you both were, then walking down the slope.

'Oh no,' I think I mumbled. You were crossing the road, heading for Tower Street. I felt the swell of panic and shot out of my hiding place, exposed like a fox on the pavement. I walked away from you, as fast as I could, then dived down a snickleway. My heart beat to an ominous rhythm and I heard your voices getting nearer.

You were talking about boxing. He boxed. My daughter with a boxer. It was getting worse! At least you had the sense to say you didn't understand how he could enjoy it. I held my breath, as if visibility was a matter of exhaling, and you didn't turn to see me. You walked on, and I followed at a distance, watching as he put an arm around you, hearing your voices but not your words, down Spurriergate and through St Sampson's Square before you disappeared back inside the college.

I went back to the car and sat there, still weary from the encounter with Mr Weeks.

You came out, after a while, an innocent girl with her cello, and I was there to meet you. You lied to me, and I let you lie, knowing that if I exposed you I would have to tackle an even greater cunning. No. I wasn't going to let it happen. Reuben had died because I hadn't known enough. With you, I was going to know everything, so it hardly made any difference whether that information came from your lips or not. And what was I going to do when I acquired all the information I needed? Well, I was going to correct the mistake I'd made when your mother died. I was going to listen to her voice. 'Terence, do something.'

Although, of course, I ended up doing far more than even I had intended.

I remember standing in the rain, in the middle of the night, and not knowing why I was outside.

It was five minutes after four, and my body was trembling from more than just cold. At first I had not the faintest clue of my whereabouts. I was at a corner, a meeting of un-peopled streets. I saw a sign. WINCHELSEA AVENUE. The street was familiar now. I knew it as our previous short cut to Cynthia's. But what was I doing there? Had I sleep-walked nearly a mile from my bed? I was fully clothed, but couldn't remember dressing.

I noticed something cold against my stomach, something tucked inside my waistband.

I pulled it out and held it in my hand: the antique percus-sion pistol I had bought after your mother died. The one I always kept behind the counter. Hastily, I hid it again, and jogged back home, taking the quiet streets. An ascending horror as I thought of the house which had caused me to feel so strange on our walk to Cynthia – number 17.

What had I done? Or what had your brother done?

I didn't know, but the question stayed with me for the rest of the week. I kept expecting policemen to enter the shop and take me down for questioning, but of course they didn't. Perhaps I should have gone back there, to 17 Winchelsea

Avenue, and found the answer out. The only reason I never did was because I didn't trust myself to stay in control of my own soul. I didn't want to risk another blackout.

And there was also an even stronger concern: if I had done something, if my hands had committed an act beyond my mind's knowing, I didn't want to risk incriminating myself. This was not a selfish fear, I assure you. It was a fear as selfless as they come.

Without me, who was going to be able to look after my Petal, and keep her safe?

Cynthia and I were having considerable difficulty moving the walnut dressing table to be closer by the window.

It was your grandmother's idea. You know what she was like about window displays. She'd stand back, pinch her lip, and analyse the whole layout with such a thorough intensity you'd think she was directing Chekhov.

'Now,' she had told me that morning, 'we really ought to make it a bit more dynamic. Don't you think, Terence? It looks a bit flat at the moment, doesn't it?'

'I don't know,' I said. After the exhausting confusion of the previous night, when I had found myself on Winchelsea Avenue, I had little more to offer. And besides, everything looked 'a bit flat' nowadays so it was increasingly difficult to compare one flat sight with another.

'Well, it does, Terence. It does. The reason you're not getting any passing trade any more is because there is nothing to engage people with in the window. All you can see is that giant oak bureau which serves no purpose but to block half the light in the shop. Honestly, it's like being in a . . . in a . . .'

'Cave?' I suggested, wearily.

'Yes, Terence. A cave.'

'Rather apt, then. For Cave Antiques.'

'It may be rather apt but the point remains that no one wants to spend money on an item they cannot see. Now, I think we need to do more with the figurines.'

So, this was her plan. Have the tall oak bureau swap places with the walnut dressing table, upon which she would choreograph a dynamic arrangement of figures. She wanted the Barrias to be the centrepiece. *Nature Revealing Herself to Science* was the name of it. A near-pornographic piece I had been reluctant to buy in the first place and had only done so upon your grandmother's urging. She had ringed it in the catalogue, along with the Arabian dancer, adding the small message: 'IGNORE YOUR PRUDISH TENDENCIES AND APPRECIATE THE BEAUTY!!'

It is easier, I believe, for a woman to make such statements. Indeed, if women could see the world through a man's eyes they would understand that beauty can corrupt a male soul quicker than any drug or doctrine. Too much earthly beauty throws the male psyche towards insanity, as it reminds him of what he must one day leave behind, and men, as eternal children, can never cope with things being taken away from them.

A man sees beauty and he wants to possess it, in the fullest sense, or otherwise destroy it, but never simply appreciate it. And so, where there is beauty there must also be violence, to correct the balance. We need to leave our ugly marks in the face of the earth in order to feel at home. We need to see palaces looted and ransacked in times of war, just as the beauty of Imperial Rome needed the murderous blood-house of the Colosseum and just as the gorgeousness of Helen's face necessarily led to the Trojan War.

I had no idea at all what a bronze, voluptuous Nature forever slipping her robes for the delectation of Science would lead to, but I knew Cynthia did have a fine eye for such items so succumbed to her judgement.

Her fine eye had also decided that full-bosomed Nature would be accompanied by two further nudes, albeit more modestly posed, and that they would all bask in the light of a gilt toleware candelabrum. Somewhere behind, as a themed backdrop, would be the old slipware dish featuring a fig-leafed Adam and Eve on either side of the Tree of Knowledge. The chest itself would be flanked by the satinwood wardrobe and that suggestively shaped art deco longcase clock, which brought further boudoir connotations to mind.

I had advocated the inclusion of a fully clothed figure, the Girl with a Tambourine, but Cynthia insisted it be left on the high chest by the counter. I was too tired to argue, just as I was too tired to be heaving that blasted table over to the window. But anyway, there we were, halfway through the morning, halfway across the floor, when Cynthia cried out with a sudden pain.

'Cynthia? Are you all right?'

She bent over, wincing. 'I'll be all right,' she said, holding her left side. 'It's nothing. It's been playing hell for weeks.' She tried again to help direct the chest as I pushed it, but she had to stop almost as soon as she had started.

'Oh, you silly woman,' she said, scolding herself. 'What's the matter with you?'

Of course, the matter was the hernia she wasn't going to have properly diagnosed for another couple of days.

'It's all right,' I said, before pushing the chest straight into a table and nearly toppling over a Doulton vase in the process.

And it was then, at the precise moment the base of that vase settled on that flat mahogany surface, that the door opened and Mrs Weeks entered the shop. It seemed like years since I had seen her, since that day I had so upset her about her son's behaviour. I had thought I must have put her off coming into the shop for good. Through my delirious gaze she looked quite a vision, in her crisp blouse and pleated skirt and shopping basket. Indeed, the sight of her neat golden loveliness was such a tonic for the ugly chaos of my thoughts that it took me a good few seconds to realise she was with George.

'Oh, Mrs Weeks, do excuse the mess,' I told her. 'We're just changing the window display.'

At which she gave a sad, regal smile and said: 'Oh, I see. No, that's quite all right, Mr Cave. George is here to say some-thing. Aren't you, George?' Her voice was delicate and her eyes, as they looked up at her son, contained a hopeful pride.

I followed those eyes up to George himself and saw he looked wholly different from the last two times I had seen him. He was smartly dressed, with a dark blue shirt tucked into a pair of corduroy trousers. His blond hair, now free from its pink fringe, was flattened and side-parted. Indeed, only his glasses remained the same. Still, as I looked up at him I was instantly reminded of the previous evening's encounter with his father, and felt a coldness run through me.

'I'm sorry,' he told the slipware dish. 'I didn't mean to trip you up. In the field. I was showing off to my friends.'

Mrs Weeks smiled as she whispered to her son. 'Look at Mr Cave when you're speaking, George. Tell it to his face.'

And he did tell it to my face, and my face did its best to show forgiveness. 'Well, George, don't worry too much. It's in the past. But you must realise that you can't go throwing your weight about. Not everyone would be quite as tolerant as myself.' A brief image of my hand pressing against Uriah's throat flashed guiltily in my mind.

Cynthia, still wincing and holding her side, released an audible breath of laughter at the use of the word 'tolerant'.

'He is truly very sorry, Mr Cave,' said Mrs Weeks, her pretty eyes wearing a sorrow of their own. 'Indeed, it was George's own idea to come around and apologise face to face. We've been away to the West Country. A lovely place near St Ives. It's done us a lot of good, hasn't it, George?'

'Oh, St Ives is – agh – wonderful, isn't it?' Cynthia was saying.

George offered an awkward 'yes' that addressed both enquiries.

'I assure you he has changed a lot over the last month, Mr Cave,' added Mrs Weeks. 'He wants to make amends.'

This fact, combined with George's altered manner and appearance, was truly impressive. Indeed, it gave me hope. If he could change so much in the space of a few weeks, then maybe you could too.

'If there's anything I can do to make it up,' said George, the eyes behind the glasses looking so timid I almost felt sorry for him, 'I'll do it, Mr Cave.'

'Well,' I said, weighing up the possibilities.

Cynthia was quicker off the blocks. 'You could help – ow – move this dressing table over to the window,' she said.

George agreed and was quickly put to his task, using his considerable weight to heave the table forwards to its intended position. All the while, Cynthia was using those pencilled eyebrows of hers to prompt me into gratitude.

'Thank you, George,' I said eventually. 'That's very kind of you.'

'We could do with a nice young man like you to help in the shop,' said Cynthia, looking in less pain than before.

Mrs Weeks gave us a flash of her smile, as fleeting as a fish darting through a stream. 'Oh, George would love to, wouldn't you, George?' she said.

'Yes,' he said, before sucking on his inhaler.

I took a moment to signify my consideration of the matter but knew it was impractical, given the state of the accounts. 'Well, unfortunately we're not looking for anyone at the moment. We simply can't afford to –'

Mrs Weeks looked at me. The smile was gone. 'Yes, Mr Cave, we completely understand. Don't we, George? George?'

'I'd work for free,' he said, to even his mother's surprise. He had his breath back now, and spoke in a more confident tone. 'It would be good experience.'

'He wants to work in antiques,' said his mother, nodding her head in a small but rapid movement.

'But, what about school? Doesn't he have to –'

'He's sixteen,' said Mrs Weeks. 'And he's not cut out for A levels. He's never been an academic type.'

She sighed and gave a distant look, and I felt a great pity inside me. I thought of her horrendous husband and their separation. I wanted to reach out to her, one stranded human to another. My glance switched between Cynthia, holding her side and wincing as the pain returned, and the dressing table, perfectly placed by the window.

I thought of the effect he might have on you. The visible change in him might act as a signpost back to the old Bryony. After all, he was one of your tribe. Or had been. And perhaps he would share the secrets of that tribe. Perhaps he knew things about you that I didn't, things that would help me in my quest to restore you.

'All right,' I said. 'We'll give it a try on Thursday. Come in at nine o'clock and I'll show you the ropes.'

Mrs Weeks smiled in gratitude. 'Thank you,' she said. 'Say thank you, George.'

George looked towards the hallway, towards the home that lay beyond the shop. 'Thank you,' he said, as I slid like a ghost across his glasses. 'Thursday. Nine o'clock.'

So, the game continued. You kept up the pretence of adhering to the rules, and I kept up the pretence of believing you. In accordance with number 1, Imogen would sometimes visit on school evenings, filling the whole place with the smell of stale tobacco.

All those times you thought I was doing the accounts, or scanning the auction lists, or repairing antiques, I would be holding the speaker to my ear and listening to your conversations with Imogen.

Out of the crackle, your voices quiet as ghosts:

YOU: I kissed him.
HER: Ugh.
YOU: It was nice.
HER: Oh my God! Ugh. I'm sorry. It's just. Ugh.
YOU: I said a kiss. Nothing else. I like him. More than like.
HER: I suppose you heard Mozart or something, when you kissed him.

YOU: Stop it.

HER: I'm sorry. It's just –

YOU: What?

HER: He's –

YOU: He's what? He doesn't live in a stately home? It's not a Jane Austen novel, you know.

HER: Go on. He's what?

YOU: Never mind. You're just prejudiced.

HER: Ha. Pride and Prejudice.

YOU: Funny.

HER: I'm not a snob. I'm just not that into boys in sportswear. It doesn't really do it for me.

YOU: He's a boxer. That's why he –

HER: Classy.

YOU: Stop it. He's nice. He's kind. You can see it. In his eyes. You know, there's a depth. It's not what he says, it's –

HER: Bryony, you are the strangest individual some-times. Do you even know what he's into?

YOU: What?

HER: Music and stuff. God, could you imagine him at the Cockpit?

You said something that I failed to catch, as Higgins had just jumped up on the bed at that point, crying for his forgotten supper.

HER: What does he like, band-wise?

YOU: I don't know. We didn't talk about it.

HER: I couldn't put my lips on a boy's face without knowing what he was into. It would be like, I don't know, going to church without knowing the religion.

YOU: I didn't plan to kiss him. It just happened.

HER: Oh my God. Your eyes are glazing over. You're falling for him.

YOU: No. I'm not. I'm not. I'm not.

HER: Denny, Denny, wherefore art thou Denny?

YOU: I'm warning you.

HER: Give me my Denny: and, when he shall die,/Take him and cut him out in little stars.

YOU: Stop it. Stop. It.

I heard the thump of a pillow and your words stopped and became laughter and then I heard her offer you something and the window opened and it was at this point I knocked on your door. You eventually opened it, and sighed at the sight of me.

'Bryony, would you be able to feed Higgins while I get on with the dinner,' I think I said.

You looked at me with disgust, but no suspicion, and Imogen left with her unsmoked cigarettes.

I have learned that in this life there are two principal types of belonging, namely the type you are born into and the type you have to prove. This is the difference between a family and a tribe. A family requires no test, whereas a tribe always expects, and needs new proof from those furthest from its centre.

I believe that Reuben lacked that essential core feeling of belonging he should have got from us, from me specifically, and that is why his focus was always out towards the tribe. And what proof did that tribe require? That tribe which Denny had also been a part of? What did Reuben need to do to show his allegiance, to show he wasn't just a middle-class boy who would cut and run at the earliest opportunity? Well, we already knew the answer in part, didn't we? But other information came, as the *York Daily Record* rushed a crowd of foreign thoughts into my brain.

The boy's face stared out from the second page. The shaven head and hard, squinting eyes. It was the one who had staggered backwards, away from the scene of Reuben's death. And then, in bold Times Roman: TEEN SUICIDE NIGHTMARE. I read on, picking up only the more crucial words. 'Aaron Tully', 'overdose', 'his mother's midweek nightshift', 'suicide note', 'I am sorry', 'on antidepressants', 'single parent', 'distraught', 'living nightmare', 'police', 'no suspicion'. And then his address, no less horrifying for being cushioned inside the last line: '17 Winchelsea Avenue'.

I closed my eyes and I saw this boy. He pressed a bottle into my chest. 'There you go, Tea-stain, take a sup on that.'

'I'm all right,' I said. 'I don't want a drink.'

We were in a living room with toys on the floor. We were in school uniform. It was daylight outside. There were other boys there too, laughing, and I felt their laughter as bats flapping around my head.

'Drink it.'

'No, not that 'un,' another boy said. The small boy who had been with Denny and Aaron the night Reuben died. The one who vomited on the pavement. 'Me mam will kill me.'

'Shut up, Cam,' Aaron said, then to me: 'Drink it.'

132

His hard eyes offered no alternative so I took the bottle and read the label. Hierbas Ibicencas. A cheap liquor picked up as a souvenir from a package holiday, no doubt.

Within the dark green glass there was a cutting from a plant which had spikes for leaves. I drank it back, and kept going. It tasted foul. Rough and hot and ancient, liquid amber drawn from the belly of the earth. I wanted it to stop. My novice tongue couldn't cope with this. Yet I was aware of my audience, aware that this was one of those times when I could prove myself to my tribe. When I could belong.

The drink burned my chest but I kept on, forcing the gulps, as some of the other boys did drum rolls on the furniture. There was a rising cheer, from everyone apart from Aaron, and the noise was inseparable from the taste and the heat I felt as it went down. And then it was over and the room spun round and I saw the other boys. I saw their faces. Gargoyles and comedy masks, nudging laughter out of the others.

The laughter was aimed at me. At Reuben.

He leaned in. Aaron Tully.

'Tea-stain's going to throw up. Must have seen himself in the mirror. The ugly ——.' He walked his fingers across my cheek, towards the mark. 'Let's go to Australia.'

The laughter increased and I saw Denny. The only one not laughing. He faded away, erased from the scene, as I sat down on a chair.

Someone was hammering out random noise on a keyboard. A cheap child's toy.

'That noise,' I mumbled (as he must have also mumbled), 'is me.'

The burning laughter kept on, and I closed my eyes and lost myself in the loud and accidental notes of our existence.

*

133

We humans love to believe the thoughts inside our heads are collected as if in some deep and private well, each equipped with only one bucket, and from which we alone are allowed to drink. We go through our life and watch experience rain into our well, and we keep lowering the bucket every day safe in the knowledge that the water we drink from is protected by a circular wall of stone. We understand that the same light or dark clouds may rain into others, but we like to think that the water running into ours is our own private supply.

But do you ever think, as Tristram Shandy did, that your mind is full of borrowed thoughts?

Do you feel ideas and images leaking in from other places?

Well, yes, I know you do. Or, at least, know you did. Back in those halcyon days, when you used to talk to me in a decent manner, when you used to always go on about peculiar coincidences. The unusual word that you would say two seconds before it was spoken on the radio. The times you thought about Cynthia just as she telephoned.

Now, imagine these little glimpses became panoramic views. Imagine you could feel another's pain as you feel your own. Then, take the next little step and imagine that you found yourself with knowledge you didn't want, knowledge so complete it gave you snatches of another's experience wrapped inside your present. Imagine if there were times when the false barriers we build between one another – even those between life and death – were suddenly washed away and there, in the merging of eternal souls, we could remember things we never knew, and feel a pain we could never have felt.

Oh, Bryony, I swear it was his memories, inside me. All of them. Aaron Tully. Mr Weeks. Uriah Heep. I could not have imagined these things. They were there, washing in to the well, every time he entered. I struggled to remember him and so he was punishing me, filling those vacant spaces with the footage of his experience. Adjusting the levels. Realigning the balance. Preparing for the final flood.

You had gone to school.

The shop hadn't opened but I was sitting at the counter with some benzene, a clean rag and a dismantled late-Victorian bracket clock. Halfway through cleaning one of the wheels I sensed a presence outside and looked up to see the gargantuan figure of George Weeks behind the glass, his pale face looking in with an intense expression I couldn't quite interpret. How long had he been there? I had no idea, as I had been fully absorbed with the clock for at least ten minutes, but once I had seen him I left it and went over to open the door.

'Hello,' he said, in a voice that seemed to come from somewhere further away than his mouth.

He was smartly dressed, with his neat hair and chequered shirt and his tie, and he quietly apologised for being early. I beckoned him inside, and he listened mutely as I ran through everything.

I concluded by showing him the auction catalogues behind the counter. 'Now, George, do you have anything you want to ask me?'

He nodded and pointed over to the wooden case that housed the percussion pistol. 'What's in there?'

'Oh,' I said. 'Just some old . . . bits and pieces. Sewing things. To help me repair upholstery . . . fabrics . . .'

'Can I look?'

'No,' I said, the word stopping his hand as it reached forward. 'No, George, you can't.'

I was already thinking this was a mistake. The whole thing. I should never have agreed to this. If only Cynthia hadn't gone and acquired herself a hernia. If only Mrs Weeks hadn't had such an effect on me.

In my mind I rehearsed the conversation I would have with his mother ('Mrs Weeks, I truly feel George's talents would be better suited elsewhere'). However, I have to say that these early doubts were slowly erased through the day. Indeed, George showed himself to be a highly interested and capable young man. He handled the till well, proved to have his mother's knowledge on a range of customer-initiated subjects (Royal Worcester, the correct application of French polish, how to identify calf leather) and he even helped clean and repair the bracket clock I had been occupied with that morning.

True, his manner was somewhat awkward, and his heavy breathing certainly disconcerted Higgins, but our takings were up and this was surely a happy omen. Indeed, even his awkwardness began to grow on me. I interpreted his long silences and shifting glances as signs of embarrassment. Symptoms of the shame he felt over his previous behaviour, when he had tripped me over in the field. I even had the confidence to leave him on his own in the shop for twenty minutes while I fetched you from school.

'I can't wait for you to meet my new assistant,' I said, as you pressed your head against the car window.

'Who is it?' you said, with only the most lethargic interest.

'You'll see.'

You kept on looking out at the streets and traffic sliding by and said nothing else.

It was becoming clearer to you, wasn't it? Your disdain for me was growing with your affection for Denny. This disdain and this affection were twin forces, which could neither be quenched nor intensified in isolation. That blasted boy had devoted three minutes of his existence to protecting you, that evening in the stables, and that had swung it for you hadn't it? Three minutes! I had spent your entire life, an entire fifteen years, devoted solely to that same task and yet I still couldn't measure up. What did that say about me? Or about you? I had no idea.

'It isn't real, you know,' I told you, as we waited at the crossroads. 'What you are feeling. For him. That boy.' I felt your suspicious eyes and decided to tread more carefully. I couldn't let you know I had overheard your conversation with Imogen, or seen you at Clifford's Tower. 'That boy who came around to see you, I only got rid of him to make things simpler. He's clearly got it into his head that he stands a chance with you and I believe it's best we nip it in the bud right now. Don't you, Bryony?'

And then out I stepped into more dangerous territory again. 'It will pass far sooner than you realise. It will only be a few days without seeing him and you will come to your senses and, once you have, you will apologise. And you will thank me for looking after you.'

You closed your eyes, determined not to take my bait. I tried to change the subject, asking how you were feeling about the festival, but you ignored me. Maybe you were feeling worried about the cello lesson you had missed. I didn't know. Even the sight of George Weeks himself, back at the shop, produced no visible response out of you.

'Hello, Bryony,' he said, as he smoothed the back of his hair with his hand.

'Bryony, say hello,' I said.

I am trying to remember your reaction. To try and detect something in your face that may have gone unnoticed at the time. You didn't say anything. I can remember that much. You

138

ignored us both and headed upstairs to practise your cello and make up for that lost lesson.

I might have grumbled to George about you.

A mistake, I realise, and one more for which I must say sorry.

Over the years I have developed a keen eye for differentiating between a counterfeit and the genuine article. When visiting furniture dealers I have learned to identify artificial finishes that only simulate age. I can detect a genuine patina, with a deep and attractive sheen on the wood, as easily as I can spot a silver mark on a piece of cutlery.

Just looking at and touching an item enables me to authenticate it. Sometimes all the validating signs can be there and you know there is something wrong, as though the object leaks an invisible shame that only those who have known and loved the genuine equivalents can detect.

Oh how I wish I had this gift with people!

How I wish I could look into someone's eyes, unblinded by my thousand prejudices, and assess the nature of their soul. If only I could have been able to know where the truth lay in all of those things.

You see, my fatal flaw has not simply been that I have allowed my soul to lose strength and weaken, and become at times wholly possessed. That is just an element of this tragedy. Indeed, the possession has only in part been an external one. The other curse has been spawned by my very own nature, and this curse has been with me for as long as I can remember.

To be succinct about it, I have never quite known how to trust myself, and this tends to thwart and twist my relations with others. Even Reuben's attacks upon me seem wholly seeded within the fertile soils of my own flawed being. Had I not always transferred my own guilt regarding your mother's demise (a guilt which leapt out of that prior, more unjustified sense of responsibility regarding my own mother's suicide) onto your brother? Hadn't I, myself, been the source of everything?

Wasn't I always liable to take truths as untruths, to mistake an Iago for a loyal Horatio?

Wasn't this how everything became so distorted? How my own will to protect became as dangerous as his will to harm?

Wasn't it, ultimately, the same thing? Hadn't it all been fathered by the same unbalanced love. Yes. I can answer it now. Yes, it was. It was.

Oh, Bryony, it was.

You stood in front of us, all our old and expectant faces that were waiting for you to break the silence.

'Look at her, Terence,' Cynthia whispered. 'Isn't she magnificent?'

As you stood there I began to worry that nerves would get the better of you, that you would cower under the pressure of the audience. The audience who watched, who waited, who shifted uncomfortably as the pause stretched further.

You glanced at your grandmother. Cynthia tried to hide the discomfort she was feeling with her hernia and reassured you with her warm, dark-lipped smile.

You closed your eyes, like Pablo Casals always had during his performances, and began to play. I closed my eyes too, in order to feel the same darkness, to feel what you were feeling. And in that voluntary darkness I heard the opening bars and imagined the music becoming an invisible fortress around you, something that protected you from the audience and from your own fears, giving you the confidence you needed.

What were they hearing, these people? Was it the waking into despair Beethoven intended or simply the soothing satisfaction gained from watching a fifteen-year-old girl playing classical music?

Someone walked into the hall, and stood at the back. I let the light back in, and you did too. I turned to see his boxer's face. And the dark eyes of a very hungry little boy admiring a feast too rich for his appetite. You fixed your gaze on him and he smiled and scratched his brow.

I felt such hatred for him then, and wished I could stop the messages you carried to him with your music. His presence was a curse that tarnished the whole thing for me. Indeed, I was relieved when it was over and the applause rained down on you and we were able to take you away from those hungry eyes. Back home, oblivious to the danger that lay waiting.

As I write this all down I notice strange recurrences, echoes and symmetries. For instance, your accident on the stairs. An accident that so vividly recalled that last image of your mother lying on the shop floor. An accident I was convinced was not an accident at all.

Now, you may well have believed it was a coincidence that the evening of your cello concert was also the evening

Higgins turned on you, but I had an altogether different understanding.

Of course, I appreciate the changeable nature of our feline friends. Indeed, I had always admired T. S. Eliot's suggestion that we should give our cats three different names, yet even you must admit that Higgins had rarely been anything other than a Higgins. He wasn't like our long-lost Matilda who, for every minute she would spend as Matilda, would have two more as a Queen of Sheba or a Mad Bertha. As you know, Higgins was never like that. We knew when he was hungry, certainly, but for the most part he had an even and gentle temperament, and kept himself to himself. This made his sudden transformation all the more curious.

I came into the living room and knew something was wrong.

'Bryony, what's the matter?'

You were wincing, holding your hands. I saw the blood, rolling like a tear towards your thumb. 'Higgins scratched me.'

The culprit sat there, fatly contented, making no attempt to disappear from the scene. 'Come on,' I said to you. 'Let's go to the bathroom. You need a plaster and some antiseptic.'

I dressed your wound. A drop of blood fell into the stain your brother had made in the carpet, when he had sought to erode his birthmark with the bristles of his toothbrush. (There, you see: another echo.)

'Thank you,' you said, as I gently pressed the plaster in place.

These moments of tenderness were fading out, like fruits out of season, and I knew they were to be cherished.

'I don't know what's got into that cat,' I said, although I already had my theories.

Of course, it was the incident a mere ten minutes later that really sounded the alarm bells. Your desperate cry reached me while I was on the telephone, having a late conversation with a furniture supplier. The moment I heard it I stood up and ran and saw you lying at the bottom of the stairs. Your mother and Reuben had died like this, I thought. Died suddenly, falling. And now it was your turn. There was a pattern to it, an inevitability, that made me think the worst.

At first you were silent, and didn't move. The terror must have leaked into my voice. 'Bryony?'

You lifted your head, saw me standing high above you, and began to whimper in pain.

'My poor girl,' I said. 'My poor darling Petal.'

I ran down to you. I helped you sit up. I kissed your forehead.

'Can you stand up?'

In your shock you were a child again. 'I don't know,' you said.

'Let's try. There. See. You're all right, you're all right.'

'My wrist,' you said. 'It's killing.'

'I think we should take you to the hospital.'

In the car you told me what had happened. You had been running down to get yourself a drink, a fruit juice, and you had tripped over Higgins. He had shot out from nowhere and caught your foot. You were worried you might have hurt him too but, as you spoke, I had other concerns.

Was it possible that something had taken hold of Higgins? A malevolent visitation? No, it was not possible. And yet, hadn't such a thing happened to me? And hadn't it happened to Turpin, also? If your brother was trying to hurt you he knew he would have had to fight hard against my love, so maybe he sought softer targets to attack you directly. Quiet, peaceful animal souls, open and undefended.

I know what you are thinking.

I had lost hold of all rationality.

Well, yes, you are right. Yet I must tell you I had lost faith in rationality the day I stared out of that upstairs window and saw your brother hanging from that godforsaken lamp post, waiting to drop.

No, long before. Study history and you will see there is nothing rational in this world. Every civilisation, from those of the ancients to our own, has sought ways of explaining our existence. Gods have come and gone, beliefs and ideologies have been fought on blood-drenched battlefields, and we are still trapped inside the same mysterious lives. All of us, like Socrates, know nothing except the fact of our ignorance. I could have been hallucinating that night I had followed Turpin and found Reuben's ghost. I could have imagined your brother had found a way inside my mind, at that Cockpit. But who could tell me for certain? What do we have to trust but our own minds? There is no truth in this world, Bryony, only interpretation. We still do not know where precisely our souls exist, when we have gone, and so we know nothing. Such were my rambling thoughts in that old rambling Volvo, thoughts broken by your nervous command. 'Dad? Slow down. We're here. Accident and Emergency.'

We waited hours, didn't we?

Hours spent staring up at the rolling news as you held your wrist. Hours among the injury-prone inhabitants of our lower society. Do you remember that drunk who sat opposite us, the one with the smashed-up face, the one who kept asking us if we had seen a chap called Melvyn? Eventually you were called, by the undead administrator behind the desk. The

Indian doctor said you had a Colles' fracture and wrapped your wrist in white cotton. I thought of Pablo Casals and the boulder that had smashed his hand and stopped him playing. That was what Reuben wanted, I realised. He had watched you at the concert and grown jealous. Yes, I was convinced of it.

'My daughter plays the cello,' I said. 'Will she be able to play again?'

'Oh yes, definitely,' said the doctor. 'A month or so and it should be fine. It is quite a mild fracture.'

He smiled at you and you smiled back. He was young and handsome, that doctor, and I sensed his interest and gentle attention was not solely professional. 'It could have been a lot worse,' he said, and I might have seen him give you a wink.

A lot worse. The phrase was a warning, I realised that. The doctor was merely a talking vessel, a messenger of fate. I had to listen to him, despite his unsavoury attraction to my fifteen-year-old daughter. I had to listen and act accordingly. You were all I had left, a glowing candle of last hope, and I was prepared to do anything – anything at all – to protect the flame.

Which all leads me to the following confession:

Higgins never ran away. I was never surprised that he did not come home for his supper, or reappear in his basket the following evening. When I told you and Cynthia that I hadn't the faintest clue where he had got to I was lying. I knew exactly where he was but concealed the knowledge from you even as you began to cry.

I must confess your tears surprised me, you could have died tripping over that cat. Still, I offered my reassurances that he would return.

Now, my Petal, for the truth.

There was a woman from Knaresborough I discovered in

the telephone book. She offered her home to unwanted cats. I phoned her up and travelled there while you were at school. I locked 'Higgins' in his transparent travel basket and placed him on the floor by the passenger seat so he couldn't see where he was going.

I drove fast, feeling those large green eyes gazing up at me the whole journey.

'I'm sorry, Higgins, if this is all a mistake, but you must understand that I have to protect Bryony. I simply cannot risk another incident. If something is . . . if there is . . . if Reuben is . . .'

Your brother had wanted a dog, hadn't he? He had never wanted a cat. 'Listen, all I'm saying is that –' A horn blasted a warning somewhere behind and I looked out of the windscreen to see a Japanese car sloping out onto the motorway. I swerved into the middle lane and narrowly avoided clips of my mangled corpse making the travel news.

I glanced again at the cat, to receive a look of malevolent and all-knowing godliness that sent a shiver through me. I said no more, fixed my eyes on the road ahead, and reached Knaresborough as quickly as I could.

The cat lady was a balding, flush-cheeked widow named Mrs Janice Cobb. Her meaty hand grasped his neck and held him at face height. 'Oh yes, he looks the villain, doesn't he?' she said, as she stared into his stretched-back eyes. And then she repeated it, quieter, in parentheses. '(He looks the villain.)'

Her house choked me with its dusty air and urinary odours. I remember noticing, amid the thousand cats, some of the most vulgar items of porcelain I had ever seen. Felines sculpted in human poses, with top hats and bonnets. Higgins jumped up to join them on the shelf.

'Down off there, (down off there,)' said Mrs Cobb, rather sternly. She landed him on that wretched carpet and he stared at me with incomprehension. He was back to Higgins again, a cautious old he-cat, reluctant to make new friends. I felt so cruel, leaving him there.

'Mrs Cobb,' I said, ready to change my mind.

'Yes? (Yes?)' A ginger mog was playing parrot on her shoulder. 'I love you too, Angus. Yes, Mummy loves you. (Mummy loves you.)'

'Nothing,' I said. 'It was nothing.'

I closed my eyes and fought back my guilt.

'Goodbye, Higgins. Be good.'

It was that night when I experienced another blackout. I had been unable to sleep. My mouth had been feeling inexplicably dry, which had caused an annoying and rather compulsive need to keep swallowing. On top of that, I kept seeing Denny's brutish face exactly as it had been in the assembly hall. It wouldn't go away. It was there, in my mind, complete with those famished eyes.

I got out of bed, ran myself a glass of water, and then went to the living room to find a book to read. I was about to pick out Stevenson's *Kidnapped*, which I had devoured as a boy but hadn't looked at since, when I caught sight of the family albums. Replacement images, I thought, to help elbow Denny's face back into the darkness.

I pulled one out and sat down, putting the glass on the table. The very first image made me cry. It was your mother, fresh out of hospital, with a baby in each arm. Her tired, joyous smile cutting straight through time as she looked out from the photograph.

'Oh, Helen, if only you were here.'

I kept flicking, and saw all those pictures of you together. The mother and her twins. On the last page there was one of the four of us. Cynthia must have taken it. You and your brother, side by side in your cots. If Reuben hadn't been crying then you would have looked identical. Wrapped up in your cream blankets like two butter beans. Your mother and I leaning over, with happy and unknowing smiles.

I pulled out another album, which had a year's break halfway through, the break caused by your mother's death. After she had died I saw little in life I wanted to record or put down for posterity. Eventually I got back on track, but never with the same frequency as when you had been babies. I went through the next album, and the next, and the next, going through your life history in photographs. Your look of amazement at the birthday cake Cynthia made you when you were four. Can you remember it, with the toy horse and the stables made of chocolate matchsticks? There was a picture of you with your Handwerck doll, Angelica, cradled in your arms. Another had you holding Cynthia's hand on the beach at Whitby. A long-forgotten Sunday excursion. Gradually, as I kept flicking through the pages, I noticed his gradual disappearance. As a toddler he was often by your side, at the forefront of the shot, but as you grew up and gained independence the bias towards you was unmistakable. He would be caught, running in the background. A distant, blue-duffel smudge. Or, later on, as you both passed double figures, he wasn't there at all. It was always you playing your recorder, or your violin, or your cello. Or at a horse event leaning over Turpin as you successfully made it over a jump. There was a couple of him looking miserable in the yard, standing by his bicycle, but hardly anything more.

I found an old school photograph, loose amid the others.

You were ten years old, wearing a dress bought from a hypermarket outside Aix-en-Provence the summer before. It had a high collar, with navy and white vertical stripes. Your hair was bobbed in the style of a Franciscan monk from the Middle Ages, your unpierced earlobes peeping out from underneath.

Your smile, your complexion (lily white except for the brush of pink on your cheeks), the eyes that I translated as happy, eager, unknowing. Sacred. The school photographer as Dutch master. In that picture, against the anonymous grey-blue background, you seemed outside of this world, somewhere special, beyond touch.

One whole album was devoted to your appearance at a York Drama and Music Festival. As I stared at a photograph of you frowning thoughtfully as you studied the sheet music, I had the most dreadful shock. It began to move. You, inside the photograph, your hand moving the bow in those slow, considered strokes.

'No,' I said. 'No, it's an illusion.'

Suddenly, inside the photograph, it was me. My side profile, staring with devotion in that same assembly hall. I was looking at myself from below, from Reuben's height in the next chair along. Then those strange sensations again. The tingles in my cerebellum. Those dancing sparks from invisible fires. I sipped my water but it was too late. The black veil was falling over my eyes and I could hardly see. Flies buzzed and crowded nearer.

'Come on, Terence, you're stronger than him. Try to pull yourself together.'

By the time I had finished the sentence I was in the park, still in my pyjamas. There was a plastic bottle in my hand. The ammonia bottle. Tipping it upside down I realised, to my ascending dread, that it was already empty.

I stepped forward, one of my bare feet pressing down on a twig. With the aid of the yellow glow from Reuben's distant street lamp I saw a black shape, scorched into the grass.

The warmth of the ground reached me as I leaned in for a closer inspection. An oval, rising to a thin point. Like a giant teardrop. I caught the faintest smell of maple.

'Oh no,' I whispered, my words silent in the night wind. 'What have we done?'

I was cooking our porridge and listening to the radio when you came into the kitchen, fiddling with your bandage. 'My cello,' you said. 'It's not there.'

'What?'

You said it again, shaking it out of your mouth. 'My cello. It's not there.'

'What do you mean it's not there?'

'It's not in my room. It's not anywhere.'

I tried my hardest not to cry. I couldn't believe it. Your cello! I thought of the scorched black teardrop in the park, and prayed you would never see it and make the connection. What was happening? Why was he doing this? Why did he want the treasured icons of the old you, the authentic Bryony, to disappear?

'Oh,' I said, my voice sounding too frail, too weak, to sound truly convincing. 'Oh, I don't know where it is. How bizarre. We'll have to buy you a new one. I'll buy you a new one. Don't worry, by the time your wrist gets better we'll have got you a new one. A better one. A Strad. We'll go to Manchester and you can choose whatever you want.'

'I don't want a new one,' you said, as suspicion crept into your voice. 'Where is it? It was in my room and now it's gone. That's beyond bizarre.'

Indeed it was. But what else could I do? Blame it on intruders, and risk getting the police involved?

'How would I have any idea where it is? Seriously, Bryony, why would I have hidden your cello? I adore it when you play.'

I was staring down into the porridge, so I have no facial expression of yours to try and recall. I imagine it as sitting somewhere between fury and confusion.

You said no more. You walked out of the room and left me

standing there, stirring porridge that was already burnt, as a man on the radio talked about the long slow death of the sun.

Oh yes, something else. Mrs Weeks came into the shop, with the apparent purpose of enquiring after George's performance the previous Thursday. She looked immaculate, as always. Neat, tucked-in, straight-bobbed, but there was something troubled about her. She nodded and twitched and clung to her wicker basket as I gave her the report. I told her that he had proved himself, despite my doubts, to be a remarkably competent assistant, one well informed on a range of appropriate subjects.

'You have worked a miracle, Mrs Weeks,' I concluded. 'You have restored the old George rather perfectly. Tell me, what's your secret?'

She kept on nodding, into the silence, as though I was still talking. Her eyes were staring in my direction but seemed to be looking through me, rather than at me, as though there was another Terence she was listening to, a metre behind this one.

'Someone attacked Stuart,' she said.

'Stuart?'

She closed her eyes and swallowed. 'George's father. He was walking home. It was outside his new place. Someone attacked him, from out of nowhere.'

A fear ran through me. I remembered seeing Mr Weeks and the tourists on their way to Clifford's Tower. I remembered his angry voice in my ear and his unmoving mouth, concealed in his beard, as I had stood inside that doorway.

'Oh,' I said, in a fragile voice. 'Oh . . . how terrible. I . . . he . . . is he all . . .'

'Yes. He was unconscious for hours, and we spent a most

dreadful night, but he is all right. The doctors say he is very fortunate to have made such a recovery after such a nasty injury.'

I wondered why she had decided to come out of her way to tell me this information. (Of course, antique sellers are third only to priests and psychotherapists as useful listeners. I believe it has to do with the shop itself, and all those old items that have silently witnessed so much over the centuries. Yet Mrs Weeks was not the type to burden you with her problems for no reason, no matter how tempted she may have been. She normally held onto them with the same tight grip as she now held onto her basket.)

The thought worried me, and pushed me towards a question. 'Who on earth would do such a thing? Have the police caught whoever did this?'

Mrs Weeks gave a quick shake of her head and I felt a relief I tried to ignore. 'No. He didn't see anything. The police say it's very unlikely that they'll be able to find the attacker. Given the time and place and the fact there were no witnesses, and no camera footage. Oh, Mr Cave, I feel so responsible.'

Her words echoed my fears. 'Responsible?'

She took a deep breath, a sigh in reverse, before trying to shed her guilt. 'You see, he had wanted to stay with us but I had insisted, for George's sake mainly, that he rethink his decision and leave. If he had been on his way back to us it would never have happened.'

'Oh, I see,' I said. 'Right. Well, don't be too severe on yourself. You couldn't have known what was going to happen, could you? The main thing is that he is going to be all right, isn't it? Mrs Weeks?'

Her face crumpled in front of me, like a fast-ageing fruit, and before I knew it she was sobbing.

'Oh, Mrs Weeks, Mrs Weeks, Mrs Weeks . . .' I came out

from behind my counter and held her in my arms, the wicker basket positioned awkwardly between us.

'I feel so ridiculous,' she said, between sobs. 'After all, you've been through so much worse this year.'

I looked over her shoulder at Cynthia's window display. At the tableau of nude figurines on the dressing table and I felt a sudden sense of shame. Alongside the sympathy I was feeling for this poor woman, I was also experiencing something else.

Oh, it is so strange. I can express to you all manner of dreadful deeds yet when it comes to that yearning emotion I felt as a result of this encounter, I feel the urge to flee from any honest account. But I know I must be honest about it. I must. I must tell you that as well as a father I was a man like many others, a man who knew that the still shores of his romantic self were susceptible to waves of longing at any moment.

I kissed her forehead. I felt her small body against mine, and the life that beat inside. I could smell the floral scent of her shampoo, and see the blurred blonde curve of her head below me. She clung tight to my body, as if it were a raft in the sea.

'The separation has been so terribly hard,' she said.

'Don't worry,' I said. 'It's all right. Time will smooth things out.'

I stood there, in the precise spot your mother had died, and held this other woman in my arms. I made reassurances only a father and husband is entitled to make.

I stroked her back, my soothing hand appreciating the divine softness of her cashmere sweater. 'Things will get better,' I said, feeling the lie's sweet comfort. 'Things always get better.'

'I'm such a fool,' she sniffed, and dabbed away her tears with a brilliant white handkerchief. 'What must you be thinking?'

'I'm not thinking anything,' I told her.

But what was I thinking? Could it have been that the desire to protect is the desire to possess? That the desire to hold is the desire to press close? That the desire to love is the desire to destroy? Amid these musings a bus rolled past the window. A double-decker advertisement for a Parisian perfume.

'*Ange ou Démon?*' asked the vampiric model, staring out into the day-lit world.

'*Les deux sont la même chose*,' came my silent response, as I kept stroking Mrs Weeks out of tears.

Now, that next morning, when I cut myself shaving. It was a lie, Bryony. It wasn't a razor, but a toothbrush. And it wasn't even me, but your brother, playing malevolent tricks with my mind.

I saw blood.

I saw drops on the brush.

I saw a speck hit the mirror.

I felt it burning, but not like the word.

Tea-stain. Tea-stain. Tea-stain.

The hand moved faster, changing brown to red, the pain pressing deep into me.

I saw the blood dripping and I looked down into the sink and glimpsed the madness of what I was doing. I kept on, as the word echoed inside me.

Tea-stain.

I heard the word as Aaron said it. With no line under it. Like it was the only name I had. He had. I had.

'All right, Tea-stain.'

'Nice one, Tea-stain.'

'See you, Tea-stain.'

And the remembered thought. If I brushed hard and deep and wide it won't come back.

'Aagh.'

I said it aloud. Through closed eyes. My whole face clenched with the pain that was too much.

I saw myself dropping the toothbrush in the sink and felt the thudding pulse in my cheek. The pain grew.

I opened my eyes and washed the weak pink blood down the plughole. I grabbed some toilet roll. Specks hit the lid and the carpet, turning black.

I padded the red wound. The paper drenched into mush.

My own voice, outside. 'Reuben? What are you doing in there? Reuben? Do you really need that much water?'

'Dad,' I said. 'I'm just . . . I . . . I won't . . .'

I switched off the tap and the door opened. It wasn't me standing there, out on the landing. It was you, in your uniform.

'Dad?'

'Bryony?'

'Oh my God! What's happened? What are you doing? The blood!'

I looked at my face now, and saw my own lined and aged skin, my Terence skin, with the blood running down it. And then I saw the damp pink tissue in my hand.

'I cut myself shaving.'

Did you see the toothbrush in the sink? Were you suspicious as to why the wound was so big? If so, you never said.

'Dad, sit down. Sit on the toilet. I'll get a flannel. I'll sort you out.'

I was delirious. I sat on the toilet, and stared into Turner's crashing sea on the wall behind you.

I remember you helping me with the plaster, pressing gently, careful of your wrist.

'My sweet Petal. My Florence Nightingale,' I said, and ignored your flinch at the words. And I flinched too, as you tapped your finger on the plaster. A sudden and specific shot of pain in the centre of the wound. It was then, I believe, that you asked me if it was all right to go to the sports centre that evening. You wanted to go swimming, you said. 'It will be good for my wrist. That's what the doctor said.'

'Yes,' I said, too weak to remember if this was true. 'Of course, I'll take you.'

*

I dropped you off at the sports centre and waited for you in the car park, my face still throbbing with pain.

I was in the lowest of spirits. I hated this game we were playing. I knew, ever since Clifford's Tower, that I had to keep it up but I just prayed that this time you weren't lying to me. Indeed, when I saw no sign of Denny, I began to believe it. Perhaps you were a normal, undeceiving daughter, enjoying an evening swim like you often used to. And perhaps I was just a normal, patient father waiting for you in the car park.

Of course, I was deluding myself. The only reason I remained in that car park was because I had to remain in that car park. There was no way on this earth I could trust you enough to stay inside that horrendous building and do exactly what you had told me.

I needed to see you disappear inside those doors and I needed to stay watching those doors in case you came back out of them too early.

That didn't happen. Indeed, the conviction that you had changed began to grow. Maybe your lies had stopped. Maybe it had all been a horrendous phase. Maybe you had seen sense and ended whatever it was that had existed between you and that boy. Maybe his late arrival at the assembly hall had embarrassed you. Or maybe you had finally realised the value of your precious soul was worth so much more than his.

But then I heard it. A roar that seemed to swell the sports centre's very dimensions. It was the roar of a mob, of a re-volution, and it frightened me to my very core. By the time that noise had died I was already out of the car, heading towards those vast windows. I leaned in close, to peep through the dark tinted glass at the swimming pool. I scanned each lane of blue water, but I couldn't see you. Perhaps you were still changing. Yes, I would wait there, outside the glass, until you emerged from the changing rooms and then I would head back to the car, switch the dial to Radio 3, and listen to a little music.

Judging from the worried glances of the swimmers, I don't think the bloodstained plaster on my cheek was doing me the greatest service. I could see what they were wondering, those slow-swimming ladies, and I tried to look as relaxed and unperverse as I could, given the handicap of circumstance.

But then I heard it again. That roar, like a violent wind. A wind that swept me towards the entrance, through those red swing doors, and to the gum-chewing sloth in the kiosk. I told her I was searching for you, and that I was worried something may have happened in the changing rooms, but I got nowhere.

'Looks like you'v'urt yerself,' she said, displaying powers of deduction that would have hardly shamed Sherlock Holmes.

Then, for the third time, I heard that wild cheer.

'What was that noise?' I asked.

''S the boxing,' she informed me, between her lethargic, bovine chews.

'The boxing?'

I turned and saw it. Him. His eyes staring out from behind his fists. One of the eight young gladiators on the line-up. North of England Under 18s Amateur Boxing League. I saw his full name, for the first time. Dennis 'Hammerblow' Hart.

Hart.

A hammer-blow indeed. Although at the time I was so determined to find you that the name hardly registered.

'Yer'll need to pay 'f you wan' watch the boxing.' The

sloth's words followed me as I walked down those chlorine-scented corridors, over that squeak-clean floor, towards the sports hall. When I got there I watched through the doors, through the crossed wire of the reinforced glass, and I saw Denny in the ring. He had that black boy in the corner, battering his guts with a series of punches that seemed to be powered by the crowd itself, gaining force with the ascending volume of the roar.

You were not hard to spot. You were the only one among that lowly mob not punching the air or screaming for violence. Indeed, you looked troubled by the bloodlust all around you. Scared, almost. My poor darling Petal, among that rabble!

Two competing impulses, inside me. The first, which we might term the 'Cynthia reflex': stay there, let you be, don't interfere. After all, I knew where you were. You still would have to leave via the main entrance and so, in theory, I could have gone back to the car and waited for you with the knowledge that you would be safe. And, after all, this was in keeping with my plan. Hadn't I promised myself not to interfere unless absolutely necessary? Wasn't this the best way to keep on top of your double existence?

Then the second impulse, boxing the other into its corner. There was something so horrendous about this scene. I felt the wild, uncivilised nature of that crowd tainting your innocence, melting it away like the last snow in March. No. It was too much. I couldn't stand back any longer. I had to change my strategy.

This was it, the last deception I was prepared to put up with. A walk through the streets together was one thing but this was . . .

No. Stop. Be honest, Terence. All right, I suppose what

really drove me into the hall was the knowledge that you loved him. I knew it then, as clear as anything. You loved him. Why else would you be sitting there, as out of your element as a kestrel in the ocean, watching the pugilist's loose interpretation of the Queensberry Rules.

I pushed open those doors and shook a man's hand off my arm.

'Can I see your ticket, mate?'

'No,' I said, drowned out by the roar. 'No you can't.'

I ran on, over towards you. A few of the crowd had begun to notice the intruder now, followed as he was by the ticket inspector, and their bloodthirsty roar started to die. By the time I was climbing the middle aisle of the bleachers the whole hall, bar the two boys boxing in the ring, had descended into a hushed quiet. Somewhere behind me the bell rang for the end of the round.

What were you feeling, when you saw me? Was there anything alongside the shame? The shame that caused you to conceal your beauty with your hands.

I excused myself past a row of knees, ignoring the grumbled profanities as I made my way towards you.

'Bryony? I thought you were meant to be swimming.'

'Go away,' you said, quietly, through clenched teeth. Your cheeks were scarlet. Your eyes couldn't look at me.

'Bryony, you lied. Now, come on, let's go home.'

'Dad, just go.'

'You heard the girl, fella,' said the rot-toothed, potato-headed specimen next to you. A man with a Celtic cross tattooed on his arm, and a low-carat gold medallion hanging over his T-shirt. 'Get out the way.'

And then the ticket inspector: 'Mate, unless you have proof of a ticket or are willing to pay for a ticket I'm going to have to ask you to leave immediately. Mate . . . mate . . . mate . . .'

The bell sounded for the next round but half the crowd were still staring at us. I grabbed your arm. 'Leave the girl alone!' said the rot-toothed man.

You saw the threat of violence, and knew you couldn't risk further embarrassment. You stood up, followed me through that roaring crowd and across the hall.

Halfway towards the door you turned to see Denny in the ring. He caught your gaze and forgot where he was. His arms hung down and his feet stopped moving across the canvas.

You whimpered in quiet pain as his opponent's gloved fist met his chin and knocked him half off his feet. We left the hall as he fell back, hooking his arms around the ropes as another blow dulled his senses. We walked down those corridors, past those pinboards and vending machines and red-faced squash players.

'Bryony, I have no comprehension what or why you feel for this boy. But I must tell you your feelings are aimed in the wrong direction. He's not right for you. You deserve better. You deserve a boy who is into the things you have always been into. Someone with an interest in culture. Someone civilised. Someone whose talents extend beyond the ability to use his fists.'

You turned to look at me and gave me such a sharp look I wondered if the violence you loved in him had begun to infect you. 'You don't know anything about him. You're just a blind snob. He's hurt now. He's hurt. Because of you. You don't know anything.'

A tingling memory of walking into a house with Denny. The putrid scent of vomit overpowering the chlorine, for that fleeting moment.

'I know Imogen doesn't like –' I stopped myself, just in time, and pursued a different route. 'If this is something to do with your brother then you are far off the mark. He didn't care about Reuben. He was there when he died. I know he let him climb a lamp post for the sake of a cheap laugh. I know that if it wasn't for him and the rest of his no-good tribe of yobs Reuben would still be alive.'

You closed your eyes and shook your head and kept whatever you knew to yourself.

'You're not a father,' you said, as we walked out into that cool evening air. 'You're a dictator. You're a weird, creepy fascist and I hate you. You could die for all I care.'

'No,' I said. 'You don't mean that. These are just histri—'

'One day you'll wake up and I'll be gone. I'll have run away and you'll never be able to find me.'

As we headed into the car park I looked at you, at your face, at the frown that dented your beauty like a chip in a vase.

'You don't mean that,' I said.

'I do. I mean it. You'll see. You'll see.'

And of course, you had never sounded more sincere.

Something I must correct:

Dick Turpin was not a man to be admired. Now, I know you and your brother loved me to tell you about him, as children, and I dare say I loved to be the teller, yet now the doubt eats at me that this wasn't quite the thing to do.

Dick Turpin was a highwayman, that is true, but there was

no heroism attached to his villainy. There was no horse called Black Bess, no twenty-four-hour ride from London to York, no care for the welfare of his victims. These were embellishments, romantic conjurings from the pens of Victorian novelists. The real Richard Turpin was a vile torturer, who held old women over their fires until they told him where their money was kept. He was a man who shot his best friend, and let his father be imprisoned rather than give himself up. He was a rapist and terrorist, who hid out in caves and preyed on the old and defenceless. A man who, for all his cunning, got caught for shooting a cockerel, who exaggerated his exploits to whatever audience he could find in York dungeon, and who paid for mourners to attend his funeral.

I was wrong to suggest a rogue could be a hero. I was wrong, on your first visit to the racecourse, to point out the spot where the gallows were, and to excite you with the famous story of how Turpin gallantly threw himself off the ladder to his own death. I was wrong to allow your horse to take his name. I wish I could have filled your ears with stories of the saints, of those who knew violence and evil for what it was, but I did not. And so I helped nurture this blindness you have, this inability to see where evil exists, this affliction I too must now recognise as my own.

I had a bit of a row with Cynthia on the telephone.

'She's lying to me,' I told her.

'Oh, Terence,' she blustered, in her dismissive way. 'She's a teenage girl. Lies are what keep her breathing.'

'She's putting herself in danger,' I said. 'She said she was going swimming and she went to a boxing match. Boxing!'

A long, Cynthian sigh. 'She needs her freedom, Terence. You can't suffocate her.'

'Freedom,' I said. 'What does freedom mean any more? Freedom's a myth, Cynthia. There's only safety. That's all. And if I don't know where she is, how can I look after her?'

And then she began to get cross. 'Do you think I always knew where Helen was? Of course I didn't. She was always out, at the village hall, watching bands. Getting up to God knows what.'

'It was a different time. And Helen was always strong. Bryony's so . . .'

'So . . . what?'

'So delicate.'

Her bitter chuckle. 'That's a man's way of talking. A father's way.'

'Well, I'm a man and I'm a father so it's no surprise. And what's your way? The way of the blinkered grand-mother?'

'All right,' she said. 'Let's say you're right. Let's say she is a delicate little thing. And let's say she has – ow.'

'Cynthia,' I asked, 'are you all right?'

'It's just this flaming hernia. Anyway, where was I?'

'Let's say she is a delicate little thing,' I reminded her, before she embarked on a rather lengthy metaphor about the art of holding butterflies that sounded like it had fallen out of a fortune cookie.

Now it was my turn to sigh. 'Is that from one of your self-help books?'

'Oh, stop it, Terence,' she snapped.

'I just want to keep her safe, that's all.' I was speaking more quietly now, aware of your footsteps above me. 'I want to stop her getting into danger.'

'You have to let her breathe.'

'Yes. But I have to make sure it's the right sort of air she's breathing. She might as well suck on an exhaust as kiss that Denny boy, the harm it's going to do in the long term.'

She laughed a painful laugh. 'Have you heard yourself? The long-term effects of kissing! Honestly! You have to act reasonably, Terence. You have to acknowledge the world you're living in. It's not the Dark Ages, you know. You can't lock her away in a tower and wait until she's twenty-one.'

Cynthia was wrong. These were the darkest ages. These were the days of dying light. 'You sound like the rest of them,' I said.

'The rest of who?'

'Them! The do-gooders. The soppy lettuces who have let us get savaged by the dogs.'

'And what's your solution? To wrap her up in cotton wool and not let her out of your sight?' She calmed herself down. 'Listen, you'll just have to let her get it out of her system. You have to just let her . . . *be*.'

I knew then, right at that moment, that I was alone. Cynthia was an ally, but she would not join me in this war.

'All right, Cynthia. All right. I'd better go.'

'All right, well, goodbye. But don't do anything silly.'

'No, I won't. Goodbye.'

'Goodbye.'

And I stayed there, listening to the dial tone's eternal hum, as the nature of my necessary task slowly became more clear.

*

When I told George I was sorry to hear about his father he nodded and closed his eyes and mouth as if a wasp was flying past his face.

He kept a lot in, that was my impression. Indeed, I admired him for it. That is how we rise above ourselves, isn't it? By leaning hard against those doors to our emotions, in the British tradition.

I put him to work on a lowboy cabinet, repairing the drawer rails and runners. He had finished by lunch, when I sent him out on another errand.

Now, let me think. It must have been ten minutes past one when George came back into the shop, breathless, with our lunch and the wax polish I had asked for. He didn't say anything at first. Indeed, I was two bites into my Wensleydale sandwich when he casually came out with it.

'I've just seen Bryony,' he said.

So relaxed was his tone that it didn't sink in at first. I nodded and had another bite, as if he was making a comment on the weather. Then the alarm sounded.

'Sorry? What?'

He swallowed his mouthful and pressed his glasses further up his nose. 'Bryony. I've just seen her.'

'No, George, I think you have made a mistake. She's in school,' I said. 'She has lunch in school.'

He shrugged, and looked over at one of the figures. The Girl with a Tambourine. 'I might have got it wrong. But it looked like her. I called her and she turned round but then kept walking. She looked like she didn't want to be bothered.'

'Was she on her own?'

'Yes,' he said, nudging his glasses further up his nose.

'Where? Where was she?'

'On the Mount,' he said. 'Walking towards –'

'The school?'

'Yes.'

A precious elixir kept in a barrel. You put a hand over the hole where it leaks but there is another, out of view, that you have missed.

I felt like a fool. Where had you been? To meet him?

I telephoned your school. I asked to speak to you. They went to fetch you and I had nothing to say. I had needed to hear your voice and I was hearing your voice but it expected words in return. It expected a reason.

'Cynthia's going into hospital,' I said.

'Yes, I know.'

George was looking at me, his sandwich-stuffed face paused in dread anticipation.

'For her hernia.'

'I know that. Why are you phoning?'

'She's got a date. The eighteenth. She called this morning and said she's going in on the eighteenth.'

'I was in French.'

'She'll have to stay the night.'

'It was embarrassing.'

'She sounded ever so worried.'

'Is that it?'

'Yes.'

You made a noise at the back of your throat to signify your frustration.

'I'll see you at four,' I told the dial tone.

George was confused.

'It's difficult,' I said. 'I have to handle Bryony carefully. There are things she hides from me.'

He nodded, and his eyes flashed wide behind his glasses as if I had made a considerable understatement.

'George? Is there something you know? About Bryony?'

He paused a moment too long.

'No,' he said. 'I don't see that lot any more.'

'Before, though. You used to know some of the same people. Was there anything?'

He took the last bite of his sandwich and shook his head, staring over at the lowboy cabinet.

'George? Was there anything at all?'

'No,' he said. And then, blushing: 'Well, not really.'

'Not really? What does that mean?'

'Nothing,' he said. 'I don't want to get her into any trouble.'

He didn't understand. 'You won't be getting her into trouble, George. You'll be helping her.'

He considered, or at least seemed to consider, and took two gasps from his inhaler.

And then, after much interrogation, he told me something I find myself unable to repeat. Something about what had happened that evening in the field. An incident which occurred after you had been drinking, between yourself and another boy, in full view of everyone. A grotesque act, which you participated in with full compliance. I remembered Uriah Heep's hand sliding down your back in that Cockpit, and I found the story all too easy to believe, especially as George trod forward through the whole thing with such slow and reluctant steps.

'I shouldn't have told you,' he said. 'I'm sorry, Mr Cave.'

The sweet chutney at the back of my throat lent the horrendous images tormenting my mind a sickly taste. I retched at the idea of you there, with those boys, allowing yourself to become no more than an object to be enjoyed. My Bryony. My innocent Petal. What had happened to you? What had happened since Reuben's death that had

169

made you lower your own value? I couldn't stop my mind. I couldn't stop the images of this girl I adored but also despised. This girl who simultaneously was my daughter and also the person who was destroying my daughter. I felt appalled. I felt like I had just watched Marcel Duchamp draw his moustache on the Mona Lisa. You were my work of art, my priceless Petal, yet you clearly viewed yourself as no more than a cheap postcard. A souvenir of the Bryony who once was.

'You pushed me away,' I said. 'George, you pushed me away.'

He nodded. His cheeks burned crimson. He understood his crime. 'I'm so sorry, Mr Cave. I just wanted to fit in. I just wanted them to accept me. I'm not like that now.'

He was nearly crying. I swear to you, there were tears glazing his eyes.

'No, I can see that,' I said. And then, realising George was now an ally in my mission, and an ally with information, I knew I could not be too severe. 'Don't worry, George. I'm just glad that you told me.'

'You won't . . . you won't tell Bryony, will you? That I said anything.'

'Oh no, George,' I said, as Reuben laughed in silence around us. 'It's our secret.'

I went to pick you up from school. Through the windscreen I watched the day girls and weekly boarders walk out of the gates laughing, talking, their voices bubbling up and boiling over with the promise of the weekend. Four hundred pupils who were not quite you. More and more of them were spilling out, heading towards waiting cars or the railway station, ready to become their other selves. The laughs became slowly more hideous, the faces more tormenting as they became less, as the crowds began to thin and the cars, one by one, drove away.

I saw Imogen, but you were not with her. I ran over to her and tapped her arm and she jumped in shock and took a moment to recognise me, a moment where I was not her friend's father but a man she didn't know coming out of nowhere to touch her arm. 'Imogen? Have you see Bryony?'

She looked at her friends, whom I had not seen before, who found something in my question to amuse them, and Imogen shrugged and said with bleak indifference, 'She had hockey, I think.'

And I remembered you had taken your hockey stick with you that morning and I remembered the still comfort of having you there, on the seat beside me before I had known about your lunch-hour excursion or the incident in the field. I was remembering your purer, morning self when Imogen walked away, and added her voice to the giggles. I wondered if something had happened between you two, something a father would not know about and would never know.

I looked around and there were only a few uniformed bodies to be seen, climbing onto bicycles, putting on their helmets, or (the other type) cupping their hands against the wind, lighting cigarettes.

Even these stragglers disappeared and I was left staring at the school building, at the tall Victorian windows and the dark archway of the entrance, the blank eyes and blank mouth of a creature that had spat out its last pupil.

I walked inside and navigated my way through the labyrinth

of corridors towards the staffroom, all the time feeling the invisible squeeze of those walls.

A face came out of nowhere. A sharp and hollow face of stern womanhood, attached to a body of long, floating clothes and mock-tribal accessories. 'Excuse me, sir?' she asked, staring worriedly at the fresh scar on my cheek. 'Can I help you?'

'I'm looking for my daughter. Bryony Cave,' I said. 'She was not there to meet me. She is always there, on time, and I am beginning to wonder where she might –'

The face tilted back, allowing my words to bounce off her chin. 'I'm afraid Bryony isn't in any of my classes, but I'll just enquire in the staffroom and see if someone might know.'

I followed her to the staffroom and was informed there had been no hockey practice today as 'Valerie' was away. I saw Mr Winter and recognised him from parents evening. 'The girls were told to wait in the library or inform their parents they were leaving school early,' he said, in a voice so cold and bureaucratic I could almost see its typeface.

'I wasn't informed,' I said. 'She didn't inform me.'

Mr Winter shrugged and closed the blue folder on his lap, 'I'm sorry, but I can guarantee that Bryony was well aware that she should stay on the school premises unless she had managed to get in touch with whoever is responsible for her. We understand our duty of care.'

My anger burst its cage. 'I am responsible for her from four o'clock. At a quarter to three she is in your care. Just as she is during lunch hour. Now, I have it on good authority that she wasn't here at lunch either. You cannot allow your pupils simply to wander out of school.'

The whole staffroom was looking at me. I was making a scene. I was, in their eyes, clearly overreacting. They did not understand the fatal danger that taints the air of this town, that rises up from the old Saxon streets to claim those too fragile to resist the follies of youth.

'She told me she had phoned you and that you were coming to pick her up,' said Mr Winter.

'And you believed her? You didn't follow her to the gates?'

'Unfortunately, we cannot offer each child their own private minder, Mr Cave. Not without significantly raising our fees.'

Someone laughed by the water cooler.

'You don't understand,' I muttered as I left the room.

'Mr Cave, I'm sure Bryony will be absolutely –'

Ten minutes later, I would be pressing my weight against a door that wouldn't open. I would be standing outside my own shop as I searched my pockets for the key. What was George doing? Why wasn't he behind the counter? I made it inside. 'George? Bryony?'

A floorboard creaked above me. I ran up the stairs and saw him there, on the landing. Not walking, just standing.

'George?'

'I needed to go to the toilet,' he said, in a voice that might have been ashamed, or angry.

'Where's Bryony? Has she come back?'

He paused, and then answered slowly. 'Yes,' he said, carefully, as though the word itself had brought you there. I moved past him and into your room and when I saw you standing in front of your rosettes, I felt so relieved that only now can I see the damp redness of your eyes.

Of course, you didn't witness this relief. You witnessed the fear, shooting out of me in angry words. 'What on earth were you thinking? Why did you lie to Mr Winter? Where did you go? You went to see him, didn't you? You went to see him. Tell me! Tell me! For God's sake, girl, tell me!'

I didn't mean to shake you, I didn't mean to make you cry fresh tears.

I want to be back there, I want to step inside that room and try again. This time, I will listen and you will tell me what I am sure you would have said, if only I had been a father and not a tyrant, if only I had trusted myself to love you the way I should have. But I did not, and you told me nothing. Inside your head, you already had it planned.

It didn't matter any more. Nothing mattered any more.

Nothing apart from him, that boy who was your world, that boy who had worked an apocalypse in your mind and turned the rest of us to dust. And so it was that I let you collapse on the bed and sink your face in your pillow, before going downstairs, with George, to reopen the shop.

Please, Bryony, understand this: the pain of a child is the pain of a parent.

I see it all, now. It was me. I was him as he was me.

I see myself at the window. I see my head busy with the accounts and I scream to get my attention. Below, they translate the scream as one of triumph and chant my name. All of them. All except one.

By the second scream I am feeling the pain in my left shoulder, a pain so sudden and intense that it becomes impossible to separate it from everything else. The voices, the terraced houses ('Gladstone Villas, 1888'), the whiskers of yellow light, my other self running across the park – all pieces of the same pain.

Still, I have to hold on. I have to wait until I am there on the street, running towards me. I watch as I step on the park wall and jump down to the pavement, landing badly.

'Reuben, Reuben!'

I see me as I push my way through the boys and know that it is time. This is what I have been waiting for, why I am here, and know I have no choice but to let go.

'Reuben! No!'

I fall, fast and heavy.

Within a second my screaming has stopped but I am still there, as there as I ever was, just leaking out from the vessel that contained me.

'Get an ambulance. Now!'

Little Cam vomited on the pavement as Aaron staggered back, away, onto the empty road.

I look at myself straight in the eyes and see the fear I know I am feeling. I turn away from me. Denny is there, silent, numb, and I see my hatred as I look at him.

'Don't go,' I tell myself, as I rub my hand, and I see the dread and confusion descend on my face. These are my last words. 'Don't go.'

I leave my body and the pain it gave me and the material world sinks into darkness. The road, the park, the shop. Every building and every object. All I can see is the dull glow of living souls, guiding me like a hundred lighthouses in the fog.

George had just left when I saw Denny walk past the window. He glanced inside but I made an overt show of not having noticed, sinking my head deeper inside the *Antiques Trade Gazette*.

Of course, the moment he had gone past I was off my stool and heading out of the door, out into an evening of crisp packets sliding along pavements, of empty sightseeing buses wheezing their way towards the Minster, of deserted climbing frames and Vikings in tattered raincoats, swigging back from golden cans.

He wasn't there. I scanned across the park, towards Reuben's lamp post and then down the length of the street, but there was no sign of him.

Cool moist air filled my lungs as I looked around. Then I realised something else was lacking from the picture: George. He had left the shop only a moment before I had seen Denny. If he was following his normal route home, he would have only reached the fish-and-chip shop by that point. Maybe he had gone inside to buy himself a cod supper.

I was about to step back inside the shop and check you were still safely upstairs when I heard something. At first I thought it was the hydraulic sigh of a slowing tour bus, although I quickly realised it wasn't coming from the road. It came again, this noise, though it was now accompanied by a kind of animal whimper. A scraping backwards breath. Shock? Fear? Sudden pain? I followed the sound and soon heard another. A cry, now recognisably human, calling out for something, someone. My mind sought to mend the mangled word but couldn't.

I kept running, to the passageway where the sound was coming from, and found them there engaged in a thoroughly one-sided physical struggle. George, the flabby giant who had once nearly pushed me to the ground, getting severely beaten by your boxer. His smashed glasses were on the ground, lying near a puddle alongside his inhaler.

Now, as I write, I remember a moment of hesitation as I stood there. Maybe I was wondering what, precisely, your boy was capable of, trying to ascertain the nature of that violence which so evidently resided within him. And it troubles me, truly, to tell you that when I saw him there, kicking an already well-battered George in the stomach, I felt a brief flowering of relief. I cannot explain it. Or maybe I can. You see, my concerns regarding your boy required this confirmation, something this substantial, for me to act upon them. It was as though the thousand doubts suddenly spoke with a single voice, and the threat he posed to your personal safety could no longer be ignored. How many times did I let his foot meet George's stomach? Many enough for me to realise that this wasn't going to end without an interruption.

Would Denny have killed him?

'Stop!'

His foot finished its final kick and he turned and he saw me but I could not read his expression given that his face was in shadow. I must tell you I had no fear of him, as I stood there. Or rather, I had no fear of what his feet or fists could do to me, or of the pain he could inflict upon my body. No, the only fear I had was for yourself, as I knew your emotions were so tangled up with this brutish rogue that any attempt to extract you from him, or him from you, would be a task fraught with danger.

Oh, why couldn't he just leave our lives? If only he had never existed! If only he had been born something else! An insect to be trod on, or a weed to be pulled out of the soil. Would it have upset the world if he had never been? Would there have been a space, a yawning lack, which you would have wanted to fill?

He stayed looking at me, a suicidal street cat in the headlights, then he turned and fled away from the scene, down the passageway, and out onto Swan Street. Once gone, I moved over to George and crouched beside him. He was in a truly horrendous state, coughing and whimpering as he held his stomach.

'George? George? George? It's me. It's Mr Cave. George, can you hear me?'

He opened his eyes, or as much of them as he could, and the sight of me seemed to have the effect of another blow.

I gave him his glasses and his inhaler. 'George? Why did he do this to you? George? We've got to get you to hospital. Can you stand up? George?'

'I think so,' he said, in a pitiful voice.

I helped him to his feet and drew my mobile telephone from my pocket to call for an ambulance. Even as I dialled the thought nagged me that I must get back to you. You were on your own, unguarded, with Denny on the loose. 'Could you put me through to the ambulance services please? Hello? Yes, we need an ambulance as soon as possible. A young man has –'

'No,' George said, raising his hand. 'Don't call them. Please, Mr Cave, I'll be all right.'

I hesitated. There was something desperate about his expression. A pleading I couldn't ignore. 'No, I'm sorry,' I told the woman on the end of the line. 'We don't need an ambulance.'

I put the mobile telephone back in my pocket. George shook his inhaler and sucked his medicine. A bruised and breathless Goliath. I couldn't help but worry about what his mother would think, when she found him like this.

'Come on,' I told him, realising he must have more information to offer. 'Let's get you shipshape again, shall we?'

*

I offered to get him a cold flannel and some paracetamol.

'What, from upstairs?' he asked me, looking worriedly to the ceiling.

'Yes,' I said.

'No. It's all right. I don't want them. I'm fine. I'm fine.'

'You don't look fine, George,' I told him.

He sighed. 'I'm all right.' He looked nervous. Understandable, I suppose. Even so, it seemed most odd the way he kept looking out into the hallway. The way he jerked every time he heard a creak from upstairs.

'Do you know that boy?' I asked, keeping my rather uncertain cards close to my chest.

He nodded, but couldn't look me in the eye. He began fiddling with one of the art nouveau figures. The Girl with a Tambourine.

'How?' I asked. 'How do you know him?'

He took a considerable time to answer, and kept turning the figure in a clockwise motion.

'Everyone knows him. Denny Hart. He's a class-A scumbag.' A certain anger rose into his voice, which seemed out of character, belonging to the George I had seen in the field and not this George. But again, given the context, I supposed it was understandable.

Then, after an even longer time, he came out with it. 'He's seeing Bryony.'

'Yes,' I said. 'I know. But I still don't get it. Why did he do this to you?'

His mouth fell open. He seemed amazed that I could know you were seeing this boy.

'How long have you known?'

'A while,' I said in a hushed tone. 'Now, George, please, why did he do this to you?'

179

Again he turned away, and looked at the figurine. 'Because I threatened to tell Bryony something. About something he did to a girl in his class at school.'

'A girl?'

He nodded and touched the swollen eye behind his glasses. 'Alison Wingfield.'

The name was familiar. I had heard it before. Maybe Reuben had talked about her. 'Alison Wingfield?'

'She was in my year. My dad taught her. That's how I found out. You see, my dad was the only person she told.'

I thought of Mr Weeks, that bullish yeti of a man whom Reuben had hated enough to miss his classes.

'Told what?'

'That he –' He moved his hand away from the figure. 'That Denny raped her.'

Raped. The word was so horrendous, so violent, it ravished the whole room. Even the Tambourine Girl in his hand seemed to have suddenly been ripped of her innocence. My doubts were rendered useless. I was staring into George's bruised and swollen face, a face which showed in itself what Denny was capable of.

'Didn't they report him to the police?'

'No. No, she didn't want to. Alison. She couldn't. Even when she –'

'When she –?'

'Even when she found out she was pregnant.'

I felt weak. I hated what I was hearing and yet I could believe every single word of it. It seemed to be a truth I already knew, buried deep inside me but which had just been unearthed again. My instincts had been correct. Denny had malice within him. He was a beast. A predatory animal, a subhuman who preyed on young girls and sought, through his primitive appetite, to ruin their futures.

'Did she . . . did she have the baby?' I gagged on the question, but got it out eventually.

'I think her parents made her, in the end.'

'Her parents?'

'Catholics. Strict, strict Catholics,' he said. I was sent back to the Vatican, back to your naked shoulders under that burning sun.

'So that's why that savage attacked you? In case you were going to tell Bryony?'

George nodded.

I leaned in towards him. 'You must tell her.'

Fear filled his eyes. 'No. I can't . . . I . . .'

'It's all right, he won't hurt you. Trust me.'

He shook his head, and panic added weight to his breathing. 'I shouldn't have said anything, Mr Cave.'

'No, you should have, you should have. Please, George, you have to tell her. You have to.'

He winced, either from the pain or the situation. And I stood up and went into the hallway. 'Bryony? Bryony?' I kept calling you, my voice loud enough to climb the stairs but you didn't come. 'Bryony?' I shouted one final time and waited a moment too long in that hallway.

I heard the bell in the shop and ran back inside. 'George?'

But, of course, he was gone.

Over our lamb cutlets I told you what I had to say. All those impure, unsimple truths. What father would have done otherwise? Of course, you didn't listen to me. Or you listened, but not in the way I had foreseen. There was that slight upward tug at the corner of your mouth as I told you about George's pummelled face, and then the drop into rage as I

181

told you about Alison Wingfield. You thought I was saying it all to hurt you. You ran through a whole century of dictators, along with any other insults you could hurl at me. You pushed your plate away and went to your room and I followed you. You were so wild and violent I had to exercise powers of restraint.

I told you a new rule, to replace all the others. You were to have no time away from me, except at school. You would be grounded for your own safety.

You screamed and raged and called me a something fascist something psychopath and you shut the door in my face. I left you alone. We had an hour before seeing Cynthia in the hospital after her hernia operation, so I went to my room and switched on the monitor.

I heard your furious breath. I heard your footsteps as you tried to walk off your anger. I heard you collapse on the bed. I heard you say something. Not on your mobile telephone, but just out into your room. 'I love you. I love you. I love . . .'

I began to question why he was staying back, in the wings away from the main stage. Your brother, I mean. My mind was fraught but it was itself. Perhaps he had gone away. Perhaps there were no more memories he needed to implant in my mind. Perhaps there were no more tasks he required of me. My optimism, of course, was a little too rash.

Now I wonder how my life will affect your own. Have I already set boundaries for you, with the things I have done? Isn't that what a parent does? Don't they settle the realms of experience their children will later inhabit? And don't the children then live inside these realms as a foot lives inside a shoe, stretching the leather but never truly breaking free?

I will answer this with a brief word about that earliest of the three unnatural deaths. I must, before I get to my ending, tell you a little of my beginning. I must, in short, say something about my mother.

She was a milliner, at the highest end of the scale. She had a shop in Piccadilly. Gardenia Hats. To you she is no more than the picture in the living room. You would think it had been taken in the thirties, judging from the dress but of course it was much later. She lived inside the past, the time of her own childhood, when hats were still the height of fashion. That picture tells a lot. The Greta Garbo mask that couldn't quite conceal the anxious, too-human face behind. Her own mother had built the business up in the twenties and thirties, selling cloche hats to the flapper girls, dressing the heads of Mrs Simpson and Lady Mountbatten. It was left to her daughter to try and keep the business fires burning and to broaden the range with fedoras and other such styles.

She gradually sank into debt, a lot of debt, and the woman behind the mask became increasingly desperate. She ended up killing herself, in 1960, after guzzling a whole jar of barbiturates. The poor woman was found in the flat above her shop, dribbling blue foam over the stubborn numbers of her account book.

*

Picture me.

The little boy in the room of hats, calling out to whatever can hear. His mother's head, not dozing on her desk; her open eyes not seeing him or the numbers in the book she was frowning over only this morning. The book that is open now, a useless pillow, collecting whatever leaks from her mouth.

Hear that scream becoming a word. 'Mother.'

She does not answer him. Her arms hang limp by her side. 'Mother!'

His first word is now his only word, the only one that matters.

He is shaking her now, and he finds her body does not move the way he is used to. The way bodies should. His scream dies, unanswered, melts into tears, but the man on the wireless doesn't even pretend to understand.

Is it an earthquake or simply a shock?
Is it the good turtle soup or merely the mock?
Is it a cocktail, this feeling of joy?
Or is what I feel the real McCoy?

The smiling voice quivers over the airwaves from another world, a voice that cannot see the woman or the boy or the wide-brimmed hats in torn-out advertisements and articles.

He tries to push her back in her chair, the rag-doll mother, this heavy and stringless puppet, but the weight is too much. She falls onto him, and then off him, her cheek skimming his shoulder.

Unnaturally, she hangs. She should be in pain, he wants her to be in pain, but she is not. It is not.

The scream is a howl now. A howl that, when the upstairs tenant Mr Steer arrives into the scene, will eventually be reduced to a heavy sob. For days, for weeks, for months, the boy will weep, and soon the sound of his own weeping will become a kind of comfort to him, the only continuity from the life in the city and the life on the Dorset farm of his adoptive parents. A new life of big skies and dung-scented air and clouts around the head from the only father he will know.

I used to blame myself for my mother's demise. I used to remember her telling me she hated me and that she wished I'd never been born. These memories are unreliable. The first one I can trust is the first one I have proof of. The one that is contained inside all the others, like the smallest Russian doll. Something I kept with me no matter how far away I got from that shop, and that home, in Piccadilly. After all, this memory had left traces. A body, an empty jar of pills, a throat that had screamed itself into laryngitis.

There was no note, though. There was no written explanation for what she did or why she did it. None of the usual suicide etiquette – 'this is not your fault', 'I am so sorry for', 'please find it in your heart to' – no, none of that. Later on, I wanted something I could hold in my hands, something I could read that would help me resolve my feelings towards this woman who was her own murderer, but there was nothing. All I had was that one simple fact.

The numbers in her account book provided her with a better argument for death than her three-year-old son had done for life.

For years, I had tried to rationalise it. My mother's suicide was not my fault. I was three years old. She was a grown woman who should have given up the business. It wasn't my fault a second world war had bombed the glamour out of the world years before.

No, not my fault. And, if I had been a rational creature, such reassurances might just have worked. Rational creatures? There are no rational creatures. Machines are rational, because they cannot love. And love, no matter what the brain scientists tell us, is not mechanical.

I felt an absence, a literal feeling, as real as the phantom limb of an amputee. You lose an arm but you can still feel the clenching of your fist. Doctors know the symptom as the 'phantom limb'. It can recur indefinitely for the rest of a life, the feeling that the arm is still part of you despite the knowledge it has gone. You get used to something being there, something you almost take for granted, that has been by your side, and you can never fully adjust to its absence. All my life, it's been there. An invisible clenching, trying to grip something I couldn't. In the process I surrounded myself with objects that belonged to the past in the vain hope I could try and reach back through time, or at least weigh it down, and stop its dread march forward.

It was too much, I realise that. And that clenched grip on the past became tighter still when I lost your own mother, and then Reuben.

All I can hope is that as my grip is released you will be able, one day, to run freer than I ever managed, and leave the unsatisfied ghosts of family to their own eternal regrets.

The Georgian houses rolled past the window as we climbed the Mount, towards the hospital. The quiet we were sharing seemed to be marginally civil, the calm after that earlier tempest.

The illusion was broken with the silence.

'How are you feeling?' I asked you.

'Why would a fascist care about feelings?' you said, pulling a thread on your bandage.

'I'm not a fascist, Bryony. I'm a father.'

'Mussolini was a father,' you said.

'I had to tell you the truth about that boy,' I said. 'What else could I do?'

'It's not the truth,' you said, and the threat of tears stopped me from pressing further.

We arrived in the ward to see her flirting with that young doctor.

When he left, to make room for us by her bedside, Cynthia looked at you and winked and made a facial expression rich with silent innuendo. I remember you laughing and I remember feeling strangely jealous of Cynthia, for being able to charm you with such natural ease.

'He'd make quite a Heathcliff, wouldn't he?' she told you, chuckling. And then in a more sombre, private tone: 'About the same age as your grandfather when I met him. Poor Howard.'

She looked around the ward and swallowed something back. Memories glazed her eyes. Poor Cynthia. All those hours she had spent in that same hospital with your grandfather, talking to oncologists or sitting by his bedside after another futile operation. Doing the crossword with him in whatever broadsheet she had managed to get hold of in the shop, as the cancer crept through and colonised every part of him.

I am sinking again, aren't I? Going backwards when I need to go forwards and explain myself. Perhaps I am reluctant to tell you yet another shameful fact. To reveal another betrayal. Yet I must. I had been in your room, that day, while you were at school. I had gone through all your drawers and bags. I found that framed photograph he had given you the night of Clifford's Tower. The belated birthday present. The picture he, or someone, had taken of Reuben. Your brother's face, smiling, no hand over his birthmark, looking down with an anonymous blue sky behind.

'Oh, Reuben, I'm sorry,' I told the picture. And after the guilt came the anger. How dare Denny use your brother to try and win you over?

I placed the picture back in your bag and tried to access your computer. I was bombarded with grey boxes and no entry signs. It was like navigating my way through the City of Perpetual Mist.

Eventually I conceded defeat and switched it off. Then, as I headed out of your room, I felt a sudden impulse to check the pockets of the coat you weren't wearing that day. The grey flannel one I had bought you last autumn. And it was there. On a neatly folded piece of paper. Denny's address, written in his own vulgar handwriting. That random combination of upper and lower case. Those ugly, ill-formed letters. I imagined your poor pen in his hand, as incongruously placed as Fay Wray in King Kong's fist.

I copied the address and I felt like I already knew it, as though it was the only possible place he could live.

If it was Reuben making me feel this, he stayed back, in

the shadows. A fleeting image of council houses curving into the distance and then nothing.

So, on with it, Terence. On with it. Yes, standing in the hospital, looking down at Cynthia's sad and unmade face. She looked so odd, without her dark-painted lips and eyes. Unfinished. Like a preparatory sketch for an oil painting. Two of her hideous am dram chums arrived. The toby jug and his wife. At their appearance the nurse returned to tell Cynthia she could have no more than three visitors at a time. And me, hoodwinking you as you had so often hoodwinked me: 'Right, we'd better be off then, Bryony.'

It worked. Your eyes stared sternly at me.

'I want to stay. I want to talk to Cynthia.'

And the toby jug, piping in: 'It's all right, Tel. I can wait outside.'

'No. No, don't do that,' I said, perhaps too hurriedly, as I walked away. 'I need to get back and see to something. But Bryony can stay here if she wants. It's fine, Cynthia. Honestly. I'll be back in an hour.'

Five minutes after I had left the hospital I was driving onto the Greensand Estate, passing the post-war semi-detached council houses. The homes for heroes that seemed to glow in the pink evening light, blushing at their present occupants. I turned left, down Leverston Road, where the newer houses shrank in line with governmental commitment. Terraced rows of pebble-dashed squalor, complete with their vulgar window ornaments, crosses of St George and mono-tonous despair.

I had seen it earlier, in that blink of an eye.

Number 35. I pulled over and sat for a moment with the engine off. The house was on the end of a terrace and looked like all the others, except for the closed curtains. Had you been there? The thought repelled me. Maybe you had been up to his room.

I got out of the car and walked down the thin path, passing the bare and abandoned patch of lawn. I knocked on the door and then noticed the bell. No one answered. I tried again and stood back, to see if there was anyone peeping through the curtains. I thought about returning to the car and waiting for him, or for his father. I was determined not to leave until I had to. After all, I had time. I knew you wouldn't leave Cynthia until I returned.

'What you after?'

I was halfway back to the car when I heard the woman's voice. I turned to see her. Dark-haired and pale, like her son, with a face that might once have been beautiful. She wore jeans and a baggy T-shirt that hung off her shoulder, like a little girl playing grown-ups. There was the vaguest sense I had seen her before.

'Hello,' I said. 'I just wondered if your son was home? Dennis. Denny. I'd like a word with him if I could.'

She offered a kind of limp smile. She was drunk, I realised. 'And what word is that? *Useless?*'

'Listen, I need to speak to him. Do you know where he is?'

She shrugged and looked around at all the other houses, even up at the sky.

'Then can I speak to you?'

The smile became a frown. 'Who are you? The police?'

'No, no I'm not. I'm Terence. Terence Cave. Your son used to know mine. Reuben.'

'Oh,' she said, in a hyperbolic gasp. 'Oh. That poor lad that –'

'Yes,' I said, shielding myself from her boozy sympathy. 'That was him.'

A group of young ruffians walked past kicking a football between them.

'Go on then,' she said, leaving the door open for me to follow. 'So long as y'ain't a copper you can come in.'

I walked into the narrow hallway and was loosely gestured through to the living room, which apart from the smell of cigarette smoke and the empty cereal bowl seemed unlived in. There was a crumpled carrier bag, as well, lying next to the chair, and some envelopes on the mantelpiece. Near those envelopes there were two small desolate pictures. A framed photograph of a boy who didn't look that much older than Denny, dressed in a soldier's uniform. And another, an older one, of a different man. A man with a dark moustache. He had his arm around a woman, sitting in another house.

'What are you requiring with Dennis?' The question broke my thoughts, and I turned to her again, to those eyes that kept widening then narrowing again, as if trying to fix me in one spot.

'It's quite a delicate issue, actually,' I said.

'Fire ahead,' she said, miming a pistol with her fingers.

'Well, the thing is, it's about my daughter. You see, I think she and Dennis might be forming some kind of a –'

'You can sit down, you know,' she said. 'So long as you're delicate.' She laughed, and I had the feeling I was either being mocked or flirted with, but I was not sure which.

'Thank you.' I placed myself down on the sofa, and felt myself weakening, losing my purpose.

'Would you like a drink of tea?' She pronounced each word carefully, like a senile aristocrat.

'No, I'm fine.'

She went into the kitchen. 'I'm going to get myself a refreshing drink of Coke. My mouth gets very dry . . .'

I heard her pouring out what sounded like two drinks, with a pause between, but she returned with only one.

'Go on,' she said, and closed her eyes for a long sip.

I looked at her and for a moment I forgot myself. The bare shoulder, the loose hair, the drunken smile. All these were weapons sent by an invisible enemy, working against what I'd come for. (Bryony, I must tell you never to confuse love with desire. There is the craving of the flesh and there is the craving of the heart, and to conflate the two is akin to mistaking a monkey for an eagle.)

I closed my eyes, and gained focus. 'Denny was there the night Reuben, my son, died.'

'Oh, it was well terrible what happened,' she said, in her true voice.

'Did he tell you about it?'

'No.' This disclosure was hardly a surprise. Indeed, it merely confirmed my worst suspicions. Your brother's death had evidently meant nothing to Denny. 'A copper came round to see him.'

I nodded, and caught myself glancing at the small mole on her naked shoulder.

'Your son and my daughter are seeing a lot of each other. Did you know about this?'

She laughed, nervously. 'Poor gal.'

'What do you –'

I looked over at her mantelpiece. At the envelopes, coloured the dull brown of state authority. I saw her name, 'Lorraine

Hart'. It came back to me. 'Denny 'Hammerblow' Hart'.

Hart. Hart. Hart.

And then I saw it.

I looked again at the photo of the couple, sitting in a different house. The woman was her. Younger, happier, more sober, but definitely her. But it was the man's face that troubled me. The moustache. The warm, deceptive smile. Those eyes.

'Where's his father?' I asked.

She laughed at this. It was hard, drunken laughter. Laughter to cover the cracks of raw emotion.

'His dad's away.'

'Away?'

'At Ranby.'

The word was a slap in the face. 'At Ranby *Prison?*'

She nodded, without shame. This was getting worse. I had the feeling of descent, as I sat there. The very real sensation of being lowered into an abyss.

My stomach flipped. Panic thudded my chest. 'Andrew Hart.'

I whispered it aloud, and saw it in my mind, the way I had seen it at the time, in local-newspaper font. And those eyes I knew so much better than the face, staring out at me from that photograph. The name swirled around me. I needed to get out, I needed to get out of that vile little house. 'You were there, weren't you?' I asked her. 'In court.'

Under the vodka-glaze there was no recognition.

'You pathetic woman,' I shouted, and felt a brief but intense pain inside my head. 'You were there. In court.'

Her smile died. 'Who are you? Here, don't talk to me like that, you nutbag. Gerrout me . . . house.'

I stood up and spoke slowly. 'Tell your son to stay away from my daughter. Tell him not to come near her. Tell him –'

Things began to grow dark. I was sliding again, away

from myself, and another of Reuben's memories invaded my mind.

I was with Denny, coming back to this house, and smelt the sick as soon as we were through the door.

'Mam?' Denny called.

We put down our bags and went into the main room.

'Mam?'

The radio was on, blaring out from the kitchen.

'Mam?'

She was lying on the sofa like something had flung her there. Denny shook her.

'Mam, wake up, wake up.'

He looked at the carrier bag where the sweet stench was coming from. There was some on the carpet, too, where she had missed. Two empty bottles of Imperial Vodka lay half covered under her denim jacket.

'Mam, wake up!'

Her eyes moved under their lids, unborn creatures about to hatch.

There was nothing for a moment but the singing on the radio.

> *If you get caught between the moon and New York City*
> *The best that you can do*
> *The best that you can do*
> *Is fall in love.*

And then she laughed and her eyes closed and Denny turned to me, to Reuben, and said, 'I'm sorry.'

*

'Tell him –' I couldn't finish my sentence. 'Get away,' I whispered. 'Reuben, get away.'

Denny's mother looked at me with wide, sobered eyes. I turned round, and walked out of that place. I saw the ruffians kicking their football against the Volvo, and shooed them away, ignoring their wild shouts and gestures as I drove off.

I was halfway back to the hospital when I saw him running, heading back to the estate. I had just turned the headlights on, and there he was, shining like a vision, pressing his sweat-glossed limbs forward up the hill. I pulled over, high on the pavement, and parked in his path.

'Stop,' I told him, winding down the window. 'We need to talk. About Bryony.'

He obeyed my command, his hands on his hips, and caught his breath. 'What?' he said. 'What do you want?'

I had to be quick about my business, as I couldn't risk any interference from Reuben. I could still feel him, you see, rummaging through the infected house of my mind as he searched for a way to switch off the lights.

I had a new plan. A new plan formed by the desperate knowledge I had just discovered.

'I can give you three thousand pounds,' I told Denny. 'Three thousand pounds for you to leave her alone.'

He looked at me with unbelieving eyes. 'What?'

I reiterated, as I felt the tingles at the back of my brain. 'Three. Thousand. Pounds. If you never see her again. I can get you the money tomorrow.'

He rubbed his hand through his damp black hair. 'Are you real?'

'Yes,' I told him. 'I'm real.' And I was real. I was as real as the patched-up tarmac he stood on. I would have paid double that amount. I would have sold the shop and its contents. I would have sold my own kidneys for him to leave you alone.

'You don't have a clue, do you?' he said, shaking his head with incredulity.

'About what?'

'I love her. I love her more than owt.'

Reuben was leaving. There was no pain, no tingling of the cerebellum. I was clear, restored. My anger had a purity. It was all my own.

'I know all about you, Denny Hart. I know all about your father. I know all about the poor girl whose life you ruined. The whole shoddy lot. Now, I am telling you to stay away from Bryony. I'm telling you to take the money and stay away.'

He was still shaking his head as he whispered his torturous words. 'I love her and she loves me, do you get that?'

A woman walked by in a wax jacket, dragged along by an eager springer spaniel. 'No, Barney, come on,' she said, as the dog leaned its nose towards Denny's salted skin.

'You don't love her,' I said, when the dog-walker had passed. 'You have no understanding of love. Love is a blessing of the mind, not a craving of the body. How old are you?'

'Fifteen.'

'Exactly. Fifteen. In a month you won't feel anything for her. You'll have moved on. She is a vulnerable girl. She has lost her twin brother and she looks for anything . . . anyone . . . to fill that gap. You just happened to come along and occupy a certain space. She'll move on, even if you don't. She'll leave you soon enough. You might as well take my offer.'

He frowned, drawing his eyes and nose and mouth closer together, like rallied troops. I thought, for a moment, he was going to drag me out of the car-window and pummel my flesh.

'Reuben were right about you,' he said.

'What?' I said. 'What did you say? How dare you bring Reuben into this. If it wasn't for you, Reuben would still be alive and you'd have to search the canalways of Britain to find a bargepole long enough for Bryony to touch you with. You destroyed his life, and I'm not going to let you destroy hers as well. Look at you. Look at you. Look at you.'

He looked down at his sweat-soaked T-shirt, and the body it clung to. A flicker of doubt passed over his primitive face. For a moment, at least, he knew I was right. He knew you were a million miles above him. He knew he deserved your love no more than a raven deserved to pluck a star from the sky.

The moment passed. 'You don't get it. I love her. We was made for each other.'

'And what cheap –'

A sudden sensation of dizziness, coupled by the usual tingles, the buzzing, the flies, caused my sentence to disappear inside a fog of unknowing. Reuben was back, stronger, trying to blank me out.

Denny had no idea what was happening and kept wading through his own delusions. 'I can look after her. After I finish school I'm going to get a job. I can make her happy. I know it. I've got it planned. I can –'

'No,' I said, fighting Reuben as much as Denny's words. 'No. Stop it. Stop it. Stop it. You'll leave her. You'll take the money and you'll leave her or I'll make her leave you. That's the proposition. Do you understand me, you ignorant –'

Denny had shaken his head and was already jogging away, taking the road with him. Everything retreated as the darkness tried to press in. I blinked it away, held it back, as the boy jogged on.

'I can do it,' I called after him, as he climbed that slow slope. 'I can make her leave you. It will be easy. You just watch. She will know who you are, Dennis Hart.'

We were driving back on that same stretch of road. The grandeur it always held seemed suddenly lost, as though it were a mere replica, a movie set. You were in the back, as was your custom these days, gazing out at a pavement Denny had passed over only thirty minutes before.

I told you – slowly, clearly, with careful spacing – the truth I had discovered that evening. Of course, I didn't tell you precisely how I had uncovered that information, as that was something you didn't need to know. What you needed to know was what I gave you. Who he was. His point of origin. The rotten tree that dropped the rotten apple. The father whose eyes had pierced my nightmares for nearly fifteen years.

'So, do you understand me? Do you hear what I am saying? Andrew Hart was the man who killed your mother. Do I need to tell you anything else about that boy for you to see sense?'

You said nothing. I watched the shadows pass your face as you kept staring. Not a flicker. Not a frown. Your thoughts were a buried book I had forgotten how to unearth.

We arrived home.

You went upstairs.

You tapped away on a computer I wished I'd never bought and I stood there, in the living room, aware of that yanking absence that seemed to be shared by the old furniture, and by your smiling portrait on the wall. I longed for the cat to rub its head against my legs. I longed to hear your cello. I longed to see Reuben – the real, living Reuben – slouched on the sofa. I longed for your mother to tell me it was going to be all right. I craved a thousand things I couldn't bring back and stood there as the room tilted and the present moment, like the memory itself, faded away.

All evening I listened, all evening I stayed there with that blasted thing against my ear, waiting for you to call him. You never did. Nor did you telephone Imogen, as you had always done before whenever I aggravated you. In fact, you never spoke a word. No, you spoke one word. 'God.' The one we are always left with, when all the others have run out.

There was nothing else, just your angry breath, and I grew tired. I lay back against the bed and placed the speaker beside me on the pillow as my eyes grew heavy.

'Dad?' It was the quietest voice I had ever heard, coming out of the speaker. He said something else, something I couldn't quite comprehend. Let me? Help me? Set me?

'Reuben?' I asked, but I was dropping now, deeper, deeper, into the dark.

I was inside your room, by your bed, but I had no recollection of either how I came to be there or how long I had been standing. My eyes were fully adjusted to the dark, to the infinite degrees of shade dictated by the soft golden light beyond the curtain. Light that stretched across the park to reach you. His light.

It was the sound of my own breathing that had restored me to myself. That faint nasal whistle indicative of my sinus trouble. I hadn't woken you, though. You lay there, lost in unknowing sleep, your neck exposed above the sheets and blanket, your head arched back, sideways on the pillow, looking so proud, so defiant, ruling the empire of your dreams.

My heart galloped. What was I doing there? Had I sleep-walked, or had it been him? I did not and could not know. Yet on the furthest fringe of my own awareness, at the precise moment of restoration, I had the last effects of the feeling that had sent my heart into this ridiculous frenzy. A strange unnameable emotion with the blinding intensity of love and hate but that was in fact neither, or was such a confusion of the two that it couldn't be labelled strictly as one or the other. The emotion seemed intricately associated with the sight of your neck, of its slender form gaining shape in the darkness. My swan. My poor, darling swan.

That Keatsian urge. That urge of artists and restorers of old furniture. That contradictory instinct, that chisel-and-thread impulse to break and repair.

Creations and destroyings all at once,
Fill'd the hollows of my brain.

The feeling retreated fast, like the tide of an unplugged ocean, and I couldn't assess it further.

*

I was in the shop the next morning when I received the call. 'Ah've changed me mind,' he said. 'Ah'll take the money. Ah'll leave her alone.'

I stared at the receiver, then pressed it harder into my ear. An old lady left the shop, with the Worcester teapot she had bought. 'Do you mean it?' I asked him.

'Yeah,' he said. 'Three thousand pounds. But now. Ah want it today. Ah'll meet you. At eleven.'

I felt no happiness at that moment. You must know that. It gave me no satisfaction to discover that this boy who ruled your heart would walk away from you for the price of a longcase clock. It did, however, confirm my suspicions.

That my reading of Denny had been more accurate than your own was now beyond doubt. You had been won over by the incident at the stables, and the framed photograph of your brother, and whatever else he had used to get close to you. You may well have seen him as rather exotic, this semi-literate street-fighter from the wrong part of town, who so obviously met with your father's disapproval. I knew, through even my darkest fears, that your yearning for this boy wasn't a physical one. I knew you weren't a Jezebel or a Lilith or a Herodias, whatever your wardrobe suddenly insisted. I knew that. Your love, built on the foundations of your vulnerable mind, was a confusion of pity and mild admiration, an unfortunate result of all that was good and charitable within your nature. Yet his love? What was that but an animal craving, an exchangeable thing, easily sold? The proof was finally there.

We set a place. I emptied the till and went to the bank to suck my accounts dry. We met on a bench by the river, like the double-crossing spies we were, and I gave him an envelope full of fifty-pound notes. He was in his school uniform, or a loose interpretation of it, and I began to worry how this might look to a passing stranger. There was no one, though. It was just us.

'If you see her again I'll tell her about this, you do understand, don't you? You must end it now. No more contact. Nothing. Like I said.'

I remember him looking at me. Oh yes, I see his face. Those eyes sporting the same incomprehensible pride as the lion beside his slaughter. I'm sure I saw the fleeting trace of a smile as he felt the envelope.

'Yeah,' he said.

'So, that's it, then? That's the end?'

He nodded, and looked out at the brown water of the Ouse, a mere metre below flood level. 'The end. Yeah. The end.'

An hour after I had handed Denny that swollen envelope I again closed the shop and drove to your school. A rather foolish thing to do, given that Friday lunch hour was one of the busiest times of the week in terms of customers, but Cynthia was still in the hospital wasn't she, so there was no one to man the fort. And I wanted to know if you were going to leave the premises. I needed to know if you were going to meet Denny, and to see if Denny would stand by his lucrative promise.

I parked and waited, in view of both main entrances. It reached five past, ten past, quarter past, but you didn't leave.

I had watched the brief rush of pupils and teachers depart within those first few minutes, but not you. Maybe I had got it wrong. Maybe I had missed you. Maybe there was another exit you could have gone through.

I left the car and circuited the perimeter of the school on foot, to see if this could have been the case. There were no other obvious exits. Perhaps you had climbed over the fence. After all, you weren't allowed to leave the school premises. Yes. The fence was certainly low enough.

The dull green grass of the hockey fields stretched out beyond the iron railing. Some boys from St John's walked by, on the other side of the road, and threw insults at me, as many as they could think of. I ignored them, raised my Second World War light infantry binoculars, and saw you sitting in the yard beyond the fields. You were on a bench, on your own. Where were your friends? I scanned across and saw Imogen, amid a menagerie of exotic-haired girls. You looked over at them, once or twice, but they refused to register your presence.

I felt relief. You hadn't escaped school to meet Denny, and you were safe.

Yet you looked so pathetic, as you sat there, pulling your hair forward and analysing its ends. I imagine I must have felt a certain pity as I watched you, alone. An island amid continents, amid the schoolyard empires of belonging. Yes, I must have felt sorry for you, but I have to confess the relief is much easier to recall. Maybe it had already happened. Perhaps he had told you it was all over. You weren't with him, that was the main thing. No, that was *everything*.

I lowered the binoculars, and found you again. A delicate grey-green speck sinking, through my unfocused gaze, into the solid orange mass of the Victorian brickwork behind you.

*

and we were inside in the red blood warmth together you and me curled up inside the space you and me before we had names you and me before we knew there were any others in the world you and me before we knew there were an outside or an inside before we knew there was anything but you and me and the beat of our hearts we did not know were hearts and we were there for ever you and me the only life in the only world you and me so close we did not know there was any difference between you and me and we did not know it would ever change and that there would be the day the light would scream into our faces and we would be held apart sucking separate milk and see our separate makers and compete for their separate love in the light white world full of empty space where people have to fight and smile and scream to feel connected and I loved you and you loved me and we were still happy because the love had no name and we had no names that we knew we just knew sounds and the faces of me and you and the faces of the makers and one face out like a light it was just him with enough love inside just for one just for you and your unstained face and he gave us words this maker and the words were other things to separate us and the words kept growing like the distance between planet earth and all its people and the distance between you and me and the love and the hate he gave us and I wanted to be back in the time I couldn't remember in the blood red warmth or the shining dark of the life before when we were the same sweet nothing you and me you and me.

*

We were at Cynthia's, the following evening. You were sitting in her rosewood elbow chair, that beautiful antique outcast in that twig-filled bungalow. You were reading your grandmother's old copy of *The Return of the Native* directly under one of Cynthia's charcoal sketches of nude flesh.

'I love that story,' she told you, a hand on her stomach. 'And your mother did too. I believe she read that same copy.'

She was right. Your mother adored Hardy. Nature as symbol. Landscape as the rough divinity that shapes our ends. She was quite a Romantic in that sense, which possibly explains why she wanted to name our daughter after a wild hedgerow plant.

'Have you read any of his others?' Cynthia asked you.

'We're doing *Tess*,' you said, in your restored voice. 'At school.'

'Ah, *Tess*,' Cynthia said, wistfully, as if talking of a friend she had known personally but who had passed away. 'Not one for a happy ending though, that was Hardy's trouble. A typical man. Wallowing in his own misery like a hippo in mud.' She gave me a sharp look at this point, which I chose to ignore.

'Listen, Cynthia,' I said, holding up the carrier bag from the health-food store and placing it on that horrendous table. 'I've brought the supplements you asked for. Shall I show you? In the kitchen?' I bounced my eyebrows in such a fashion that she gathered I wanted a quiet word. We left you to Egdon Heath and went into the kitchen.

'It's over,' I whispered, placing a jar of hawthorn tablets down on the unit. 'With her and that boy. It's all over.'

She eyed my glee with suspicion. 'What did you do, Terence?'

'Do?' I said, mock-insulted. 'I didn't *do* anything. I think she's finally seen sense that's all. Anyway, does it matter what's happened? It's over. It's over.'

She closed her eyes. 'Poor girl. Is she upset? Has she said anything?'

I felt as though Cynthia was missing the point. 'No. She hasn't. And I don't think she's upset, really. She seems quite her old self. You know what youngsters are like, it was probably just a phase.'

'But, Terence, I don't understand. How do you know it's over?'

'Because it is,' I said.

She winced in pain and held her stomach. 'So, what are you going to do now? What are you going to do when the next boy comes along? Are you going to lock her in a cupboard? Put her in a glass case and interview prospective suitors, like an old king?'

'Oh, Cynthia, stop it!' I told her. 'If you knew what I knew about that boy you would be as relieved as I am.'

The pain seemed to leave her. She inspected the dietary information on one of the jars I had bought. 'So, why don't you enlighten me? What was he like? Terence? Terence?'

I was looking past her, to the magnets on the door of her fridge-freezer. You know the ones. The miscellaneous collection of words that you and Reuben always used to rearrange. Four of the magnets were together, an even line amid the chaotic jumble all around them.

petal   wants   a   horse

'It doesn't matter,' I said. 'I'll tell you another time.'

Again I was in your room. Again I had no idea of how I got there. Again you were lost in oblivious sleep. Again that withdrawing Keatsian urge.

One difference, though: a pillow – my own – held in my hands.

'Oh, Reuben,' I whispered, once I was back in my bed. 'What were you doing?'

Stillness, broken only by the tick of the clock. I clenched my eyes closed and bit into the sheets, fighting back the unborn heat of your brother's guilty tears.

It was the following Monday, wasn't it, when I was meant to go down to Horncastle? I had been reluctant to close the shop, but as Cynthia was still bent double from her operation, and as it seemed too much to ask George, I decided it was worth the gamble. After all, I hadn't made a significant Monday sale since the drop-leaf table I had parted with the day Reuben had died, and now I knew Denny was out of your life I had decided to try and restore a degree of normality. I didn't have a stand, this year, but it was still worth going to catch up with the competition, and bargain-hunt among the collectors' stalls.

The plan was thwarted, though, due to the blackout I experienced on the motorway. I had only been on the road for ten minutes when, without the usual warning, time stuttered forward. One moment I was in the fast lane, trying to shorten the journey as much as possible (I was trusting you with lunch hours now, but still wanted to be back at those school gates for four o'clock). The next moment I was sliding diagonally across the road. Cars honked long and thudding elephant notes behind me, as

I cut them up. A lorry driver leaned out of his window, waving an obscene gesture.

'Stay back,' I pleaded, with your brother. 'Leave me alone.'

I made it to the lay-by, parked and composed myself. I switched on the radio and Beethoven's 'Moonlight Sonata' slowly restored my mind. A few steady breaths and a decision was made. It was too dangerous to try and carry on with the journey. What if Reuben tried to take over the wheel again?

No.

I would drive the shorter distance home, and be attentive to any darkening of vision or strange cerebral sensations.

Of course, nothing happened. I made it safely back, with the help of Beethoven and a quieter road. Now, having the full knowledge of time, I realise he had no further reason to interfere. I was heading home, as he wanted. Yes, as he wanted.

I entered from the shop side but locked the door again. The truth is I was still feeling rather worried about what had happened on the motorway, and didn't want to weaken myself further by facing customers.

Instead, I decided to reupholster the George IV mahogany dining chair I had been intending to repair for weeks. So I went into the back to fetch my scissors and ripping chisel and, having found them, suddenly heard something from upstairs. Music. Faint, faint music. I stood still, for a while, because I was sure my ears were deceiving me. It was Beethoven's 'Moonlight Sonata', coming from upstairs. It was on your London Philharmonic album, I was sure, yet the truly peculiar thing was it was the precise same part I had heard on the car radio. The beautiful lament that comes towards the end of the first movement, that 'tender poetry beyond all language' as Berlioz put it.

Maybe the radio had been left on upstairs, but if it was the radio why was it playing exactly the same refrain it had already played minutes before. With the chisel in my hand I trod my way carefully upstairs. Halfway up I wondered about returning to the shop and fetching the pistol, but I dismissed the idea. After all, why would an intruder be playing Beethoven?

Outside your door, I waited. I heard something above the soft piano – a slow and rhythmic thudding. Most curious, given that I knew the piece was devoid of a percussion section.

'Bryony? Bryony? Is that you? Petal?' You didn't answer, so I called you again, 'Bryony? Are you there?'

Maybe this was just another delusion. Another aural hallucination. After what had happened in the car, it couldn't be ruled out. I leaned my ear against the door and heard nothing now but the dying moments of the first movement.

Adagio sostenuto.

Of course, you know what happened next. With the chisel in my left hand I opened the door with my right. I saw you there, just you, on the bed. Your tender body clothed in only the sheets.

A second later I scanned left and he came into view, already in his jeans, pulling a white T-shirt over the rest of him.

Denny.

I kept blinking him away, but he was still there: this sweating animal, this predator inside my own home. He looked at the chisel in my hand and wondered what I was capable of. I stepped closer.

'What have you done to her?' I asked, but I could see the answer all around me. Hear it, smell it.

209

'Nothing,' he lied, addressing the chisel. 'We were doing nothing.'

I stepped closer towards him and kept my eyes fixed on his face. 'You made a promise,' I said. 'I gave you –'

I couldn't say it. I couldn't let you know what I had done, not then.

'Dad, stop it,' you said. 'It's my fault. It wasn't Denny, it was me. Please, Dad, you're scaring me. Please.'

The second movement began. Those strange, unsettling, opening bars intensifying the mood.

'Nothing,' I said, picking up on Denny's word. 'That's all she is to you, isn't it?'

'No,' he said. 'No, she's not, she's –'

'Shut up. Jesus Christ, shut up!'

'Dad, please.'

What was I going to do? I had no idea. In truth, I wasn't thinking. I just kept conjuring pictures of him, on top of you, a scene that should have been beyond my worst imagining.

'Do you think, Petal, that you can heal a boy like this with music? Do you think, Petal, that you can take this lump of stone and turn it into something more dignified? More worthy of your own nature? Well, you can't. Look at him. There's nothing there.'

I wasn't looking at you. It was impossible to look at you. Instead, I was looking at the quiet fury in his eyes, as my own anger began to dissolve. An image flashed in my mind. Not of him and you in bed but of something else. I saw him fighting another boy, with a face I couldn't see. There were toys strewn on a carpet. It was a flash, nothing more, but it triggered a sudden weakening of my will. My body stood there, a hollow object, and the chisel dropped by my feet.

*

210

The room crept slowly out of the darkness, like an old layer of paint under a blowtorch, and both of you were gone.

I telephoned your school. You were there. You had arrived late, at half past ten. Apparently you had told them your grandmother had just been taken into hospital.

The lies were so easy for you now. So natural. You could shed the truth at any given moment, as easy as slipping unwanted clothes.

A day of empty, monotonous horror and then the return journey from school.

We said nothing of what had happened. Indeed, we said nothing at all. I felt you looking at me from the back seat. You were clearly suspicious of the silence, but didn't question it. We were both lost in our own plans, formulating the secret and opposing schemes we thought would set us free.

and I was inside his head and I was pressing all the lights keeping them all pressed all the time as I looked out of the windows that weren't windows and down at you and it was so hard pressing all the lights that I could hardly hold on inside there but when he steadied I looked at you down from the watchtower and saw you lying there and saw you PLEASE GO *no I saw you and I saw through your unhatched eyes the dream of you* STOP *and I saw you and you saw the time we went for tamsy beetles little green tamsies and you saw and the lights kept flashing but I kept smoking them out and you remembered* STRENGTH *you remembered when he wasn't looking at us when he had his back in front of us and I grabbed your mouth and you bit my hand* REUB *and I pushed you and I left you on the nettles and I felt the hundred* EN *stings you felt trying to get out and he saw and you told on me like the green goody grass you always were and I felt him smack me and I felt the pinkness and the shame of your bite and your bites he made me look at and the sadness when he put the penicillin on you and the smell of pink milk back when we were home* LEAVE ME *and the lights kept shining and I kept looking behind his eyes and raised his hands and walked slow towards your bed and I was so close from making it happen so close to freeing you from his love but I stopped and lost the power to stay inside the solid tower of him and the lights got brighter and brighter white as the sun like the lights that shine now and the hands fell by his side and he stood still as I left him as the light burned me out of the lies and into the truth and speeding me fast around the earth getting so foggy all the time and I couldn't get back couldn't find his light* LEAVE ME *and I went again to the place I go now without you* ALONE

Through the whispered crackle of the baby monitor, I heard you speak to him on your mobile telephone. You were planning to see him. You were meeting him at the shed at Rawcliffe Meadows and you were going to run away that night. Rawcliffe Meadows! Rawcliffe Meadows! Oh, Aristotle himself would have grimaced at such pathos. Rawcliffe Meadows. Where I had once taken you and your brother to hunt for tansy beetles. Was that your idea, to meet there? I didn't know. I didn't know where you were planning to go next. Maybe you were intending to stay hidden in the wild, catching rabbits and fishing for polluted carp in the river. I didn't know. All I knew was the time and the place.

You stopped talking. You opened your door.

'Bryony?'

Your feet stopped, but your mouth said nothing.

'Bryony? Petal? Is that you?' Ridiculous question, un-answered. I went out of my room and saw you. 'What do you think you're doing?'

'I'm going out,' you told me. 'And you can't stop me.'

'No,' I said. 'No, you're not.'

'Dad? What are you doing? Get out of the way!'

I shook my head and stretched my arms out. A makeshift crucifix, blocking your path. 'I'm sorry, Bryony, but you are not yourself. And until such a time has arrived when I am confident that Bryony is Bryony again then I am very much afraid to say that your actions are under my command. You do understand that this is for your own good, don't you? You do know that the most irresponsible thing for me to do right now would be to let you walk out of this house? You do know that I can't let you see him, don't you? That animal.'

'What?'

'That animal. Denny. I can't let you see him. Not after what I saw in your bedroom.'

'What are you on about? I'm going to Imogen's.'

'Stop that,' I told you. 'Stop those lies.'

'I'm not lying.'

'You're not going to Imogen's and you know it. You're not friends with Imogen any more.'

Was it then you pushed past me and reached for the door? Was it then I took your mobile telephone out of your pocket? Was it then I grabbed your arm and pulled you upstairs towards the attic, while you screamed like a banshee. You scratched my arm, do you remember, as we climbed the last few stairs? You even pulled my hair, causing me to treat you more roughly than I would have intended, and I apologise for that.

'What are you doing?' You spat the words. 'Where are you going?'

'Never mind where I am going,' I told you. 'The important thing is you are not going anywhere.'

You looked at me in disbelief. 'You can't lock me in the attic, you Nazi psycho.'

'I assure you I can and I will.'

'That's abuse. That's illegal. You're mad. You need a hospital.'

'It's for your own protection.'

'I hate you,' you said and I know you meant it. Your mouth, your eyes, and your kicking legs – you all meant it.

I pushed you back. 'I'm sorry, Bryony.' And then I locked you inside there, amid the old boxes and your mother's and Reuben's belongings.

Your feet and hands thundered against the door. 'Let me out! Let me out! Fascist!' I must confess I feared you then, feared this force inside you, as people fear the most violent and unpredictable weather. Yet it was my only choice, and I had a new courage in my actions. The door would hold. The thick Tudor oak would take its beating, and the iron lock wouldn't give. Closing my eyes, I placed the key in my pocket, and let it be.

> *I dare do all that may become a man;*
> *Who dares do more is none.*

I knew precisely what I had to do. It was as though, all of a sudden, the future had become as solid as the past. I was being guided by something outside myself, as though I was being written by another hand, caught inside a story I couldn't quite control. Not Reuben's story, and not my own, but someone else's. It was impossible to tell if I was the hero or the villain of this narrative, and it made no real difference, for my actions were already written.

'I am going out, and I will open the door on my return,' I said, above your kicks and wails. 'I will be three hours at the most. There are some old books in one of the tea chests. An early *Alice in Wonderland.* The eight hundredth ever printed. Or somewhere around there. It's got the number on it still, I believe, on the inside cover.'

'Open the door!' you screamed above my words. 'Open the door!'

I stood there in the hallway, still baffled by the force of your emotion. A possession I knew I could never grasp.

Your scream melted into tears. 'Open the door.'

'Goodbye Bryony,' I said, too soft for you to hear, and trod my way downstairs to the shop.

*

The mahogany case was open and that old gun lay before me, the engraved steel of the trigger-guard shining in the dark like a waking eye. It looked so beautiful, so exquisitely crafted, it was almost impossible to believe it could perform the task I had in mind.

I picked it up. I took the old bullets from their tin box. I loaded the pistol.

As any father would, I tried to keep you safe. Every waking moment I thought about it, the ways I could ensure you a long and happy future. Yet it occurs to me now that every single attempt I made had a reverse effect. Each time I tried to interfere in your life I pushed you away from me, and lost a little more of your trust and respect.

Even when my actions were hidden, and you saw the puppet but not the strings, they were equally futile. It was as though there was an enemy within my own mind, a double agent who was willingly jeopardising every task. Of course, this is not so far away from the truth.

Indeed, over the past few weeks and months I have come to a greater understanding of the invisible forces that thwart our best efforts. I see that there is not such a great difference between the psychic and physical landscapes. Both, in their separate ways, are continuous narratives within which the actions of the living are determined by those who have gone before.

In our own city, with its Roman foundations, with its Saxon streets and Norman defences and Victorian railway, we understand how things connect. How the old and antique contains the present and how, in turn, that present manages to seal our futures. You live and walk and breathe among these layers.

Minds are the same. They are not cities shaped in our own image. They are cities shaped by the whole human experience, by all that has gone before, all this knowledge that has been built by those who exist in memory, in books, in possessions.

Yet if minds are cities they can be vulnerable to attack, invaded by forces coming at us in the night, when we are weak, when there is no one manning the towers.

You see, Bryony, this is what has been happening. Everything I have done to protect you has only served to aggravate him, and stir his unrested soul in jealousy. As I have been watching you, I too have always been observed. If I had done things differently, shown you a little less attention, displayed to him a little more grief – then perhaps I would never have gained this new knowledge. Perhaps I would never have been forced to realise that our minds are no stronger than those of animals. They are territories that can be invaded and taken over the same as any other.

Yet only now do I realise there is a way to calm his soul, and quench its horrendous thirst. In doing so, I truly believe he will love you again, and rest in the peace we prayed would be his. It is my last hope, and will prove to be my last action. I will raze my mind's city to the ground, and create a fresher, clearer space, where avenging spirits float through without pause.

It was quite a walk, but I had time. Once I had crossed the park, and passed under Reuben's lamp post, I headed towards the river. I went the quiet, longer route, via the cycle path, so there were fewer eyes to witness my journey. On and on, in the dark, with the pistol weighing against me. Onwards, over Lendal Bridge, and further down Stripe Lane. I could smell the wild flowers, the hedgerow plants, and heard the skylarks, and knew I was getting closer. What was the plan? Were you going to stay the night there, before heading north to Beningbrough and catching a morning train to somewhere else? Or were you going to stay living out in the wild, like Neolithic hunters, outside our civilisation?

My suspicions grew. Why had he wanted to meet you in

the middle of nowhere? I had seen what he had done to George. I had heard what he had done to Alison Wingfield. I knew only too well what his father was capable of. Maybe he was meeting you there to do unthinkable things, more unthinkable than I had already seen – things he could get away with, knowing everything was constructed to look like two teenage lovers escaping happily into the night.

A mute swan blocked my path. I didn't see it until the last moment and then there it was, wings outstretched, hissing its warning. He may have had a family to protect but as far as I could see he was a sole operator, a highwayman swan, looking for spoils I couldn't provide. There was something of a stand-off. To my right, the river. To my left, the copse. As the swan showed no sign of moving I was forced to venture into the dense, low woodland and steer around.

When I was back on the path I heard a voice behind me.

'Daddy? Daddy? Look.'

The swan wasn't there.

It had disappeared completely.

In its place was a young boy, about seven years old, with a birthmark on his face. He was holding out his hand. 'Look, it's on my finger. Look!'

I crouched down and he came over to me. It was fully dark now, but the luminous bottle-green beetle crawling over his hand could be clearly seen, as could Reuben's young eyes. That intense look he used to have, sternly inquisitive, his eyes pressing me to respond.

'Reuben,' I said.

'Is that a tamsy beetle? Have I found one?'

'Reuben? Why are you here?'

His voice became cross. 'Is it a tamsy beetle?'

'Yes,' I said, and got caught in the memory. 'But it's tansy. Tan-sy.'

He looked sad. 'I didn't mean to push Bryony in the nettles. I'm sorry, Daddy.'

'It's all right, Reuben. Bryony's fine.'

He frowned at me, as though I was lying. 'She's gone.'

'No,' I said.

'We've lost her. In the dark.'

'No. She's safe. She's at home.'

'She's gone invisible. She's not here.'

I became cross. Not with Reuben, but with myself, with the nervous mind that had conjured this apparition. 'No,' I said. 'You're not here.'

'Where am I?'

I tapped the side of my head. 'In here.'

'Where's the beetle?'

I kept tapping. 'In here as well. You're not real. You're not real. Now, I've got to go.'

'Don't leave me, Daddy,' he said. 'Don't leave me, don't leave me, don't leave me . . .'

The hallucination began to cry. I closed my eyes and begged reason to stay with me. 'Oh, let me not be mad,' I said. 'Not yet.'

I could not afford for the possession to take hold tonight so with clenched eyes my hand reached out slowly, cautiously, towards that imagined face. Of course, I expected to feel nothing at all. I expected my fingers to glide through empty air and confirm it as a delusion. Instead, I received a sharp and most painful bite.

You must remember I was already crouching down, and so the action of yanking my hand away, combined with the sight of the swan returned to where it had been standing, caused gravity to gain the best of me. I dropped backwards to the ground.

Given that the swan was violently beating its wings and hissing like the Devil, I desperately tried to scramble to my feet but was still too slow. Trapped in this awkward position the wild bird was upon me, its neck thrusting forward, its wings full-stretched beating my legs.

There was no stopping this creature.

Again I tried to get up but received such a winding blow to my chest I was knocked down, lower than before, landing in mud. He would have killed me, I am sure, and with hindsight we might see this as having been God's intention (or whatever unseen author was still shaping my quest), yet I needed to make you safe and survive a few more hours. So I reached inside my coat, drew my pistol, and while my other hand wrestled helplessly with the bird's neck I shot him in the breast. After that loud, echoing clap there was a final hiss and then the neck collapsed. Dark blood leaked fast out of him, glugging almost, and I was momentarily paralysed by the sight. Life cut away very quickly and after the smallest of fits the poor bird fell limply across my legs.

Now, in a rotten panic, I carried the bird to the river and tried to keep any more of its blood from staining my clothes. When I saw its previously unseen family in the shadows, asleep in their watery nest, I felt such a terror fall over me that I cannot describe it to you. Oh, Bryony, it was such a hideous feeling! Those blameless, unclaimed animal souls. Once the bird had been washed away on the current, half sinking, I vomited amid the rushes and tried to clear my mind by inhaling that chilled air, but it was no good. If I was ever to live past this night I knew that pale swan would haunt me, as the albatross did the old mariner, for the rest of my days.

*

At the end of the copse the path thins out and makes way for the hay meadow. As I could see the shed from there, I decided to stay back, hiding among the last of the bushes.

The incident with the swan had taken longer than I had realised. My watch told me it was ten past nine. Denny would have arrived. Yet I stayed amid the blackberry bushes and creeping thistle, and waited for him to appear. It was there I caught a smell. Something overpowering the wild flowers. A burnt, toffeeish smell. In the distance smoke rose from the sugar factory, erasing stars. A night shift. People would be there. They might hear the gunshot and come to inspect before I had time to discard the body.

I saw a dark shape pass across the shed window. It was him. I could recognise the outline of that hideous padded jacket I had seen him wear when he had met you at Clifford's Tower. A dark swollen chrysalis. It disappeared back out of view. My thoughts became questions. What was he doing in there without a light on? Had he broken in? Did he know someone who owned that shed? What was he getting prepared? How long would he wait for you before leaving? And where would he step out from?

I couldn't see a door. There obviously was one – which had probably been forced open – but I couldn't see it from this side.

Oh please, picture me there.

See me amid those bushes. Crouching in the dark. Damp with swan blood and mud-water. A trembling antique pistol in my hand. I want you to understand the rapid madness of my thoughts. The creeping doubts that weakened my resolve. The familiar sensations in my brain, bringing the alien images of other experience.

*

I saw him, in my mind. I saw Denny, with the others, on East Mount Road. He was looking at me. 'Don't do it,' he said. 'You don't have to do it just 'cos of Tully.'

And my mouth began to whisper Reuben's words. 'I'm not doing it 'cos of Tully.'

And Andrew Tully himself, laughing and looking around at the other boys, and their laughter scorching me the way it must have scorched Reuben.

And Denny shaking his head at me. 'You'll kill yourself.'

I shook the memory away. It was false, I told myself. It was as false as all those other hallucinations. It didn't happen. Denny was as responsible as the rest of them. Of course he was. Yet I could feel it happening, the changes inside me.

I was about to lose myself again, my soul destroyed by those fires raging inside my mind, at the worst possible time.

'Stay strong, Terence,' I told myself. 'Stay Terence.' My name sounded hollow, as if it meant no more to me than it did to the surrounding plants and trees, yet I still had clarity.

Denny was going to hurt you. I could not question it. At some future place and time he was going to reveal his true and hideous colours and do to you what he had done to Alison Wingfield. Reuben was playing with my mind. He wanted Denny to hurt you. Of course he did. Reuben himself had been trying to hurt you, through his various methods, since he had died. I followed the horse and it had led me to him – that had been the first sign. And then the Higgins incident. He had found ways to get inside their minds, as he had found a way into my own. His jealous spirit couldn't settle while you were still with me, so for you to run away with this violent rogue would have been most desirable.

I had to act fast, as Reuben was still pressing in.

I stood up and walked onto the plain.

The moment I was out there, treading across that ancient earth, I was no more than an empty vessel. Reuben would have been able to come at any moment and steer me away, but he didn't. It was just me, watching myself, this Terence with his pistol down by his side, trying to stay out of view from the window.

Terence picked up speed and tried to think away his own footsteps, and the pain that throbbed through his left leg.

He could see the door. A dark rectangle of wood swinging slowly away from the side of the shed. He stood still. He raised his gun. He stayed there, silent as the waiting wolf. He felt the bushes and the low trees retreat behind him, sensed the river sliding further to his right. The boy appeared, wearing his padded jacket. A silhouette that seemed too small for the distance between them, as if perspective was melting away.

Had the boy seen him? Terence didn't know. All Terence knew was the pistol in his hand, the pistol he now raised and fired.

He had missed. He was sure of it. For a moment the boy was still standing, and made no sound of pain.

Terence was searching his pocket for another cap when the boy fell back, holding his shoulder, and his scream came. Then there was someone else, another silhouette. A boy the same size as Denny. No, bigger. A man, crouching over the fallen body.

*

It was so confusing in the dark. Terence, whom I can see falling into myself again, began to panic. Who was this other man, dragging Denny behind the door, out of my sight? I didn't know. I had to leave. A thousand black flies swarmed up my body and buzzed their angry murmurs around my head.

I heard something else. A baby crying, screaming, somewhere behind, within the copse. I turned and walked – jogged, hobbled, stumbled – towards the sound, the crowd of flies keeping speed. Behind the bushes but before the trees: two babies lying, writhing, on a bed of nettles. He was wailing like he always had done, and you were silent by his side. 'Shhh,' I told Reuben. 'Shhh. Please. Shhh.' I went to pick him up, closing my eyes and mouth against the flies. The buzzing stopped. And the crying. There were no babies.

It was then I headed home. Through the low wood and towards the footpath, feeling the silent scream of nature from every tree, every insect, and every living thing.

You are sitting down, aren't you? Are you at Cynthia's? I can see the look on your face, I can see it as if you were here with me, frowning as if looking at a piece of music. Something you'd never played. Your eyes narrow. Flinching, almost.

Please don't be scared. I can't cope with the idea that I have become something else to be scared of, even from my grave.

My grave.

Oh, I feel it already. I feel the daisies growing above me, as Keats did in the days before he died. It's so strange, you know, sitting here. Writing in this car, straining to see in the dull light. Knowing that tomorrow I will be nothing, knowing there will be no more to add to these words, knowing I will not be knowing. Or maybe gaining a different kind of knowledge. Reuben's kind.

No.

I must stop this, right now. This pathetic weakness. This fear that –

Never mind.

Imagine my panic. Imagine, for a moment, how you made me feel when I came back, opened the attic door, and discovered an uninhabited room and an open window.

It was in such horrendous desperation that I searched behind the door, under the old sleigh bed, among the boxes, hoping that this was just another delusion. A reverse hallucination: your presence masquerading as an absence. Then I noticed a torn page on the floor.

'Advice from a Caterpillar.'

Other pages too, ripped apart, lying on those old green-painted boards like a foreign map, an unfamiliar archipelago of text and tea-party illustrations.

'Bryony? Where are you? Petal? Petal? Petal? Where are you? Bryony? Show yourself.'

It must have been at this point that I walked over to the open window and began to contemplate your only route of escape. I still do not quite understand how you managed it. To have risked your life climbing out of that window and onto those loose tiles, your feet teetering on the gutter rail, the awkward hang down to the roof of your bedroom, the horseback shuffle along the ridge, getting tangled up with the ivy as you descended the trellis. The mad and blinded action of your love.

For a moment, I was convinced you must be dead. I saw a missing roof tile and imagined it slipping under your foot, causing you to fall. As the adrenalin flooded into me I ran down those flights of stairs. I picked up the keys I'd left in the shop, again catching my hip against the chest and nearly losing the Girl with a Tambourine.

Outside I saw your wet footprints treading away from the puddle, fading as they left the passage. Relief you were alive was quickly swallowed by concerns as to where you had gone. The street held no clues. The park, the street lamp, the growl of indifferent traffic. I strained my eyes in every direction but it was clear that I was too late. You had disappeared out of the scene.

And then, the faintest of sounds. The telephone, the shop line, at that late hour.

My ears were at a high hum from the gunshots, but there was no mistaking the dread ascending with each ring.

'Yes?'

At first nothing.

'Yes? Hello? Hello?'

The fuzzy sound of breath.

'Yes? Who is this?'

And then his voice.

'Mr Cave?'

I looked around me, at the objects in the dark – the figurines, the vases, the drawing tables, the longcase clocks. They were closing in on me. It was an ambush. I was General Gordon at Khartoum, besieged by the Mahdists.

'Yes, this is Mr Cave. Who is this?'

I knew the answer before he spoke.

'It's Denny.'

I took the receiver away from my ear. 'Mr Cave? Mr Cave? Mr Cave?'

Perhaps my shot had killed him and this was another ghost. First Reuben, now Denny. The manifestations of guilt, nothing more.

'No,' I said. 'No, you're not Denny.'

I picked up the nearest figure. The Girl with a Tambourine.

'It's Bryony. She's been . . . someone's . . . she's been shot.'

I said nothing. Images flashed in my mind. The empty attic. The torn-up *Alice* book. The sinking swan. The figure in Denny's coat, falling to the ground. The man over the body. The babies lying on the nettles.

'She's . . . in hospital.'

He was crying, this ghost.

'She's in hospital. They're operating . . . We were there. At Rawcliffe. At Rawcliffe Meadows. Ah had the money you gave us and we were going to run away. Ah'm sorry . . . But someone shot . . .'

'Someone . . . someone . . . someone . . .'

'George Weeks. Ah think it was George Weeks. He attacked Bryony. That's why ah –'

'No,' I said. 'You're the attacker.'

I remember George standing upstairs, on the landing, and your frightened face. What had he done to you? And why hadn't you said anything? Didn't you think I would have been able to sort it out? Did you think that running away with Denny was going to be the answer?

I hung up, and telephoned York General Infirmary for a weary night-shift voice to put me on hold. A tinny Mozart serenade tried to calm my nerves.

I remembered George in the shop, his bruised and damaged face staring at the figurine. My heart beat at tremendous speed as I tilted the figurine in my hand and looked at the base.

Alison Wingfield, 1932.

It slipped from my grip, and smashed. I cowered down, to the waltzing strains of Mozart's river music, and surrendered to the ambush.

And then it came. The cacophony:

I saw the ghost walk come to an end. I saw that blond yeti turn his head and nearly see me. I saw him shrug to himself and carry on his way, beyond the walls, and on to the quieter streets. I saw him take a short cut through the bowling green and towards the library. I saw the bottle in my hand. I jogged past the library, getting ready to meet him on the other side. One strike in the dark and he was on the floor, his face in the grass, as quiet as the dead.

I was staring at the water. The drops, falling down over all the petrified objects. It was the middle of the night. I had driven miles and climbed over two fences to get here but I still couldn't see it. I walked further along, passing the top hat and the tea towels and the wellington boots until I was at the wristband. I held out my hand and felt a kind of relief at the touch.

The cold water that could defy time running over my fingers. 'Look, Dad,' I whispered. 'I'm –' A dog barked, somewhere in the distance. I saw a torchlight flicker through the trees. Two male voices, getting closer. An unpeggable wristband. It dropped and I lost it in the pool. I reached my arm in but the cold stones all felt the same.

I held your Handwerck doll. I gazed a moment at the delicate stitching on the cape, at the intricate floral pattern on the dress, and felt the rage that wasn't mine. I twisted off the bisque head and left her body under your bed. I walked in quiet, small steps towards the kitchen and placed the head inside the bin, those eyes looking up at me as she lay on the carrot shavings. 'Goodbye, Angelica.'

I saw Denny in that living room, on the day Reuben was forced to drink that revolting drink. I saw him walk across that toy-filled carpet and slam Aaron Tully against the wall.

'Leave him alone,' Denny said.

'Tea-stain's all right, aren't you, Tea-stain?' said Tully laughing.

'He's called Reuben, you ———.'

The fight started as the boy on the keyboard kept on playing his random music. A toy castle was crushed as Denny swung Aaron to the ground. He slammed his fist into his face and I saw that small boy called Cam saying 'Stop! Stop!' and then my Reuben self just sitting and looking at the empty bottle in my hand.

I stood there, at night, alone in the park. I turned towards the flames. The plastic bottle that had contained ammonia dropped by my side and I stepped closer, shielding my face with my hands, and felt the same heat that was devouring your cello. And I stayed there, listening to that wild, crackling music, until there was nothing but a large black teardrop scorched into the grass.

I saw the gun pressed into Aaron Tully's sleeping head. I heard my voice telling him to wake up. I saw the fear in his young eyes as I delivered the threats.

The jar of pills by his bed. Blue pills, like my mother's barbiturates.

'Who are you?' he asked. He didn't make the connection.

'You know me,' I said. Or my voice said. 'I'm Tea-stain.'

'What? What? What?'

I saw him getting out of that bed, in his T-shirt and underpants.

'Me mam's –'

'Your mum's on her night shift.'

I saw him take the pen and paper I had taken from the sideboard. I heard me giving the words. 'I'm sorry. I can't live with myself.' His hand trembling, slow to shape each letter.

I held the pillow and gripped it tight. I stared down at your perfect, sleeping self and felt what he felt, that yearning to be with you, that desire to be with you alone, away from your father. To be as you once were. Together. Equal. At peace.

And then the cacophony faded and I was on the floor. Strange dark forms surrounded me, in the ticking quietness. Tiny figures stared down from wooden cliffs, working out their next move. I was a giant in an unfamiliar land, a fallen Gulliver, waiting for Lilliputian armies to take me hostage.

I couldn't move. I lay there, not asleep and not awake, not Reuben but not quite Terence, as the darkness outside the shop made its slow concessions to the day.

Just then I looked in the mirror and found not Gulliver but Robinson Crusoe staring back at me. 'What has happened to you?' I pondered.

I came from a civilised place and now I'm an ignoble savage.

I used to believe in this world. I used to treasure its old objects. I repaired fine things, made by human hands.

I believed this was the essence of our species. This desire to preserve what has gone before, to restore the past and then to learn its lessons. This is what makes us human, what separates us from all the other animals. Ever since Neolithic times we have been building something up, a kind of moral ladder that takes us higher and higher away from the apes and sharks and wolves we share this planet with. Yet it is we who have got it wrong, isn't it?

There is no difference, is there? At the bottom of it, we are the same as every other animal. The only difference is this tragic need we have inside us to understand this world, to represent it in art and to dissect it in science, and then to compensate for our lack of true understanding with material possessions. The clocks and dolls and inkwells that kill our true selves as surely as pistols.

Oh yes, I see it now. As I face that infinite sea of infinite souls, I see all our errors.

I see that we have lived the biggest of lies. We collectors, we restorers, we foolish fathers. We search for an understanding that forever slips our grip. We believe we have that understanding, and that this understanding separates us from the rest of life, as we like to believe our minds are separate from each other. And I believed it more than most. But I was wrong. We are all together, all of us, in the same boat, sailing the same infinite sea. There is no high and low. No them and us. No you and me. Our friends and enemies are all inside us, as we are inside them. We know this as babies, as I know this now, but we lose this understanding. We topple, and fall apart, like Babel towers.

Born civilised, we come to understand how knowledge makes lonely primitives of us all.

Before I left this morning I went to visit George.

Poor Mrs Weeks looked most confused when she answered the door. 'I thought you were the postman,' she told me.

I imagined, briefly, another life.

I imagined I had done nothing to hurt you.

I imagined I wasn't coming to talk with George, but to see Mrs Weeks.

I imagined my author had another narrative for me.

In this story I would look into her sea-blue eyes and ask if she wanted to accompany me to the theatre. Cynthia had told me about a production of *The Cherry Orchard*, coming to the Playhouse. We would go along, myself and Mrs Weeks, and we would dissect the performances, and nod and agree about the bold stage direction. We would arrange to see each other again, for a meal this time, and I would dab the side of my mouth with a napkin and tell her how lovely she looked. Intimacies would be shared. I would call her by her first name and she would tell me how comfortable she felt in my presence, how safe. Over time, we would tell our children that the relationship was serious and you would be pleased for us. We would all live together. You and George (who was the George I had once imagined, not the real

George) would fly the nest, but Mrs Weeks and I would attend all the fairs together and she would paint her portraits. And slowly, through the shortening days, we would restore each other's happiness.

But alas, I got the narrative I deserved.

'Mr Cave? Are you all right?' Her eyes scanned me up and down.

'Yes,' I said, slowly, returning to my task. 'I am here for a word with George, if he's home.'

She looked quite lovely, standing there, her golden hair and pristine white shirt lending a heavenly lightness to her appearance. 'Yes,' she said, 'he's here. Please, do come in.'

She opened the door and I stepped inside, into the tiled hallway. I could smell coffee. Music was playing in the background. There was a portrait on the wall. A blond boy with a fringe and glasses, five or six years old, a large careless smile across his broad face.

'George? George? Mr Cave's here to see you. George?'

A heavy footstep creaked the Victorian floorboards above me. I had kept my nerve, up to that point, but when I recognised the music I cracked.

'Beethoven,' I said, and couldn't help but laugh as I realised. '"Moonlight Sonata".'

'Yes indeed,' she said, giving a glimpse of that rare smile of hers. 'I love the first movement.'

'Oh yes, the first movement is wonderful, isn't it?' I said, my words gaining sudden speed. 'The first movement is sublime, I would say. Of course, Beethoven didn't think so. In his mind he had created an unfathomable monster. It had a will of its own, packing out concert halls across Europe, and Beethoven had no comprehension why it should be his most popular piece.' I struck an exaggerated but philosophical pose, my index finger resting on my chin. 'But that is the thing, isn't it, Mrs Weeks? That is our tragedy, isn't it? We all want the world to be bent to our own image. We want things to be seen the way we see them. We want to have control over what or who is loved when really we can't even have control over our own minds.'

Mrs Weeks' smile had been usurped by a twitchy frown. 'Mr Cave, are you all –'

My raised palm blocked her enquiry.

'And when we realise this we begin to wobble,' I went on. 'We begin to feel the "hot terror" poor Ludwig felt. As though our own souls are caving in, giving way. A lot of the great poets felt something similar. Keats, for instance. An annihilation of the self. Not a lack of identity as such but rather an absorption of other identities, Mrs Weeks. An absorption that stretched beyond the realms of empathy into . . . ah, George, there you are.'

Mrs Weeks turned to see her son standing behind her on the wooden staircase. Raised above us, on that third step, he cut a colossal figure, his equatorial midline marked by the tight brown towelling of his dressing-gown belt. Judging that he was still in his pyjamas, coupled with the state of his hair, it was clear he had just hauled himself out of bed. Yet he instantly seemed aware of the significance of my visit. Indeed, the bruised eyes behind those thick lenses viewed me with what I can only describe as a lethargic dread.

'Hello,' he said, in his faraway voice.

I cleared my throat, and tried to speak calmly. 'Yes, George, I'd like a word. I think we should have a little chat. On our own.'

Mrs Weeks turned to me, mouth agape. 'What is it you would you like to speak with him about?'

I took a breath, then announced it. 'About a certain Alison Wingfield.'

George went pale, and seemed to shrink before my eyes.

'I'm not sure that now is a very good time, Mr Cave,' said Mrs Weeks. She noticed my trembling hands. 'You seem like you need some –'

'It's all right, Mum.' His tone was sheepish now. 'I'll talk with him.'

'George, I don't think it's –'

He closed his eyes. 'I'll talk with him.'

Mrs Weeks seemed taken aback by her son's insistence, and most concerned about my own. I wondered what lie George had given her, to explain his bruises. Eventually though, Mrs Weeks stood aside and I followed George into the living room, which was stuffed with familiar antiques bought in the shop. The pine mule chest was there, and the Arabian Dancer was positioned on a small side table next to the sofa along with Barrias' Winged Victory.

Mrs Weeks disappeared into the garden, but kept peeping in through the rear window as she hung out her son's laundry.

'You lied, George.' My voice was quiet, quieter than his breath as he began to panic.

'Please, I know. Please, I can explain. I'm sorry, Mr Cave.'

'Who are you, George?' I asked.

His waking dread. 'What?'

'I mean, who are you? Who are you? A loyal Horatio? No, I don't think so. Iago is nearer the mark. I'm just trying to see where everything fits into place, that's all. What do you want with her? With Bryony?'

'I don't want anything,' he said, his palms facing me in surrender.

'Then why did he attack you? Why did Denny attack you?'

'I don't know, Mr Cave. He's mad.' He couldn't look at me.

I remembered something else. 'That day I came back to the shop. I found you upstairs. What had you done to her?'

He was wheezing now, looking around at the old furniture. The chest I had helped carry out of the shop with his father.

'Nothing,' he said. 'Honestly . . . I didn't . . . I . . .'

'That's not what Denny told me, George.'

I caught Mrs Weeks' sharp glance as she pegged George's checked shirt to the line. I gestured to the French sofa, out of her sight.

'Sit down,' I told him, above the delicate piano music. 'Catch your breath.'

He descended onto the sofa in a slow and careful movement, which still seemed to exhaust him. I stayed standing, but turned so Mrs Weeks wouldn't see the rising anger marked on my face.

'I need my –'

'You wanted to work in the shop to be close to her, didn't you? You hurt her, didn't you? She was your Alison Wingfield, wasn't she?'

'No,' he said, holding his chest. His eyes bulged with panic. 'No . . . I didn't . . . please . . . I . . . my inhaler . . . I can't breathe. I need . . .'

'What?'

A limp point upwards, like Plato's in *The School of Athens*. (I see your face in Rome, viewing the one artwork that truly impressed you on our visit to the Vatican museums.)

'Bedroom,' he said, between desperate breaths, the scraping sound of each inhalation getting louder all the time. He began to change colour, the speckled pinkness in his cheeks spreading, turning purple.

'Be quiet, George.' I remember saying it, over and over, as

I moved closer. 'Be quiet, be quiet.' As I reached for the cushion and pressed it over him. As he grabbed at my sides and tugged desperately at my clothes.

'Be quiet. Be quiet. Be quiet.'

So easy, now I couldn't see George's face, to ignore what I was doing, to cancel out the pathetic crumble of his glasses as I pressed further. A hundred quiets and she was there behind me, screaming like the animal we all are, ripping her hands like claws into me, pulling on my collar, drowning Beethoven.

My arm swung back and caught her chest with my elbow. She fell and landed against the corner of the chest as I let go of the cushion.

I knew what I had done. The dark act I had committed through my blind possession. Terence Cave. Myself. Alone.

'Mrs Weeks? George?'

But it wasn't them. It wasn't them, Bryony. I tell you I couldn't see them.

I looked on the sofa and saw your brother, lying precisely where George should have been. The same glazed eyes that had stared up at me from the pavement. I could see the blood leaking down his face. Not a fading ghost but a solid form, creasing the fleur-de-lys pattern of the fabric. And as I turned to the body on the floor I didn't see Mrs Weeks, but your mother, wearing the blue shirt with the rolled-up sleeves she had worn when the intruders came, lying in the same awkward pose she had died in fifteen years before.

*

Your face was so pale and smooth, lying on that thin hospital pillow. I prayed for a frown, for a chip in the vase, for life to fracture your beauty.

'Please, Bryony,' I begged you, as I had once begged your brother.

A thin slab of light shone across the blankets, curving as it acknowledged your presence underneath.

'Please.'

Denny was somewhere else, talking to the police.

I was unwatched, except by the nurse. The nurse who had asked me if I wanted a drink. I had said 'No', despite my dry mouth. It seemed a crime beyond all the others, to sustain my body as yours lay so helpless. The nurse gave me a soft, undeserved smile and she trod in quiet footsteps back to her desk and the paperwork that awaited her.

I sensed you were going to die and so I had no incentive to leave you. The police were going to identify the bullet soon enough, and trace it back to me, even if Denny didn't give it away. The Weeks' bodies would be found at any moment and further evidence provided. But I didn't care. Nor did it seem to matter whether or not Reuben returned to infect my soul with his own. If you were gone, what further damage could he cause?

I glanced briefly at the other patients in the unit. Those sliding souls, engaged in their own silent battles with death. Old, wasted and fully-lived bodies, so different from your own.

'Leave her.'

I looked back at your face, the source of the whisper. I had imagined it, surely. You were still unconscious. Still undented. Maybe it was another imagining. My mind so frail after those events at the Weeks' house.

I leaned in towards you. 'Bryony?'

My nervous hand touched your arm. The thin slab of light dissolved into the blanket. I looked over at the nurse, filling in a form at her desk, and was ready to tell her you might be waking.

I was beginning to realise what was happening here. I understood that everything was still hanging in the balance, and that the victor of your own silent battle was still far from decided.

I took a deep breath. 'Reuben, tell me, what is it you want? What is it? I'll do anything. Please.'

The nurse stopped filling in her form and looked over at me. I offered a weak smile, and my hand retreated from your arm. The nurse frowned and deliberated whether to leave her desk, but eventually went back to ticking boxes.

'Reuben?' My voice was barely audible, even to myself. 'Reuben? Please, don't hurt her. Please. You love her. She's your sister. None of this is her fault. It's my fault. Everything. All of this. It's my fault. It's about me, not her. Please. I didn't want to hurt either of you.'

'Leave her.'

The slab of light returned, and with it the realisation. Suddenly it became clear. I had left him. For fifteen years I had left him, blaming a wailing baby when I should have blamed myself. All his jealousy, all his frozen anger, it had come from me. And if I had caused it, then I could end it, and that is what I vowed to do. I would return to him.

A flicker, at first. So slight it might not have been there at all.

'Petal?'

And then a second time. A movement behind your eyelids. Dreams on the boil, bubbling away beneath the surface.

Your nose twitched, your frown arrived, your mouth chewed

the last of its sleep. And then the eyes blinked open and you were there, my darling girl. Alive and awake, staring tiredly up at me.

'Dad?' The thinnest of voices.

'Bryony? Petal? Don't worry. You're in a hospital. You've been hurt, but you're going to be all right.'

You looked frightened. 'Denny?'

'It's okay. He's okay. He's fine. He'll be back in a moment.' And you seemed to understand so much in these words.

'I have to go, Bryony. But I'll be back.' I delivered the lie at the last moment, as I leaned to kiss your brow, so you weren't able to assess my eyes. 'I must leave, Petal. You will be all right. Everything will be. You'll see.'

And I walked away from your bedside, and told the nurse you had woken. She left her desk and went over to check that I was right, speaking words I couldn't hear. At the door I turned to have one final look at you. You frowned as you watched me, and something about that frown told me you would be fine, whatever else happened. You would survive all the dents my life and death could inflict, because you were as tough as your mother had been, and you would tackle life as it should be tackled. The pain and the shame I had caused would eventually fade, and become caged safely in the past. You will go on without me. Surviving. Yearning. Loving.

Living.

I hope. Yes, I hope.

I used to imagine how your life would turn out. Oh, it was a beautiful existence that I saw waiting for you – you would marry the right kind of man, you would live in the country, you would play in an orchestra – and my job as your father was to help navigate your way through the dangerous territory that lay en route.

I now realise my own folly. I understand that like the amateur restorer who rips the canvas he is trying to repair, I have ruined this portrait. Your future will be textured differently to how I imagined, and it has every right to be. The only purpose of living is to accept life itself. To trust our children to find their own course, and realise there isn't a single one of us who has the right answers. How can we, when we haven't even discovered the question? All I pray now is that your life is devoid of the mistakes that have blighted my own course.

I hope that if and when you have children you will note their differences but love them equally. I hope you know that we can create new life but never own it, and that we should never let our desire to protect become the will to possess. I hope you will know that children have achieved the whole world just by entering it, because we live and breathe its glories in every waking moment.

And there is glory in abundance up here, with the vast sweep of the land in front of me. I remember walking these moors years before you were born, standing here and looking out at a whole wild atlas of green and purple. This was in July, when the heather was in flower, and so different from this evening. It holds a bleaker beauty now, but a beauty nonetheless. A beauty I can breathe inside me, as I sit out here, away from the car, and bring my task to a close. Bryony, I am so tempted to linger but I know I will be found before too long. I feel them getting nearer, with the night.

Two small final requests. Please tell Cynthia I am sorry for leaving her that note – she must have had a terrible fright when she opened it this morning. I know she will look after you in the proper way, and help repair the damage I have caused.

Also, the old picture of my mother in the living room. It is on the wall, tucked behind the door as you walk in. You know it. The one where she's looking out rather crossly, with Greta Garbo's face painted onto her own. I want you to keep it. I know you owe me nothing, but if you are still reading I might be able to presume you would be willing to do this one task. So please, if you could, keep it safe. You don't have to put it up on your wall, but keep it. Somewhere, anywhere, but make sure it's safe.

Now, it is over. That is everything. The paper has been filled, and I am so close to the finish that the fear is leaving me. There is nothing further to be afraid of, even as I look ahead and see them. All of them.

They stand in front of me, their silent spirits. Those I have lost, those I have killed, with Reuben one step forward. His hand beckons, but he looks finally at peace.

I have no fear as I reach the end. I will offer him the love he needs and I will watch you in this beautiful world and let it shape you as it plans.

The day's last breath brushes my face, and tells me it is time.

I will go to him.

Goodnight, Petal.

Goodnight.

Acknowledgements

I would like to thank:

Caradoc King, my agent, for his complete and unflinching enthusiasm for this novel from the start.

Dan Franklin, my editor, for letting me head into the dark without insisting I bring a torch.

Alex Bowler, Rachel Cugnoni, Alison Hennessey, Chloë Johnson-Hill and everyone at Jonathan Cape and Vintage.

Elinor Cooper, Judith Evans, Christine Glover, Louise Lamont, Naomi Leon, Teresa Nicholls and Linda Shaughnessy at A.P. Watt.

Alan Moloney and Tim Palmer at Parallel Film.

Matteo Moretti and everyone at the Hotel Art in Rome.

Michel Faber, Toby Litt, Scarlett Thomas and Jeanette Winterson, for providing me with advice and assistance at various points over the last few years.